TORN

Torn

Copyright © 2019 S. Nelson

Editor:
Hot Tree Editing

Cover Design:
CT Cover Creations

This is a work of fiction. Names, characters, places, and incidents are a product of the publisher's imagination. Locales and public names are sometimes used for atmospheric purposes. Any resemblance to actual people, living or dead, or to businesses, companies, events, institutions, or locales is completely coincidental.

Torn/ S. Nelson. – 2nd edition

ISBN-13: 9781734302318

TORN

S. NELSON

To all who are yet to follow your dreams, do so with a lightness in your heart, a drive in your soul and a determination to conquer the world.

PROLOGUE

*T*he outside world whizzed by, my breaths never seeming to catch up to each other as the scenery made me dizzy. With each tree, each stretch of highway, each blur of the passing vehicles, my chest tightened in anticipation for what I had planned. For as much as I willed my body to relax, to calm down before perpetuating into some sort of heart attack, I was powerless to stop the barrage of feelings washing over me. Perspiration coated my palms, causing my hands to slip from the wheel every few minutes.

Suspended anxieties racked my body. Drawing air into my lungs, holding for a five-count, then releasing, and repeating several times did nothing to sedate my apprehension. And no matter how much liquid I forced down my throat, my mouth remained dry.

I'd heard it was normal for a man to feel such things before he asked the biggest question of his life, but the reassurance didn't help. Visions of what was to come only caused my muscles to tighten, so much so, I thought they were going to split apart.

Resting my right hand on the top of the bottled water, I ran my thumbnail along the ridges to calm me. Repetition often soothed my wayward thoughts, and even though the scraping sound masked my uneasy breaths, my mind flooded with too many thoughts to be rational.

What if she said no, buying into our families' concern that we were too young to be this serious? Would I be able to live with the rejection?

The closer I approached, the more my heart sped up.

Thump.

Thump.

Thump.

My entire life was going to change, and that was either a good thing or a very bad thing, depending on the outcome. I'd practiced what I planned on saying and it sounded convincing when I spoke the words to my mirror image. But how would they sound to the one person who set my heart ablaze? Who held my happiness in the palm of her hand?

Repeating *calm down, man,* over and over to myself, I finally came to our street. As soon as I made the left-hand turn, my pulse boomed in my ears. Our apartment building loomed ahead, taunting me.

I tried like hell to think of something else for the next few hundred feet until I parked, but it was useless. *Thank God I'm only doing this once.*

Shutting off the engine, I opened the door slower than I ever had before, needing those few extra seconds to get my head right before I saw her. Wanting tonight to be a surprise, I needed to act like it was any other Friday.

The ring I'd purchased was tucked safely away in the back of my closet. She never ventured onto my side of the shared space; she complained it was a mess and couldn't stand to look at it, let alone search for anything.

A few steps later and I stood at the main entrance to our building. Our apartment was tucked away at the end of the hallway on the first floor, giving us enough privacy from our neighbors, the closest one being Mrs. Hannigan, an eighty-year-old woman who was hard of hearing.

Thank God for that because there were some nights we were anything but quiet.

When I reached our door, I inserted the key then took a breath. "You can do this," I mumbled to myself before taking a step inside the dark living room. I flicked on the light, and at first, I thought it was odd she wasn't home yet.

Excitement flooded my veins for the first time in hours. All I wanted to do was rush into the bedroom, fight my way through the closet, grab the ring, and place it on her finger. All the while babbling incoherently about how much I loved her and wanted to spend the rest of my life with her.

As I walked through the small rooms, flicking on one light after another, something was off.

The air seemed different.

Tense.

Chalking my uneasiness to nothing more than nerves, I walked toward the kitchen to grab a bottled water from the fridge. Midswallow, I saw a piece of paper on the kitchen table. At first, I didn't think anything of it, until I leaned in closer and saw my name.

People say to listen to your gut, that everyone has a sixth sense that should never be ignored. And my instinct told me something heartbreaking was written on that damn piece of paper. I snatched it up and scanned the page, the words drifting through my mind but never settling in.

Goodbye.

I'm sorry.

I can't do this anymore.

What the hell was I reading? It was the love of my life's handwriting, but the words weren't hers. It didn't make any sense.

None of it.

The letter was vague, never giving me a reason as to why she wasn't coming back. As to why the hell she'd left me.

I will always love you.

Don't try and contact me.

By the time you read this, I'll be long gone.

Twenty minutes passed before I finally broke out of my daze. The first place I went to was her mother's house. She told me her daughter had left California, and it was best to let her go, that I would never find her. Although her mother tried to remain stoic, I saw tiny cracks of compassion seeping out, her strained smile whispering she wanted to tell me everything but couldn't.

I visited her home every day for six months, and every day it was the same. Her mother never wavered, and when I'd finally had nothing more to give, I hardened my heart and vowed to never love another woman as long as I lived.

ELI

*T*he bed creaked underneath our weight, the sound ripping through the silence of the room numbingly comforting.

"Harder," Beth panted, reaching back and digging her nails into my thigh, attempting to anchor us together. Pushing further inside her, my muscles strained, and my resolve to hold out longer weakened with every thrust I propelled into her tight heat.

With my body molded to hers from behind, I bruised her hip with my hold, punishing her for nothing… and for everything.

Beth Stanton was someone I occasionally hooked up with, and every single time I reiterated I was only interested in sex, nothing more. I made her verbalize her consent before we went any further. The last thing I needed was for her to become clingy, creating some twisted fantasy that I was her boyfriend or some shit. But I wasn't stupid. I saw the defeated look in her eyes every time she said yes, knowing damn well she wanted more from me but didn't want to risk me cutting her off completely.

In the end, I did her a favor because I was incapable of

having a normal romantic relationship, not only with her but with anyone. Only one woman had stolen my heart. But then she crushed it into a million pieces when she abandoned me. The only thing that remained afterward was a cold slab of muscle pumping inside my coiled chest.

I vowed never to open myself up like that ever again.

That Eli was long gone.

"You want it harder?" I bit the sensitive spot beneath her earlobe, and she tensed in anticipation. "Are you sure? You know what I like."

My fingers danced around the edges of her breast, teasing until she pushed back against me and moaned. Then I pinched her puckered nipple, twisting until the sounds that fell from her lips turned raucous. I tossed her into a world that rocked between pleasure and pain, my hold on her fierce, all the while fully aware of how far I would push her.

Over the years, I formed a proclivity for rough sex, loving the fine line between pain and pleasure. I'd dabbled in some BDSM, but it wasn't for me.

If I'd taken the time to stop and question why I preferred sex the way I did, I supposed there could have been a plethora of reasons.

To punish myself and the women I was with, to a certain degree.

To drive out my own anger and demons.

Because I was simply wired this way and hadn't realized it until I was more mature.

Whatever the reason… I enjoyed it.

Immensely.

I wasn't a heartless beast or someone who got off on a woman's tears, but I didn't do soft and tender, either. I always made sure the woman fully understood what she was getting herself into, taking it slow in the beginning until I'd built up to exactly the way I liked to fuck.

While I'd had countless sexual partners over the years, I tended to stay with the same one for a short period of time. It was a challenge to find a woman who I was not only attracted to but who also shared my appetites.

"Please," she begged, arching her back and pressing her ass further into me, enticing me. Little did she know it wasn't going to take much, especially after the shitty week I'd had at work. Too many deadlines and obstacles had barreled down on top of me.

I need this release.

"As you wish." I pulled out and moved her from her side, grabbing her hips and positioning her how I wanted her, on all fours. Right before I buried myself balls deep, I slapped her ass, the sting of my palm making my dick harder.

Beth gasped, the sound floating through the air like the sweetest melody.

"I love your huge cock," she moaned.

"You do, do you? Do you like when I do this?" Tangling her long, blonde hair around my fingers, I yanked her head back, rutting inside her with a fierceness that surprised even me.

Her answer was a loud squeal, her hands clutching the sheets in excitement as the headboard continuously knocked the wall. The only thing on my mind was coming, first her then me.

The bedroom was the only place I could lose myself and not have to think.

Just feel.

Take what I wanted, giving back everything I could only with my body. Only ever with my body.

The moment my fingers circled her clit, her body shuddered. "Right there. Please," she cried. "Don't stop. Please…." She barely had time to pull air into her lungs before she cried for me to fuck her harder, to make her come.

"You have such a greedy cunt," I rasped in her ear, driving

into her over and over again. Seconds later, she clenched around me, her breaths expelling in short spurts.

When her orgasm finally waned, I released her hair and positioned my hands on her waist for leverage. I slammed into her, trying to go as deep as possible. She reached back and grabbed my wrist, pushing back against me as I drove forward, the sounds of her ass slapping off my skin fueling my need to come.

The sound that erupted from deep within me was guttural, the familiar tingling jolt spreading from my balls up to the base of my cock. I was close, seconds away from exploding. My muscles screamed with tension as I rushed over the edge, leaning over Beth and sinking my teeth into her shoulder, careful not to break the skin while I expelled all the frustration I'd endured for the entire week. And it was in those few precious seconds afterward that I pretended I wasn't still messed up inside, that I wasn't a shell of my former self, looking for the light at the end of a never-ending tunnel.

As my heart slowed from its erratic pounding, I slipped from her body and hopped off the bed, pulling off the condom as I walked toward the bathroom. When I glanced back at her, she was lying on the mattress, completely satiated. I never did anything half-assed, sex being no exception.

When I reentered the bedroom, I grabbed my clothes and quickly dressed.

"Where are you going so soon?" Propped up on her side, I had full view of her nakedness. Beth was an enticing woman—her tits perky and more than a handful, her ass deliciously round and her pussy warm and tight, but I didn't want anything more than the occasional romp.

"You know I don't cuddle. Nor do I stay afterward." Pulling on my suit jacket, I reached for my keys and lessened the distance between us, placing a quick kiss on her lips. When I tried to turn around, however, she grabbed my arm to stop me.

"What are you doing tomorrow night?" The hopefulness I heard in her voice irked me; she knew better than to try and take our tryst outside the bedroom. "I was thinking we could grab some dinner. Maybe a few drinks after."

If my heart had been left intact years ago, I might've taken her up on her offer. But I wasn't whole.

I was broken.

Therefore, our *relationship* could never be anything more than sexual gratification.

"I can't," I responded. Her mocha-colored eyes closed half-way, disappointment written all over her face. "I have a family dinner to attend."

"I could go with you, if you want." She was about to spout out some other crazy shit, but I interrupted her.

I removed my arm for her grip and stepped back. "You know exactly what kind of arrangement we have. There is nothing beyond this room." The only way to shut her down was to be completely honest... and blunt. "If you don't think you can handle just having sex, then maybe it's time we end this."

Scrambling to the edge of the bed, she wrapped the sheet around herself, shielding her vulnerability from me, in more ways than one. Her eyes darted from me to the floor and back again. She was the only woman I was seeing at the moment, so I hoped she didn't end things, but if she wanted more, then I would search elsewhere for sex. If I was any kind of gentleman, I would've backed out right then, realizing she had feelings for me that went beyond our agreement.

But I was selfish.

She fidgeted with the bedsheet, refusing to look at me when she answered. "No, please. I don't want to end this. I'll take whatever you can give me, Eli. I'm sorry." She lifted her head and brushed her long locks over her shoulder. When she finally stood, shuffling up next to me, she rested her lips over mine, her bottom one trembling.

Shit!

She was more into me than I realized.

Deciding not to deal with our new predicament right then, I returned her kiss and backed up. Flashing her a smile, I told her something I didn't truly believe. "I'll call you in a few days."

I disappeared from her bedroom as quickly as I could, never giving her a chance to say anything else.

ELI

"Are you coming tonight or not? You missed the last two weeks, and Mom is on my ass to find out why." Cal grilled me, and it was the last thing I needed right before I was about to close a deal for a huge client. But he was right. It wasn't like me to continuously miss the weekly dinners.

I enjoyed hanging out with my family, allowing the week-long stress to evaporate with a stiff drink, and some healthy sibling rivalry with my three younger brothers, Dray, Dex and Cal. Besides, our gatherings gave me ample time to tease Dray. Since he'd married Essie and they'd had their twin girls, Isla and Emma, I loved to antagonize him. All I had to do was stand a little too close to Essie or kiss her cheek in greeting, and Dray rushed to her side, glaring at me to back up. He was so easy to rile, and I took full advantage every time. I was just doing my part in reminding him to be grateful for his new life.

Tragedy struck Dray's life years back when his fiancée, Elizabeth, was killed in a car accident, an incident he'd blamed himself for. It wasn't until Essie unexpectedly came into his life that he started to live again, his carefree personality emerging, something I hadn't witnessed in years. He was still a moody bastard, but I gave him a pass for his sullen moods, which were the direct cause of worry over his wife and children, who he loved something fierce.

"Yes, I'm coming. Tell Mom to calm down. I'll be there."

"Are you bringing anyone this time?" he asked, a different tone to his voice.

"No, and don't start."

"Mom said—"

"I don't have time for an inquisition right now, Cal. I have a bunch of shit I have to get done before I leave work." To sound harsh wasn't my intention, but I was tired of my family constantly asking me when I was going to settle down with someone. I had no wishes for that shit, and neither should they. I was perfectly happy with the way my life was going.

"Fine. Whatever." An elongated pause met me on the other end of the phone.

"Listen," I started, "it's not you. I'm just stressed. That's all. I'll see you tonight, okay?" I did my best to keep my tone light. It seemed to do the trick.

"Yeah, okay. See you then." He hung up before saying good-bye, which was his way of telling me he didn't appreciate being the middleman.

Hunching over my desk, being the last remaining partner at the firm for the night, I reflected on everything I should've been grateful for in my life. Although I wasn't the same person I was before *her*, I had many blessings to be thankful for.

My family was wonderful and supportive, although a touch nosy and intrusive. I was still close with a few buddies from my youth, who I met up with for a guys' night every other month, and I had a great job, albeit stressful most of the time.

When I was young and naïve and decided to specialize in corporate law, I thought I'd chosen a less demanding field. Boy, was I wrong. If I wasn't busy ensuring the legalities of many of the firm's commercial transactions, I was advising corporations on their legal rights and duties, including the responsibilities of their officers. Boring to most, and while tedious and repetitive sometimes, I actually enjoyed my work when it didn't suck every ounce of vigor from me.

Some days, I'd come home so exhausted I barely had the energy to strip out of my clothes and flop on the bed only to close my eyes and pray the next day would be less hectic.

Saving the spreadsheet I'd been working on and locking my desk, I shut down my computer and headed for the door, my arms free from the bundle of work I usually brought home. It was pointless since I'd be back in the office in less than ten hours.

As I walked toward my car, I kept reminding myself my life was full. Rewarding. Fulfilling. That I was happy with the way everything turned out. Kicking over the engine, I shook my head and mumbled, "All lies," right before hitting the gas and tearing out of the parking lot.

"Umcle Ebvis! Umcle Ebvis!" my three-year-old nieces, Isla and Emma, yelled, launching themselves into my arms as soon as I walked through the door. Normally, Isla was the shyer of the two, but tonight, she seemed as vivacious as her sister.

Good thing Dray was close because he grabbed the beer I'd brought before it hit the ground, the force of my nieces' excitement nothing to laugh at. Except, I did. They were so filled with life, their enthusiasm made me jealous. To know only love and happiness was something I once had.

Refusing to dwell on the past, I lifted them up, the hem of their matching blue and white polka dot dresses draping over my forearms while I alternated kisses on each of their cheeks. They weren't identical twins but they loved to dress alike, their appearance more similar than not with dark hair and pale blue eyes. The only noticeable difference between them was their hair texture. While Emma's was curly, Isla's strands was slightly wavy.

"Hello, my lovelies." My voice dropped lower, my faux evil tone making them laugh until they squirmed to get down. They were beautiful, and I didn't envy the shit Dray would have to deal with once the boys came sniffing around.

Once their feet hit the ground, they took off running toward the kitchen, the aroma wafting from the room one of the reasons I'd come tonight. I was starving for a good meal as well as the distraction from my life that my family would provide.

Walking behind my brother, I took in the sight of his house, smiling because I was happy he'd finally found someone who brought out the best in him and his previously stuffy domain. Before Essie arrived, the rooms had been sterile with too many neutral colors, and while the look and feel was masculine and classy, it lacked warmth. Now, splashes of color painted the walls in way of abstract art, and in the simple addition of pillows littering the sitting areas. Patterned curtains hung from the rods, the tieback thingys certainly Essie's idea. If it had been up to Dray, we would've been fine holding on to the taupe drapes that used to adorn all the windows.

Turning the corner, Essie came into view, her arms opened wide as she strode toward me. Her dark blonde hair fell over her shoulders in waves and she looked as lovely as ever. "Eli, how are you?" she greeted, drawing me in for a big hug. My brother walked behind her, and as I returned her embrace, I winked at Dray over her shoulder. He shook his head, but I saw the faintest smile drift over his face. While I wasn't a threat to him, he still didn't appreciate any other man touching his wife. He was tolerant of his brothers, but only barely.

When we separated, Dray walked toward the kitchen and I pulled back to look at the woman who'd changed my brother's life. The first time we met was here at the house, in the library to be exact. Although we'd been strangers, our interaction that night had been effortless, as if we'd known each other for years. Her beauty attracted me, there was no doubt, but the ease of our conversation and the way she seemed to lift my dreariness, even if for a time, captured my laden soul. But from the moment I realized Dray was caught up in her—although he didn't dare admit such a thing at the time—and that Essie was in love with him, I backed off, never extending another invitation for her to go out with me.

Now, I loved Essie like I did Bridgette and Dela, my other sisters-in-law. The only difference was that I enjoyed goading Dray. At times I'd whisper something in her ear, usually about him, or kiss her cheek, and we'd both laugh because not seconds later he'd be standing next to us, irritated and tucking his wife under his arm. "One of these days," he'd say, and to this day, I had no idea what he meant with those four words.

"I'm good. How are you?" Her infectious smile put me in much better spirits.

Before she could answer, her girls ran back up to me and threw their arms in the air for me to pick them up again.

"Didn't I already say hello to you two?" I questioned, finding it odd they wanted to greet me again so soon but loving their attention all the same.

I bent down and grabbed hold of them both, pulling them back up with me when I stood to my full height.

"We love you, Umcle Ebvis," they sang in unison, their little fingers holding on to my face.

"You know you can call me Uncle Eli, don't you?"

"Daddy says you like Umcle Ebvis." They laughed, and when I looked over at Dray, he grinned like a fool. He knew damn well I didn't like being called Elvis. I had no idea why my parents chose the name, but as soon as I hit first grade, I told them I wanted to be called Eli. Now, other than my nieces teasing me, the only time anyone called me Elvis in seriousness was when my mother was frustrated with me and used my full given name.

Looking into their sweet, little faces, I decided not to correct them. If they wanted to call me Uncle Elvis, then I wouldn't cause a fuss.

"Can I tell you a secret?" I leaned in close and whispered softly, "You two are the only ones allowed to call me Elvis. No one else. It's our thing." Their mouths formed the cutest O shape, but their attention span lasted all of five seconds before they wriggled so much in my arms, I feared dropping one of them if I didn't put them down.

"Give them to me before we have an incident," Essie said, reaching for her daughters. Once they were safely on their feet, I passed through the living room, greeting Dex and Cal before rounding the corner into the kitchen.

My stomach growled when I walked up behind my mother, inhaling the delicious aroma of the spicy sauce she stirred.

The familiar smell threw me back into the memories of when we all resided under one roof. Not too many of them included my father, however, because he'd left several years after Cal was born. He'd had an affair; my mom had found out and kicked him out. End of story. He never looked back, and I never wasted any emotion as to why. Because my brothers didn't have a father figure, they vowed to be the best dad they could be when they had kids of their own. And they stayed true to their word, every last one of them.

"Honey, I'm so happy to see you." Mom smiled, placing the ladle on the counter before coming over to me. Even dressed in dark-colored jeans and a pale green top, she exuded elegance. Every blonde hair on her head was styled in place, and for the life of me, I couldn't ever remember a time where she didn't look like the picture of perfection.

Before she drew me in for a hug, she slapped me on the arm, her much shorter stature doing nothing to diminish the authority she held. She looked up at me, her brows drawn tight. "It's been too long since I've seen you."

"It's only been a couple weeks," I corrected.

"Like I said... too long." Her hand caressed my cheek as she gazed adoringly at me. "Why don't you shave, Eli? You have such a handsome face. Why do you want to hide it with this scruff?" Her question was serious, but her tone indicated play-fulness.

I remembered a time when I consistently kept my face free of hair but that was years back when I was a different man. Needing a change, not wanting any reminders of my time before, I'd grown various stages of beards, from light scruff to full on mountain man, which was only worn when I was on vacation.

Essie strode into the room as the back of my hand drifted over my chin. I pulled her close and rubbed my face against her cheek. "Because the ladies love the scruff, Mom. Right, Essie?" My sister-in-law laughed right before she stroked my short beard.

"We certainly do." She was pulled from my arms before she could say another word.

"Get your own woman to molest," Dray growled, looking incredulously at his wife. "Don't encourage him." His blue eyes darkened right before he kissed her. Essie laughed when he tugged her toward the other side of the kitchen, and far from me. Glancing back over her shoulder, she winked and flashed me a heart-stopping smile.

He mumbled something in her ear, but I was too busy popping the top off my bottle of beer to pay much attention. Just as I swallowed the first sip, two of my nephews barreled right into my legs.

"Whoa! Calm down before you guys hurt yourselves." They ignored me, running past and into the adjoining room. As I opened my mouth to ask where my other sisters-in-law were, they both appeared, Cal's wife Bridgette being the first to embrace me, rubbing her fingers along my jawline just like my mother had done moments earlier. She kissed my cheek before snatching up one of her sons, who tried to run after his cousin.

I locked eyes with my mother. "See, the ladies love the scruff." She offered a bemused smile before turning her attention back to her spaghetti sauce.

"How are you, Eli?" Before I could answer, Bridgette shot off another question. "When are you going to bring someone to dinner?" I was stunned, not from her question, because I'd prepared myself for some sort of inquisition, but because she'd been the one to ask it. Bridgette was the quiet and reserved one, her fiery red hair belying her personality.

By some miracle, my more brazen sister-in-law Dela saved me from having to make up yet another excuse. "Leave him alone. He'll bring someone when he's good and ready." She paused for a second, tucking a strand of her blonde hair behind her ear, then tapped her finger against her lips. "Come to think of it, Eli, I can help you with that. We hired a really nice woman at the shop. I think she would be perfect for you." Leaning in closer, she half-whispered, "I can arrange everything."

Dela and Essie owned a bakery together. It had started off small but had flourished as soon as Essie started working for her. They eventually became partners and expanded the business, buying the building next door to the shop for more room.

No matter how much I loved my family, there was no way I'd ever let any of them set me up with a stranger.

"Thanks, but no thanks. I'm fully capable of meeting women on my own."

"None of whom are the type of woman you would bring home to meet us. The chicks you hook up with are... how shall I say this... easy to please." Dex appeared out of nowhere, joining right in and putting me on the spot, more so than usual.

"I like my women easy to please." I wiggled my brows,

earning myself a pat to the back of the head from the matriarch of our family.

"Elvis Holden Warner," my mother enunciated. "I don't want to hear any of that. If you boys want to talk about sex, do it in the other room." My mother was far from a prude, but I doubted she wanted to listen to us talking in such a way. I didn't blame her. Hell, I didn't want to talk about it, but my brother left me no choice, resorting to deflection with jokes and puns in order to stop the conversation from becoming serious. I had enough on my mind with work, and my impending "breakup" with Beth. She'd become too attached and I had to end our arrangement before her feelings for me developed any deeper.

"How about you people choose another topic, huh? Don't worry so much about my life. I'm perfectly content." I smiled big, hoping to convince them I hadn't just lied. After a few grunts and groans, the subject switched to vacations, kids, and work.

An hour later, as we all sat around the large dining table, I leaned back and took it all in. Glancing from one person to the next, several conversations blending together mixed with the chaos from the kids, I counted my blessings yet again. My family meant everything to me.

Too bad they'd never have the opportunity to see me with someone.

That ship had long since sailed.

KALISTA

*M*emories from my youth flooded in as I drove down the same tree-lined roads I'd traveled so many years ago before I abruptly left everyone and everything behind without an explanation.

Passing the pizza shop Eli and I had eaten at more times than I could count made me wince, the pang of lost time solidifying the unease I felt the moment I'd arrived back in town. Next was the theater where he always let me pick the movie—a small but selfless act on his part because I knew full well he didn't want to sit through another romantic comedy, but he allowed me to choose because he loved me. The final clincher down memory lane was the park that was just a five-minute walk from where I grew up. We stayed out many a late night there, talking about our hopes and dreams for our future.

The plush lawn had cushioned us as we declared our love for each other over and over. Although we were young at the time, our chemistry and passion were electric. All Eli had to do was touch my hand and I swore a current traveled through me, a desire I'd only ever felt with him enrapturing me. We were head over heels and even though some of our friends and family thought we were too young to be that serious, we didn't care.

We'd met our freshman year of high school when he'd accidentally knocked me over while rough housing with some of his buddies. The moment he helped me to my feet, I was a goner. I had a huge crush on him and while we became the best of friends, I never once revealed my secret. Then one day, everything changed. We were at a party for one of my girlfriends and the new guy at our school struck up a conversation with me. He put his arm around my shoulder and even leaned in to kiss me. I didn't stop him because a part of me wanted to make Eli jealous. Either way, the kiss never happened because Eli came out of nowhere, pushed the guy aside and dragged me out of the party. When I opened my mouth to yell at him for being so rude, he sealed his lips over mine. After that night, we were inseparable, moving in together right after graduating high school.

It was the best time of my life, and I'd screwed it all up, believing I was doing the right thing. If given the opportunity, I would've hit the rewind button, traveled back and changed the only choice I felt I had then. I would've never left the love of my life.

Time had given me an invaluable perspective, one I wished I'd had when I was twenty years old.

My mom was thrilled when I'd told her the news of my return, her only child moving back home something she'd wanted since the day I left. She often talked about regrets and how they were a waste of time, yet something told me she was anxious to make up for the ones that still might haunt her.

Growing up, she provided me with the basics of shelter, food, and clothes, but hardly ever her time. Because she was a single parent, she worked long hours at a prestigious law firm as a legal secretary. And when she wasn't working, she was dating a few of the eligible lawyers. She hated being single, yet she never wanted to settle down with any one man, flitting from one guy to the next. I supposed it was her means of driving away the sting of lonely nights without ever fully giving herself to someone.

While I didn't love being alone, I hadn't dated much over the past fifteen years, only having one other serious relationship. There was no one in the world who could ever replace Eli or invoke a fraction of the feelings I held toward him, so it was pointless to even try. I settled before ever searching. In a lifetime, I believed we were gifted one big love, and I stupidly threw mine away years ago.

Only one time when I was younger did my mom have a talk with me about my relationship with Eli. She told me to be careful, that if I ended up pregnant, my life would be over. I remembered the guilt that tore through me because, while she loved me, I couldn't help but feel I was the reason my mother wasn't able to find her true happiness in life. My father—or rather, the sperm donor—up and left the second he found out I was coming into the picture. Turned out, the bastard was married with a whole separate life. He'd lied to my mother to get her into bed and being the gullible twenty-one-year-old she was, she fell for every one of his lies.

After I was born, I spent a lot of my earlier years with my grandparents while my mother earned her degree. She went to school part-time because she still had to work to support us both. For as much as she was absent, she did install a strong work ethic in me from an early age, which was good because I found solace in hard work, the late hours distracting me from my loneliness.

ELI

I'd been burning the proverbial candle at both ends for as long as I could remember, and it was finally catching up to me. I couldn't focus on the brief I'd worked on for the past three hours for one of the firm's biggest clients. All the words jumbled together, not making a lick of sense. While frustrated, I reminded myself I'd signed up for this shit when I accepted partnership in my firm.

Deciding the best plan of action was to stop for the evening and head home, I did just that. The slow descent of the elevator to the parking garage gave me a few moments of peace, the hum of the car oddly calming. That was until the sound of my cell burst my serenity. Pulling the device from the inside pocket of my suit jacket, I saw Beth's name flash across the screen.

I hit the Reject button, sending her straight to voice mail, barely possessing the energy to walk to my damn car, let alone to deal with a woman who had become attached.

Just thinking about my schedule the following day exhausted me. Three conference calls, a lunchtime appointment with a potential client, followed by endless hours of paperwork and research wasn't ideal, but when it was all said and done, I loved my job most days. Thankfully, when I became overly stressed, I had a great way of releasing that tension. At least, I did. After I ended my arrangement with Beth, I was going to be one pent-up bastard until I found someone else to take the brunt of my frustrations.

Financially, I'd been smart with my money, and while I owned a nice home, had a closet filled with designer suits, and drove the newest model Mercedes, I'd invested wisely. Being smart with my money was something I learned early on because if life had taught me anything, it was that circumstances could change in an agonizing split second.

With the window down, the air perked me up enough to make the half-hour drive home, but I swore as soon as I pulled into the garage, exhaustion stole my last bit of energy. Practically crawling from my car, I entered my house, the silence that greeted me always bothersome. There was no one to welcome me, no one to share my life with—not in any way it counted, anyway. I'd contemplated rescuing a dog a couple years back, but I worked such long hours, my absence wouldn't be fair to the poor animal.

Whenever I was this tired, and... lonely, my thoughts drifted to the one woman who'd changed me forever, pushing through the fog I tried every day to asphyxiate in. Most of the time I was successful in escaping the past, but there were instances, like right now, when I couldn't stop the onslaught.

Her image flashed through my mind and stole my breath, the ache in my chest a dull thud since the day she left. The last time I'd seen her, she looked happy, her beautiful green eyes lighting up when I kissed her goodbye.

It was hard for me to remember any of the good times we had together, her abandonment desecrating every memory we'd ever created.

Her betrayal stung.

It sliced.

It tore through me like the sharpest of blades.

Hoping a hot shower would relieve me of the torment I put myself through, I disappeared inside the tiled enclosure and turned on the water. I succumbed to the torrent of the heat raining down on me; my head hung low as the water prickled my skin.

I tried to think about my hectic work schedule, or about my family, but her face shoved everything else aside, and soon, my body betrayed me. Conjuring the memory of the last time we'd had sex made my cock thicken. Even though it'd been fifteen years, the memory was almost as vivid today as when it happened.

We'd arrived home to our apartment after a fun night out with friends. We were both tipsy and fumbling to remove our clothes. Deciding the bedroom was too far away, I pinned her against the door, pushed up her dress and tore off her panties. The haze of lust in her eyes when she looked at me while I buried myself inside her had always been my undoing. Our movements were quick, rushed, both of us too consumed with the other for the sex to last long.

We'd fallen to the floor shortly afterward, laughing as we lain there in a crumpled mess, limbs entwined, fingers tracing heated flesh and lips promising the world with words and kisses.

My grip became fierce. I hated myself for jerking off to her memory, but I needed a release, a moment of pleasure in an otherwise joyless existence. Stroking myself with a vengeance, my balls drew tight. I hated she still had the power to affect me, even after all these goddamn years. My fury wasn't enough to stop the onslaught, though; I was too far gone. As my cum spurted forth and mixed with the water, my heart hammering inside my chest, I released not only my pent-up frustration but my anger as well.

I couldn't continue to live life thinking of her, even if it was sporadic. And while my family was probably right in trying to push me to settle down with someone who could temper the lonely nights, I realized that feat was impossible.

When Kalista ripped my heart from my fucking chest, my life had ceased to exist. She overshadowed my thoughts often enough to keep me trapped in the past and unable to move forward.

ELI

"*P*lease, tell me you're not going to blow me off again, man. I've let you get away with canceling way too many times. I need a drink, and I know you do, too." Mike exhaled, his annoyance loud and clear on the end of the phone. I'd canceled on him the past three times, all without good reason. I used work as the excuse, although I suspected he knew I was bullshitting.

Closing my eyes, I reclined in my seat, needing a moment to contemplate his offer. He was right; I did need a stiff drink, or two, knowing my impending conversation with Beth would have to happen soon. And this way I could use my friend as a sounding board, although I wasn't sure he'd be much help since he slept with anyone with a pair of long legs, men included. But I didn't judge. To each their own and all that happy shit.

"Hello? Did you hang up on me?" he asked, his voice drifting away from the phone as he spoke, no doubt checking if the call was dropped.

"No. I'm still here. I'm trying to decide if I can meet you."

"You know you can. Stop being a pussy and live a little. You're gonna be old and decrepit before you know it." Funny thing was he was right. Minus family dinners and the occasional rough sex romp, all I did was work.

The words tumbled from my lips before my brain could stop them. "Sure, why the hell not? Give me another hour to finish up here and I'll meet you. Same place?"

"Cool. Yeah, same place. See you soon."

After our call ended, I teetered between calling him back to cancel and following through and meeting him. I ended up choosing the latter.

Mike Hawkings and I had been friends since our freshman year of high school, so there wasn't much we didn't know about each other. From the love of my life flipping my world upside-down, to the death of his younger brother, to him coming out to me that he was bisexual. We were as close as two friends could be. In fact, my own siblings considered him one of the family. Hell, even my mother thought of Mike as one of her children, accompanying me to many family dinners and serving as a distraction to ensure my family wouldn't hound me to death about not bringing a woman.

In exchange for a home-cooked meal, he agreed to be interrogated by Vivian Warner. My mother wasn't going to be happy until everyone was married off and breeding like bunnies, close friends of mine included in her crazy, but loving, plan.

THE INSIDE of The Royal was dimly lit, the atmosphere of the upscale bar inside the Hotel Regency reserved for knocking back a few, hooking up, and taking the party to one of the numerous suites upstairs. Mike loved coming here because he could easily *close the deal*, what with the rooms being only an elevator ride away.

I caught sight of my friend tucked in one of the booths in the corner, chatting up a pretty brunette. A faint smile kicked up the corners of my mouth, finding his shamelessness amusing. Being secure in my masculinity, I could see why women and men alike were attracted to Mike. He was an inch shorter than my six-one frame, broad-shouldered, and in good shape. We often worked out at the same gym, so I knew for a fact he took care of himself. He'd kept his style of dark curls since I could remember, simply because of the number of compliments he received. He was all too aware of his looks, using them along with his charm and wit to draw in his conquests. "One and done" was his motto. When we were younger, I thought it was a lonely way to live, never connecting with someone, but I'd come to believe he had the right idea.

Don't get close to anyone and you can't get hurt.

Mike caught my eye as I approached. The brunette was sitting on his lap, laughing at something he'd said before I walked over. His left hand tightened around her waist as he gestured for me to sit with the other. Recognizing the possessive sign he cast immediately, I inwardly chuckled. All men were cut from the same cloth. We all had a bit of caveman lurking around inside us, staking a claim on the person of our choice, warning all others to stay away. It was a subtle movement on his part but one that didn't go unnoticed. All males understood the code and when those lines were crossed, the inner beasts often emerged. Thankfully, my inner caveman had not been tested in a very long time.

"It's about time you got here." He whispered something to her before focusing on me. "I thought I was gonna have to come looking for you," he mumbled, his hand disappearing beneath the woman's shirt and working his way to her breast.

"Are you sure you don't want to be alone?" I suddenly felt like the third wheel. I understood his primal need to get laid, but I thought he wanted to hang out, just the two of us. At least that was the story he sold to me earlier, when he all but harassed me to come out with him, going so far as to make me feel guilty for blowing him off the time before.

Without responding, he leaned into his guest and said something else in her ear, something that caused her cheeks to flush before she stood, walking away without a glance back at him.

"What did you say to her?" I asked, motioning for a waitress so I could order a drink.

"I told her what I was gonna do to her later on if she was still around when you and I were done." A cocky grin tipped his lips as he ran a hand through his curly hair.

Locking eyes with the pretty blonde waitress as she sauntered over calmed me because a drink would shortly follow her arrival. She stumbled as she closed in, glancing between the two of us, and whatever vibe I gave her made her focus her attention solely on Mike. And the horny bastard that he was charmed her, even though he'd had another woman practically humping him not two minutes earlier.

"What can I get for you both?" she asked, making eye contact with me first, then going back to eye-fucking my buddy. I wasn't offended. In truth, I was grateful she wasn't hitting on me because I didn't have the energy required to participate in such a dance.

"I'll take a scotch. Single malt. Neat. Give me the best you have."

"Make it two," Mike announced, gripping the waitress's hand as she turned to walk away. "And can you hurry? My dear friend here hasn't been laid in a long time, and I need to loosen him up some so he can wipe away the cobwebs." Her eyes landed back on me, and she smiled but turned away from us before I could say anything in my defense, although I had no idea what that would have been.

"You're something else," I huffed, but I wasn't surprised. Mike never tired of trying to shock people, hardly ever holding anything back. And it was for those exact reasons that he often got the brunt of my mother's chastisement. A light tap to the back of his head, a slap on his arm, or even a tug on his ear was often what happened when he opened his mouth around my family.

"What? You *do* need to get laid." Drumming his fingers on the table, he studied me for several seconds. "When was the last time you had sex? And with *yourself* doesn't count."

"Not that it's any of your damn business, but it was two nights ago."

Where the hell is my drink?

"Yeah? With who?"

"With the woman I had sex with," I retorted, arching my brow in mock annoyance.

"Uh-huh," he mumbled, continuing to strum his fingers on the polished wood.

When our waitress finally returned, I snatched my drink from her tray and swallowed a hefty amount, the liquid slithering down my throat and coating my nerves. It was no Glenmorangie, but it would do the trick for the evening.

Craning my neck from side to side and slinking further into my seat, I was finally beginning to relax. Mike, on the other hand, fidgeted, his focus all over the place.

"So," I started, taking another sip of my drink, "what did you want to talk about?"

"What makes you think I want to talk about anything?" I should've expected him to rebuff my question. He barely talked about himself, other than who he'd taken to bed, of course. His interest flicked around the bar, but I saw the small crack in his façade. The face he liked to show the world slipped, and he tried his damndest to put it back in place. But I knew him well. "I just needed a wingman."

I barked out a laugh. "A wingman? Nice try." I'd seen Mike walk up to two women and their guy friend, blurt out his bullshit and then disappear inside the men's room with all three of them. There was no way in hell he needed me to be his hench-man. "Out with it, Hawkings."

We stared at each other for countless seconds, time crawling by as we tried to read the other.

Deflecting yet again, he asked, "So, who is this mystery woman you shagged two nights ago?"

"Shagged?" I laughed. "What, are you stuck in the seventies?"

"What's wrong with shagged? Would you prefer boned? Or banged? Or maybe you like horizontal mambo?" He laughed louder the more my face contorted with every one of his lame phrasings.

"There's something very wrong with you, my friend," I said, our waitress suddenly appearing and standing directly next to Mike. The top two buttons of her tightly fitted white shirt were undone, her cleavage on full show, either for tips or to ensure that the man she had her sights on reciprocated her lustful attention. Or both.

Mike pulled her close, his gaze sinking into hers. "Sweet-heart, do you find my friend attractive?"

Heat ricocheted through me, heightening the thrum of my pulse. I swore I was gonna punch him as soon as she walked away. Typically, I wasn't an excitable man, but putting me on the spot like that was enough to make my fists clench.

Flicking her eyes to me, she surveyed me before licking her lips. "Of course, I find him attractive. I have eyes, don't I?" The last thing I wanted to do was encourage him, so I kept my mouth shut, which was a hard feat to accomplish.

"Would you have sex with him?" he repeated.

"Many times" was her blatant response. She returned her attention to Mike, hoping in some way her answer to his ludi-crous questions had pleased him. His mouth twitched, and it was at that point I became more uncomfortable. Was his goal this evening to hang out and drink with me or was he going to try and convince me to embark in a threesome, an exploit he'd bragged about on numerous occasions, oftentimes with men and women alike. He knew I'd never slept with more than one woman at a time and told me outright I was missing out.

Keeping one woman from falling too far for me was hard enough, let alone two. I wasn't conceited by any means, but I spoke the truth. I was aware I was attractive; some would say very. Did I use it to my advantage sometimes? Sure. I *was* human, after all. But I didn't think I was God's gift to the female population.

I cleared my throat. "Are you done now?" My question was poised to Mike, but he didn't respond. Instead, he smacked the waitress on the ass before dismissing her with a wave of his hand. Once she was out of earshot, I leaned forward. "Pull that shit again and I'm gone."

"What's got your panties all bunched up? You never cared before."

"Well, I care now." Swallowing the remnants of my drink, I slammed the glass on the table, the sound putting my friend on alert. He leaned back in his chair, the corners of his brown eyes crinkling.

"All right. All right." He surrendered, throwing his hands in the air. "I'm sorry. Obviously, you're not in the mood to be messed with tonight."

"Obviously not," I retorted, keeping my eyes on him when our server returned with fresh drinks. Glowering at him drove home my earlier point that I didn't want to be the butt of his antics, and while I intimidated people when necessary, my demeanor wasn't working full force on him tonight. He loved to go toe-to-toe with me, and it irritated me most of the time.

"Listen, I'm sorry I was such a dick. Honestly. I'd rather rile you than deal with—" He lowered his head and grabbed the back of his neck, taking a moment before continuing. "I don't know what to do."

His raw emotion was a rarity to witness, so whatever bogged him down was grave. "What's the matter?"

"I don't even know where to begin."

"Start at the beginning then." We didn't have serious conversations often, choosing to keep our banter on the surface level, but one look at his change in demeanor told me he needed my support. I mentally kicked myself for avoiding all his invitations to hang out over the past couple weeks, and before I chastised myself further for being a shitty friend, he opened his mouth and blurted out two words.

"She's pregnant."

ELI

*I*f I'd been in the middle of swallowing my drink, I would have spit it out all over the table, my surprise genuine. My first thought, of course, was that he'd finally managed to slip one past the goalie, but then I remembered him telling me, on several unwanted occasions, that he made sure to wrap it up, especially since he barely knew the majority of the people he had sex with. But before I got ahead of myself, I asked the most obvious question.

"Who's pregnant?"

Mike pounded his fist on the table, our glasses rattling and drawing the attention of several nearby patrons. "Sierra." Slumping his shoulders forward and resting the weight of his head in his hands, he repeated, "Sierra is pregnant. My baby sister went and got herself knocked-up. She's only twenty-two, Eli." Taking a deep breath, he groaned, "twenty-fucking-two. She's a baby… having a baby."

"Well, she's not *that* young." He leaned in, the murderous look in his eyes screaming I chose the wrong thing to say. I showed him my palms. "Sorry. Go ahead."

While he geared up for the rest of his rant, I signaled for our waitress, who had just dropped off a tray of drinks two tables over. She sidled up next to Mike and gleamed when he winked at her, his mood switching on a dime. "We're gonna need a few more, sweetheart," he confessed, steeling his mask until she walked away. He didn't say anything else until she came back with the alcohol, and I didn't pressure him to continue until he was comfortable doing so.

Once we were alone, he started back in. "She refused to tell me who did this to her." He relaxed against the seat and stretched his arm forward on the table, gliding his glass back and forth in a way of distraction, but it didn't help. "Fuck." His teeth worked furiously over his bottom lip.

Mike had been taking care of Sierra since she was ten years old, him being thirteen years her senior. Their parents had died in a tragic fire, and he'd assumed responsibility for her soon after, ensuring she graduated high school before enrolling in college. Any financial problems she encountered, he was right there to help fix them. He was more of a father to Sierra than a big brother, and in taking on that role, he also tried to keep her away from guys like him. He'd chased away many a boyfriend, which only resulted in weeks of radio silence between the two of them. In the end, he never apologized for protecting her, and because she loved her brother fiercely, she always ended up forgiving him.

"How is she doing with the news? Is she happy about it? Upset? Is the guy willing to stick around and do the right thing, or was he a one-night stand?" He flared his nostrils and shot me a death glare when my last questioned registered.

Grinding his teeth, he seethed, "She's goddamn happy about it. Said the bastard is a good guy and they're in love." Drowning some of his rage with a hefty gulp of his scotch, he looked more defeated than angry. "I threatened to camp out at her apartment until she told me his name. And you wanna know what she did?" His question was rhetorical, of course. "She kicked me out of her place. Can you believe that shit?" Finishing off his drink, he reached for mine, and I didn't say a word because he needed it more than I did.

"She knows you're going to beat the shit out of the poor guy. It's why she didn't tell you his name."

"'Poor guy'?" he asked incredulously. "He knocked up my baby sister. He deserves a pounding for that." His face contorted with another wave of fury.

"Listen, I totally understand where you're coming from, man. I do. But the only thing you're going to do is push her further away from you if you keep acting like a hothead. Is that what you want?" A pause ensued. "Do you?" I repeated.

"No!" he finally admitted.

"Then I think you know what to do." He looked at me as if I'd spoken a foreign language. "You have to apologize, let her know that you'll be there for her in any way she needs you to be."

He scoffed and shook his head. "Not gonna happen."

"Then you can kiss your relationship with your sister good-bye." Being blunt and to the point was the only way Mike would listen, not sugarcoating shit. Besides, Sierra was as stubborn as he was, and if he didn't initiate the first step, they wouldn't end up talking until his niece or nephew was old enough to intervene.

"Shit." His lip curled in disgust. "I'm still gonna mess him up once I find out who he is."

"Well, not too badly because he just might be your brother-in-law someday."

"Not funny," he responded, but a hint of a grin lifted the corner of his mouth.

Since his mood had dissipated, I let him in on my original thoughts when he initially uttered those two words.

"I thought *you* got someone pregnant."

"Are you out of your mind?" His brows were practically buried in his hairline. "No way am I having kids."

"Well, then. There's your silver lining to this whole situation." We clinked glasses.

"I guess so."

SEVERAL DRINKS LATER, Mike and I were feeling good. We could handle our alcohol, had enough experience in doing so with many a late night under our belts. We were in the middle of reminiscing about some shit we did in high school, when a woman standing by the bar caught my attention.

"This is all I need," I mumbled, drawing his focus.

He turned his head in her direction and released a low whistle. "Some hot chick is staring at you, but if you don't want to be bothered, I'll take one for the team."

"Don't you think you have enough people on your team?" I stammered, more aggression in my tone than intended.

"What's wrong with you?"

"Nothing." I dared to look toward the bar again, and sure enough, she was still looking my way. "Remember I told you I had sex two nights ago?"

"Yeah."

"Well," I gestured with my thumb, pointing toward the bar, "it was with her."

"And you don't want a repeat?

"It's not that. I've been sleeping with her for almost three months and now I have to end it."

The crooked smile that appeared on Mike's face irritated me because I could predict what he'd say next, simply because he said it on several occasions.

"What's with you and that damn three-month rule?

"What's with your 'one and done' stature?" I threw back at him.

"Touché."

Winning that argument did nothing to dampen the level of unease that twisted me up inside. I wasn't heartless. I didn't want to hurt her, but our arrangement had reached the end, for me, at least. "She wants more, and I can't give it to her."

"You don't *want* to give it to her. There's a big difference. Ever since—" He had the decency to look away for a moment, careful not to mention her name. "You've just shut down, punishing women for the sins of one." My gut churned at the reminder, but anger coiled deep within me, and before I could stop myself, the alcohol I'd consumed spurring me on, I lashed out.

"Maybe you should psychoanalyze yourself before you try that shit on me. You have plenty of your own issues, pushing people away so you don't get too close."

He refused to argue, a sentiment I very much appreciated. "Your woman is walking this way."

I barely managed to calm myself enough to appear unaffected, the mask I often showed most of the world. My family and Mike were the only ones who saw the cracks in my illusion from time to time.

The moment Beth approached, my vision hazed, and I choked on a deep pull of air. The last thing I wanted to do was talk to her, especially in the state I found myself, but her arrival gave me no choice in the matter. I sensed her eyes on me before I looked up at her, needing the tension-filled seconds to hash out what I was going to say. Mike rose from his seat and extended his hand in greeting, his politeness reminding me that I was never this rude, slightly intoxicated or not.

I stood seconds later and offered her a seat next to me. Her face lit up at the gesture, her stare raking over me in appreciation, urging me to have the talk with her the very next day.

If I wasn't so wrapped up in the content of our impending discussion, I could've appreciated the way her red dress accentuated the plumpness of her tits or the way the fabric hugged her curvy body. Her blonde hair was down and poker-straight, a style that suited her.

Her hand found mine and she gave me a slight squeeze. "How are you, Eli?" Her question was simple yet loaded, her brown eyes scouring over my features, looking for any indication I was happy to see her, or if I was still upset with her for pushing me about doing something outside the bedroom.

"I'm good." With resigned annoyance, I blurted, "What are you doing here?" She flinched but recovered quickly, ghosting me a smile before looking down at her hand resting on the top of the table. When I glanced at Mike, I saw the disapproving look on his face, but instead of silently warring with him with raised brows and scowls, I turned my attention back toward Beth. I made a small noise with my throat and she met my eyes.

"A few friends wanted to come out for a drink. After a lot of nagging on their part, I finally gave in." She leaned closer. "And I'm glad I did." I hadn't noticed when she first walked over, but Beth was tipsy. A few of her words slurred when she spoke, and her eyes had a glassy sheen.

Realizing I was in a bind, Mike spoke up and saved me.

"It was nice meeting you, Beth, but Eli and I were on our way out. We have an early meeting tomorrow and this one," he said, jabbing his thumb in my direction, "needs his rest. It's important he's on his A-game."

Beth ran her finger down my arm. "I was hoping you could meet some of my friends, then we could go back to my place." My friend wasn't going to save me twice.

"I can't. Mike's right. I have to be well rested before the meeting tomorrow. Another night perhaps," I lied, hoping she wouldn't push the issue. Her face fell, but she tried to smile anyway. She failed. The slight quiver of her bottom lip screamed it was my cue to leave.

Shuffling out of the booth, I gave her my hand to hold while she transitioned from sitting to standing. I threw several bills on the table before ushering her back toward her group of friends. Looking back to see if Mike was behind me, I saw him still seated, sandwiched between the woman who'd been sitting on his lap when I first arrived and our waitress. Man, he worked fast.

Once I'd walked outside, the night air did nothing to relieve me of all the scrambled thoughts in my head, from the upcoming week's workload to Mike's issue with his sister, to Beth. Because I'd had too much to drink to feel comfortable driving home, I reached for the back door of one of the many cabs the hotel had on reserve for its guests.

The entire way home, I contemplated ways of getting back at Mike for pulling some of his slick shit earlier, as well as reminding myself to thank him for my escape plan.

KALISTA

"There you are," Mom sang, bouncing into the kitchen as if it was the best day of her life. Reaching for a mug, she filled it to the brim with the coffee I'd just brewed, inhaling its aroma before taking a sip.

It was still early in the morning, but I hadn't slept well the night before. Being back in my hometown messed with me. I feared seeing Eli every time I left the house, even though the probability of running into him were slim. That was as long as he continued to be oblivious that I'd come home.

Over the years, I'd asked my mom about him, wanting to know how his life had turned out without me. While my heart hurt every time we had those conversations, I was pleased to eventually learn he had become the youngest partner in his law firm. A fraction of the guilt I'd felt about leaving him dissipated because there was no way his life would've turned out that well had I stayed.

I loved him so much back then I was willing to sacrifice my own happiness, and while I still cared for him, seeing him again would tear me apart, even after fifteen years.

"Sweetheart?" Mom waved her hand in front of my face. I

hadn't heard a thing she said, too wrapped up in the memory of long ago.

"Sorry. I guess I'm not awake yet." The smile I gave her was weak at best, so many things wracking my poor brain, I couldn't decide which one to give consideration to first. So, I swung my attention back to her.

No matter what time of the day it was, she always looked radiant, this morning being no exception. Her dark hair was pulled away from her face in a high ponytail, the simple style making her look more like my older sister than my mother.

"Where are you off to at this ungodly hour?" Dressed in black yoga pants and a fitted light blue sweatshirt, complete with matching sneakers on her small feet, my question seemed asinine. She'd never liked gyms, and there was no way she'd run errands in her workout outfit so that only left one viable option. "When did you start walking?"

"Actually, I jog. It's good for the soul."

"Yeah? And does this soul have a name?" I poured myself a cup of hot joe before leaning my hip against the counter. My mom hardly ever did anything that wasn't motivated by a man, a trait I was thankful I hadn't inherited.

"Kevin. And before you grill me, he's a really nice man who I've been seeing for close to a month now."

"And where did you meet this Kevin?"

Justine Ellington was beautiful, and men shamelessly flirted with her all the time, so I wasn't surprised she'd confirmed her sudden interest in "jogging" was due to a man. And while she had the right to live her life how she wanted, I didn't think it was healthy for her to flit from one guy to another, a habit she'd done my entire life.

"At the grocery store. Can you believe we reached for the same pineapple?" She tilted her head to the side and stared off into space, remembering the moment, I was sure. My mother...

the hopeless romantic. Or glutton for punishment. I wasn't quite sure.

"Just be careful. I'd hate for you to get hurt. Again." I felt the need to throw in my two cents, even if she hadn't asked for it.

"Enough about me," she said, waving her hand in the air. "What are your plans?" She widened her stance and bent over at the waist, moving from side to side to stretch each leg before her run.

"I'm going to visit some schools and ask about enrollment. Then I'm off to look for a job." I bit my lip in trepidation, the day's errands already making me nervous. Intuition punched me with unease, but I chalked the anxiety up to being home again.

After standing and stretching her arms above her head, she stood next to me, resting her hand over mine. "Kalista, I know that look. You think I haven't paid you much attention, but I know my own daughter. Calm down. The chances of you running into him are slim to none. He doesn't live around here anymore. Granted, he doesn't live far away, but you shouldn't have to deal with seeing him until you're ready." Her words solidified my nervousness, yet they oddly appeased me as well. She was out the door after her words of wisdom, leaving me to stand there alone with my rampant thoughts.

Not until I was ready?

Would I ever be ready to see him again?

EXHAUSTION DEPLETED the last of my energy as I dragged my tired limbs into a local coffee shop, needing another caffeine boost in order to make the drive back home. After placing my order, I found an empty table near the back and out of the way of the other patrons.

I'd been at it all day, visiting four schools and touring their grounds, trying to decide on the best one. Afterward, I'd taken to searching for employment. Another tiresome venture.

Several of the hospitals I'd applied at had postings for a radiologist technician, the position I'd held back in Vermont. Now all I had to do was wait to hear back about an interview.

Lost inside my own head, mulling over my mental checklist of things I still had to take care of, I almost missed the woman behind the counter calling my name. When she saw me walking toward her, she smiled and held out my coffee, but before I reached to take it, someone else snatched it from her. Swiveling my head to the left, a surprised gasp fell from my mouth when I saw who had stolen my drink.

Mike Hawkings stood next to me, looking much the same as he had the last time I saw him fifteen years ago. The only differences were a few extra lines around his eyes, and his dark curly hair was slightly longer than I remembered.

"Kalista Ellington? Is that really you?" A salacious smile tipped his lips. "Holy shit, woman! It's like looking at a ghost."

"Hi, Mike." I'd finally found my words, the shock at seeing him slowly dissolving. "How are you?" He and Eli had been as thick as thieves growing up, and I couldn't help but wonder if they were still in contact, although I would never dare ask such a question for fear he'd say yes. And that would mean Eli would be alerted to my arrival back home, and I wasn't ready to face what that would mean.

His smile widened, showcasing his dimple that had made many a girl swoon. When we were younger, Mike had been a walking hormone, hitting on every female who interested him, including me, although he'd only made that mistake once. His crass words earned him a punch in the face from Eli. Mike had laughed as blood poured from his nose, but he'd realized right then I was off-limits.

"I'm good." His eyes raked the full length of me. "I still can't believe it's you." He gave my arm a gentle squeeze and I relaxed some. Uprooting my life had taken a toll on me, and seeing a familiar face just helped to ease some of my tension, even though he could heighten my apprehension with the mere mention of a certain someone. "How long has it been?"

"Too long," I confessed, reaching for the coffee he still held. "Do you want to join me?" I asked, gesturing to where I'd been sitting.

"Absolutely."

After we were seated, I averted my eyes every few seconds, my leg bouncing nervously under the table. Taking small sips of my hot beverage, I contemplated which topics would be safe to discuss, but most memories I had of Mike and me involved Eli.

"So," he started, tapping his fingers on the table, "does he know you're here?" *Nothing like getting right to the point.*

"Who?"

Mike cocked his brow and leaned back in his chair, his demeanor telling me he thought my question was asinine.

Fidgeting in my seat wouldn't deter him. He enjoyed seeing people sweat, always had. He was blunt, full-force, and no-holds-barred, often spewing whatever he wanted just to get a reaction, even if his words landed him in hot water.

"I don't know who you're talking about." Right after my lie, my right eye twitched, which was my tell.

"Uh-huh," he mumbled, crossing his arms, the fabric of his black T-shirt stretching over his chest. He was still in great shape, and for as much as I wanted to appreciate his looks, which had become even more handsome with age, my mind drifted to thoughts of Eli, wondering what he looked like after all these years. "Come on, Kalista. You know me well enough to know this is happening. I'm not letting you leave here until you talk to me."

My breathing had suddenly become as erratic as my heart-beat, my mouth dryer than it was a second ago. Although I dreaded our talk, I decided honesty was best.

"I only moved back a week ago." I slumped in my chair because I knew where this conversation was headed.

"Are you staying at your mom's?"

"For now."

Seconds passed before he asked his next question. "Are you planning on reaching out, to let him know the woman who tore his heart from his chest is now back in town?" A slight tremor shook his voice. He attempted to appear aloof, but his protectiveness over his longtime friend seeped through.

"You're still in touch with him?" I asked, desperate to steer his attention away from his question.

"Of course. I didn't abandon him like you did." His voice rose on the last word, his angry eyes boring into mine. Composure seemed to be a struggle for him.

I squirmed in my seat, but no amount of unease would release me from answering. Mike would push me until I either shouted for him to stop or fled the shop, neither of which was ideal.

"Can we please not do this right now?" My voice shook, and while I silently implored him to let me off the hook, tears welled in my eyes and threatened to spill over. I realized Mike was the lesser of two evils, and even though I wanted to say something, anything, my mouth clamped shut while the tension bloomed heavily in the air between us. After a minute of neither one of us speaking, he slapped the top of the table, causing me to jerk back with the surprise.

"You might not want to have this conversation with me, sweetheart, but it's better than having it with Eli. Don't you think?" His condescending tone angered me, and while I thought we could have a civilized discussion, I realized how wrong I'd been. I reached for my keys sitting on top of the table, but Mike snatched them away from me.

"Give them back," I demanded, my outstretched palm face up.

"Not until you answer my question."

Deciding not to prolong the standoff any further, I answered. "No, all right? No," I said louder. "I haven't told anyone I'm back home. Are you happy now?"

"Happy? No. Pissed? Yeah, pissed pretty much describes how I'm feeling." The muscle in his jaw ticked before he continued. "It took Eli years to get over you. And now you're back to fuck things up again and send his head in the wrong direction."

"That's not my intention. Truly. I have no plans to contact him. I know what I did hurt him, even though I had my reasons at the time."

"Yeah? And what were those?"

"None of your damn business." I was tired of him trying to make me feel like shit. I'd done it enough to myself over the years. Nothing anyone could say to me would lessen the amount of pain I'd inflicted on myself since the day I'd left.

"You know I'm gonna have to tell him, don't you?'

Instantly going into panic mode, even though I knew it would come to this, I stammered over my words. "Pl-Please, don't s-say anything to Eli."

Shit! Why did I have to wander into this damn coffee shop?

Finally, Mike rose from his seat and tossed my keys on the table. "Do the right thing," he said before walking toward the door. The moment he was gone, I was left feeling worse than I had in years.

ELI

*W*ith deadlines fast approaching, I barely had time to sleep, let alone talk to anyone who wasn't a client. Mike had called me often over the past two days, his voice mails vague, telling me he had to talk to me right away, yet he never said what about. And every time I remembered to call him back, I'd gotten distracted with one thing or another.

At first, I couldn't fathom what would be that urgent, then I remembered his baby sister was pregnant. Even though I warned him to behave himself and not get into any trouble over the situation, Mike always did as he pleased. I only hoped he hadn't done something that would have caused him to get arrested, like beating the shit out of whoever knocked up Sierra.

Dismissing the thought as ludicrous, knowing damn well I would have been informed if he'd been arrested, I saved the document I was working on, picked up my office phone and dialed his number, waiting for the call to connect.

It rang once.

Twice.

Before it rang a third time, the door to my office flung open, a disheveled Mike looming in the doorway, his hair ruffled more than usual. An exasperated look overshadowed his sullen features while he braced his arms on each side of the frame.

"What the hell, Warner!" he yelled. "Don't you know how to answer your damn phone?" Within seconds, he was next to me.

While it was clear he was annoyed with my lack of communication, there was another emotion lurking behind his eyes. He chewed on the corner of his lip, doing his best to disguise his reaction as pure irritation.

"Sorry, man, but I've been busy." A sudden rush of agitation washed over me as I watched my friend. His eyes darted from me to around my office and back again. When he took to pacing, I leaned back in my chair and studied him further.

"Do you have anything to drink?" he asked, never waiting for me to answer before he moved toward the small liquor cabinet in the corner of my office. He tipped the decanter and poured himself a scotch, swallowing the contents in a single gulp before pouring another.

"Does your mood have anything to do with Sierra?"

His eyes locked on mine and he sipped his second drink with reservation. "I wish."

"Wow. That bad, huh?" My chuckle fell flat when he poured more scotch, but that time into a different glass.

Mike broached the space between us and shoved the drink at me.

"You're gonna need this."

Doing an about-face, he walked toward the leather sofa and sat down, his glass dangling from his fingertips. He avoided looking at me, and the more time that passed in silence, the more my heart sped up.

"What the hell is wrong with you?" I tried to keep some semblance of composure, but his downtrodden state freaked me out.

Raising his head, he grimaced, the pained look on his face telling me everything and nothing at all. "Thank God you're sitting down. Although, I wanted to tell you this after we'd had a couple of these," he grumbled, raising his glass in the air. "It would have made it so much better. Well, not better... but easier. Shit, that's not right, either. Not easier, but...," he rambled on.

"Mike!" I shouted, the boom from my voice reverberating loudly around the room, causing him to flinch in surprise. "What are you trying to tell me? Out with it already!"

His breath rushed out of his mouth with force. "She's back, Eli." He dropped his gaze from mine and repeated, "She's back."

I knit my brows so tight I almost gave myself an instant headache. My lips parted to speak, but he beat me to it, explaining what he meant by *she's back*.

One single word dropped from his mouth, destroying the carefully orchestrated world I'd built for myself over the past fifteen years.

"Kalista."

One name and I was rocked to my core. The air in the room stopped circulating and my breathing slowed. Hell, my heart stopped beating for what felt like forever.

I'd tried for years to rid myself of that woman's memory, failing at every turn, but I'd at least gotten to the point where I didn't think about her every single day.

Until recently.

Hearing her name again brought back all those emotions from years before when I'd discovered she'd left me. My vision tunneled with hurt, pain, and anger, and I was so consumed with the past that I hadn't realized Mike stood by my chair, his hands wedged deep in his pockets.

He was motionless, which only served to spur the onslaught of fury that boiled my blood. Where my heartbeat had slowed moments ago, it now slammed against my ribcage, threatening to arrest if I didn't control the adrenaline coursing through me. I gripped the arms of my chair so tight, my knuckles turned white. When the muscle in my jaw pulsed, I realized my dear friend was going to witness my explosion in T-minus…

Three…

Two…

One…

Jumping up, I shoved him hard, yelling in his face because I had no one else to direct my anger at. "What do you mean she's back? What are you telling me, Mike?" My hands connected with his chest once more, shoving him as far from me as possible. I needed to expel my confusion and rage, gifting my brain those few precious seconds to compute what he told me, to figure out exactly what they meant.

Clenching my fists at my sides, I took a menacing step toward one of my oldest friends, but he side-stepped me and walked around the desk to move out of the eye of the storm. He knew what was coming because he'd witnessed it once before.

When she deserted me all those years ago.

I'd been so clouded with rage afterward, I didn't know how to react except to freak out, Mike catching my right hook to his jaw when he'd tried to tell me to calm down.

"Eli," he warned. "I will hit you back if you put your hands on me again." He retreated another step before continuing. "I understand you're upset, but you need to take a breath." Mike wasn't afraid of me. He was simply refraining from contributing to my volatile behavior. "Eli!" he boomed, finally breaking through my brief snap with reality. Focusing on his face, I saw him, really saw him for the first time since he'd told me what I never wanted to hear.

Or did I?

I'd tried to prepare myself in the past, longing to hear such news but refusing to ever believe she would come back. I'd become numb realizing I would never be given the closure that might have helped me to move on. I wanted answers, but she'd taken them with her the day she left.

Tipping his head to the side, he gauged whether he should approach. I nodded, indicating I was fine. Well... not fine, but well enough to continue our conversation in a non-threatening way.

Swallowing the drink Mike poured for me earlier, I refilled my glass and finished that one in two gulps, making myself a third. I plopped down on the couch afterward, resting my head against the back and closing my eyes. My mind warred between hearing what Mike had to say and drinking myself into oblivion before he uttered another filthy word.

Countless heart-breaking, silent minutes passed before I opened my mouth, my lids remaining closed to block out my reality.

"How do you know she's back?" I waited in deafening silence until I heard him draw a breath.

"I ran into her at that coffee shop near my garage." I felt the couch dip, finding his weight next to me somewhat comforting. "I was shocked, to say the least. Thought I was seeing a ghost." Hearing him swallow some of his drink, I relaxed in the knowledge that my buddy would get rip-roaring drunk with me, if that was the road I chose to travel.

Finally prying my eyes open, I turned to focus on him, who, to no fault of his own, ripped me apart with mere words. I hadn't even heard the whole story, yet my nerves clawed at me from the inside. But I needed to know every detail, slow and steady, then decide what to do afterward, if anything.

Jerking my chin for him to continue, I braced myself for the details of their surprise run-in.

"We sat down for a few minutes, simple pleasantries at first, but I couldn't hold my tongue for long. She fucked you up, man, and I let her know about it. She didn't say much until I informed her I was gonna tell you she moved back home. Then she got nervous. Antsy even."

My heart skipped a beat. "Wait. She's back for good? Like,

living here permanently? She's not just visiting?" My palms started to sweat in anticipation, a heat spiraling through my core.

Maybe it's the alcohol.

"That's what she said. She's staying at her mom's for now." He tipped back the rest of his drink, his eyes on me the entire time, assessing my reaction and probably preparing himself in case I lost my temper again.

Dreading the answers, I asked my next questions. "Is she married? Does she have kids?" Holding my breath did wonders at calming my erratic heart, if only for a few seconds. If I wasn't breathing, I wasn't living. And if I wasn't living, heartache couldn't rip my life away from me yet again.

He shook his head while uttering, "Not that I know of. I didn't see a ring on her finger, and she never mentioned having any ankle biters, although I didn't give her much of a chance to talk. I pretty much read her the riot act before I left. But I know one thing, she didn't want me to tell you she's here."

"Yeah, I'm sure running into me is the last thing she wants because then that would mean she'd have to explain herself." I slumped forward on the couch, my arms resting on my thighs. I swore my head was too heavy for my shoulders, the weight of what he'd told me too much to process.

Mike said she didn't make any mention of having children, and he didn't see a ring, but that didn't mean either one of those scenarios was true. Without warning, memories bombarded me with the times we used to sit up late at night, wrapped up in each other after making love, and talking about one day getting married and having a boatload of kids.

"How did she look?" *Please, don't tell me she looks good.*

"Sorry to say this, man, but she looks even better than she did back then. Something certainly agrees with her." We both winced at his choice of words. "Sorry," he repeated, raking his fingers through his hair.

A little while later, after we'd downed another drink, Mike asked me his final question.

"So… what are you going to do now?"

Instead of answering, I walked toward the wall of windows on the other side of my office, bracing myself against the pane and looking out at the world below. My only acknowledgment of his question was a painful shrug.

That *was* the million-dollar question, after all.

KALISTA

$\mathcal{F}$orty-eight long hours had dragged by since my run in with Mike and I couldn't help but wonder if he'd talked to Eli yet. Oh, who was I kidding? He probably called him the second he left the coffee shop. For all I knew they could be plotting to surprise me, catch me off guard and make me answer for my betrayal.

Dramatics were all I had, but I had hurt Eli, Mike attesting to such. Not that I needed his acknowledgment. When I left that note for the man I loved, I was a coward. I should've told him I was leaving face-to-face, but I couldn't risk him talking me out of it.

Over the years, I often wondered if Eli had moved on.

Did he ever think about me?

Did he hate me?

Had he found someone else to love?

I had so many questions, and I wasn't sure yet whether I wanted them answered.

After a much-needed long, hot shower, the day's worries seemed to drift to the waste side, waiting until the break of dawn to come back and haunt me, I was sure. I was midstride into the center of my bedroom when the chime of the doorbell surprised me. Glancing at the clock on my bedside table, I saw the time was just after nine at night. Remaining motionless, as if the person standing on the porch could detect me in some way, I slowed my breathing while I contemplated what to do. As I moved toward the window to see if I could see anything, the large maple tree sometimes obstructing my view of the street, the bell rang again, only this time the sound was followed by three raps on the solid wood of the door.

Quickly eliminating my mom from the equation because she was staying overnight at Kevin's, I ran down the short list of possibilities. I'd told Mike I was staying here for the time being, so it could be him. Or Eli could be standing there instead, furious and wanting answers.

Another knock on the front door and I quickly threw on a pair of white lounge pants and an old Southern University of Vermont T-shirt. Walking down the hall and past the bedroom on my right, I closed the door completely, fearing the sounds were going to disturb him, causing an even graver situation for me, depending on who was here. He hadn't been feeling well so he'd turned in early, otherwise I was sure he would've raced down the steps to answer the door before I could.

Each step I took down the stairs heightened my worry. Bombarded with all different scenarios, I tried to concoct answers and excuses, but the problem was I didn't know the questions, too many to pinpoint just a few.

Why had I left?

What was I thinking?

When had I turned selfish?

Was there a specific reason why I took off?

When I finally reached the bottom of the staircase, the door several feet in front of me, I hoped and prayed the person on the other side wasn't Eli. There were too many variables at play, things I still needed to think about before we saw each other again.

With my hand braced against the side of the window, I slowly pulled back the curtain, hoping to catch of glimpse of the mystery visitor before I opened the door, and as luck would have it, the person took a step back at that exact moment. My momentary relief was replaced with a pang of guilt.

Jasmine Stacks, a dear friend of mine from years back, stood on my front porch. The past flooded in when I saw her, remembering the two of us had been glued at the hip whenever I'd been apart from Eli. We'd formed a bond much like that of sisters early on and my heart had broken when I'd left her behind. I'd never contacted her and told her why because I'd feared she'd tell Eli.

I didn't know what her reaction would be once we laid eyes on each other. She could yell at me for taking off without so much as a word or she could pull me into a hug and cry. I was going in blind, but I owed it to Jasmine to see where our encounter would lead. Forcing myself back into the moment, I released the curtain and wrapped my fingers around the doorknob.

As soon as the barrier between us swung open, my former best friend stepped back, her posture rigid and her eyes wide in shock.

"Kalista? Is that really you?" she asked, launching herself at me before I could form any sort of response in my head, her small frame crashing into me while she wrapped her arms around me to pull me closer.

I swore she hugged me for a full minute before she pulled away, never averting her eyes from my face. Jasmine looked even more beautiful—the years certainly having been kind to her. Shorter than my five-eight frame, her blonde hair was cut to just below her perfectly shaped ears, a fitting style for her features. She remained willowy in stature, her physique the envy of many I was sure, myself included.

I reached for her hand to pull her inside, pieces of memories filtering in at the connection.

"Jasmine," I finally spoke, "how are you?" The past fifteen years slipped away as if we'd never been apart. A smile tipped her lips, but it was the glassiness of her eyes that pained me.

She stepped forward and brought me in for another hug, this embrace quicker than her initial one. "I can't believe it's really you." When she stepped back, she stood tall and smacked me on the arm, more playful than hurtful. "Why didn't you tell me you were back?" She pursed her lips and frowned.

"I haven't told anyone, Jas. I'm not sure how to deal with everything that's going on just yet, and I suppose I was hoping for more time to figure it out." Mine was a lame excuse, but it was my truth. "How did you know I was here, anyway?"

"Melinda saw you around town the other day, and of course you know she loves to talk." She scrunched her face slightly, and I remembered what a gossip Melinda was. "I would've come earlier, but I had to wait for my husband to come home to watch the kids."

My eyes dipped to look at her left hand and saw two rings on the designated finger. I was excited for her that she'd found someone to settle down with and have children yet saddened I'd missed out by not being here to celebrate with her.

I guided her toward the living room to take a seat before disappearing into the kitchen to retrieve a bottle of wine and two glasses.

We'd always been able to sit in easy silence, but right then, there was an uncertainty zinging between us, and I prayed I possessed the comfortability to speak with her like I'd once been able to do.

"So, where have you been all these years?" she asked, breaking the quiet and accepting the glass of wine. Leaning back against the sofa, she crossed her legs and looked relaxed, although her tense expression belied her body language. She was full of unspoken questions, and I only hoped I could give her the answers she wanted, all without revealing too much too soon. I had to be smart about what I said; otherwise, I could end up creating more stress for myself.

I didn't need to reflect on my actions because they haunted me day in and day out. Not only had I abandoned the love of my life, but I left my best friend in the dust as well, casting her aside without another thought. At least, I was sure that was how she perceived my actions, although it was anything but.

I'd lost many nights of sleep because of the war of emotions raging inside my head.

"I moved to Vermont," I answered, my voice sounding defeated, and I'd only just begun. "I needed to pick somewhere he wouldn't think to look." I closed my eyes, remembering the day I'd left like it just happened. The moment Jasmine placed her hand over mine, my lids flew open, my eyes becoming glassy at witnessing the pain in hers.

"I've missed you so much." She pulled me into another hug, where we stayed wrapped in each other's embrace until we had both calmed. "I'm so angry with you," she mumbled, right before reaching for her drink. I didn't say a word while she sipped generously at her wine, or when she narrowed her gaze at me, realizing she had every right to take her time in telling tell me whatever she wished. I owed her that much, at least. "I can't believe you took off without telling me. Not a word, Kalista. I thought I meant more to you." A lone tear slipped down her cheek and gutted me.

"You did." I swallowed hard. "You do." The air between us suddenly became stifling, but I had earned the right to be uncomfortable while in her presence. My punishment for deserting her. "If it makes you feel any better, my decision to leave has tortured me every single day since." Having Jasmine with me right then made me happy, grateful she'd taken the initiative to seek me out, but at the same time, my past decision reared its ugly head, strangling me with an immense amount of guilt.

She wiped away another tear. "Well, it *does* make me feel a little better. I ain't gonna lie." Her short laughter was appreciated.

Over the next two hours, I found out about all the events in her life that happened, my regret amping to a whole other level. Jasmine married a man she'd met in college, and they had two children, a boy and a girl, both with the same shade of blonde as her own. They were beautiful, as was evident in the many pictures she showed me on her phone. While I was happy for her, I was sad I'd missed out on celebrating the milestones in her life. Her wedding day, her pregnancies, and every day in between and since.

I did my best to veer the conversation to her and her alone, but eventually, I had to answer her questions. Starting with what I'd done to support myself and ending with brief accounts of the few men I'd dated over the years, two of them not lasting more than several weeks.

There were some details I wasn't prepared to share with Jasmine just yet, but the decision was stolen from me when I heard his bedroom door open. Footsteps sounded above us, drawing not only my attention but hers, as well.

"Is your mom home? Did we wake her up?" I wished with everything in me that was the case, but she was about to find out it wasn't.

The noise overhead drifted down the stairs. I could have lied and told her it was my mother, run to the stairwell, and helped to protect my secret a little while longer, but after spending time with Jasmine tonight, I decided that I needed her support and understanding. Besides, this might be the first step to helping me rid some of my remorse.

Rooted in my seat, I waited for him to come around the corner.

"Mom? Who are you talking to?" He shuffled forward, his dark hair sticking up in the back and making him look so freaking adorable. He hated when I called him that, but I couldn't help myself. *"Adorable is for little kids,"* he would say. All of fourteen and he viewed himself on the verge of adulthood already.

As my son came to stand beside me, his hip resting against the arm of the sofa, I saw him glance from me to Jasmine, fully awake now as he smiled at her. He was handsome beyond belief, every bit his father.

His full name was Holden Eli Ellington. The decision not to take his father's last name had been difficult, but in the end, it was what I deemed best.

"Holy shit," my friend exclaimed beside me, grimacing when she realized she'd cursed. She inched forward to garner a better look at my boy.

Looking confused, Holden nudged me with his arm and jerked his head in her direction. I'd totally lost my manners, and he'd just called me out on it. "Sorry, honey, this is my friend Jasmine. She stopped by to chat."

Leaning over me, he extended his hand in greeting. He was forever the young gentleman. While I was all too aware he was growing up, only four years from becoming a legal adult, he would always be my baby. "Nice to meet you. I'm Holden." He grinned, his smile infectious as Jasmine beamed from ear to ear.

"Nice to meet you, too, sweetheart."

Patting his arm, I said, "Why don't you go back to your room? I'll be turning in soon." Realizing my friend was going to interrogate me as soon as we were alone again, I wanted to get it over with as soon as possible.

"Okay." He bent down and kissed my cheek before repeating, "Nice to meet you," to Jasmine.

"You, too, Holden."

As soon as he was out of earshot, she turned her body toward me. "Out with it, Kalista. All of it." She settled back into the sofa for my tale. "I have so many questions. Jesus, woman, he looks exactly like him." With wide eyes, she waited for me to start talking.

Holden *was* the spitting image of Eli, but to hear someone else acknowledge it, other than my mother, of course, shot me straight through the heart. Guilt and regret melded together to make me feel even worse.

The few times my son asked me about his father, I'd simply told him we'd separated when I was still pregnant with him, and I hadn't heard from him since. Of course, I left out a lot of details, the shame eating at me every single day. I hated I'd taken the chance away for both to get to know each other, but I'd thought I was making the right decision at the time. The thoughts of a twenty-year-old are much different than those of a thirty-five-year-old woman.

When silence was no longer an option, I parted my lips, hoping some sense of relief would flood over me once I started talking. I'd learned the hard way that secrets burdened the soul, the only solace being able to expel the weight of it all.

"What do you want to know?" I waited, watching her mouth twitch and her eyes squint, clearly thinking of her first question.

"Why did you leave? Why did you take off and not tell anyone where you were going?" She placed her glass on the table before nestling back into the cushions.

"It's complicated, Jas. The only excuse I can give was that I wanted what was best for Eli. And at the time, that meant removing myself from his life." A deep crease formed between her brows. "The way his eyes lit up when he talked about going to law school… well, there was nothing like it. His dad left when he was young and wasn't active in his or his brothers' lives, and I think deep down, he wanted to prove something to him, although he'd never confessed such a thing to me. When we were together, we'd talk about where our lives were headed, making big plans. When I did broach the question of what would happen if our dreams didn't come true, he'd shake his head and always say the same thing. 'Nothing will get in the way of our dreams.' He was only being positive, pushing us both to accomplish everything we'd talked about, but his resolute response was stifling, especially after I'd found out I was pregnant.

"Knowing a baby would throw the biggest wrench in our plans... his plans... I made the decision to leave. I took the coward's way out and left him a note. If I'd told him face-to-face, he would've convinced me to stay, ruining his dreams. And I couldn't live with that kind of regret." I took a breather, grateful to have someone other than my mom to talk to about what happened.

"But didn't Eli want to see his son?" she asked, but the contortions of my features gave everything away. "Oh, my God! He doesn't know?" Shaking her head in disbelief, she stared at me for several long and agonizing seconds. "Please, tell me Eli knows Holden exists, Kalista." Her plea brought tears to my eyes.

"No, he doesn't." Before another word slipped from my mouth, I broke down and sobbed, my confession both a relief and a burden. I'd been carrying around my secret for what seemed like forever, and now that someone else knew, I could breathe. But as quickly as I'd said as much, having another person know compounded the secret. Just one more person who knew before Eli.

She gathered me in her arms, offering me the comfort I was so desperate for. "Shhh...," she calmed, stroking my hair as she gently rocked me.

"I don't know what I'm going to do." The tears came fast and hard. "I ran into Mike the other day, and he told me he was going to tell Eli I'm back in town. It's only a matter of time before he sees Holden. And you saw my son. There is no denying who his father is. No denying," I repeated. I pulled back in an attempt to regain some of my composure.

"Just take some time. I'm sure you'll figure out what's best." I appreciated her words more than I could ever express, her compassion and understanding the heady concoction I'd needed right then.

A short while later, when we were both more than exhausted, we agreed to meet up again soon, rekindling our lost friendship a necessity.

Now all I have to do is figure out how to tell Eli Warner he's a father.

ELI

A whole week had passed since Mike told me the woman who'd destroyed me was back home. Still in shock by the news, I'd done nothing besides work and lose myself to fucking Beth. I had planned on ending things with her, but after what I found out, I needed someone to be the recipient of my sexual demons.

Every time I buried myself inside her, Kalista's face filtered in, the one I remembered, at least. I hadn't laid eyes on her in a decade and a half, and although Mike said she looked good, another blow to my ego, the only memories I had of her were when we were twenty.

"Are you up for a little something extra tonight?" I asked, circling Beth like prey. And I supposed, in a way, she was.

The eagerness in her eyes encouraged me because I felt exceptionally frustrated tonight. Before she answered, I snatched her arm and pulled her close, my grip tightening and making her wince. The flare of excitement that flashed over her face told me she loved the aggression.

Too bad she had to go and develop feelings for me.

"Answer me." I dipped my head and grazed my teeth over

her shoulder, latching on before biting down. I was careful not to break the skin, but there would be a mark afterward. Her response was a gasp, right before she leaned into me.

"Yes." Her eyes fluttered in delight. "Anything you want, Eli. You know that."

"Good answer," I replied, whipping her around so I didn't have to look at her. The only woman I wanted to see right then was Kalista. I wanted to punish her, fuck away all my anger.

Lifting the hem of her blue dress, I tugged it over her head and threw the garment to the floor. When Beth turned her head and attempted to reach back to touch me, I halted her with a harsh "No." She complied and faced the bed once more. I removed her matching black bra and panties, leaving her completely bare for me to do as I wished.

As I needed.

With my hand in the middle of her back, I pushed her forward until she fell on the bed, ass up and waiting for me to lose myself. "Don't move," I warned, shedding my clothes quickly so I could rid myself of my persistent hurt. If I was a better man, I'd show Beth the door and jerk off until I was satiated, but I was weak tonight. I needed someone with me to take the brunt of my anger.

My hand connected with her plump ass, the pain singing out not only from her groan but from the sting of my hand. "Tell me you love it," I demanded, needing to know she was still on board with what I had planned, although I hadn't told her as much, my vague question opening all sorts of doors.

"You know I love it, baby." Her blonde hair fell forward and shrouded the side of her pretty face from me. *Perfect.*

I'd learned over the years the only way for me to get off was to fuck, the days of making love long gone.

Slow and gentle didn't excite me.

I preferred aggressive and hard.

Sheathing myself with a condom, I ran my finger through

her folds to make sure she was ready for me. Only when I found her slick and needy did I line up and thrust inside her in one quick motion, rooted to the hilt. I watched as her fingers clenched the covers, her breaths short and stuttered. Because I was well endowed, I normally waited until she'd adjust to the fullness, but I didn't care right then. All I wanted to do was rut like an animal until all my fury had been released.

I gripped her hips and pulled her back toward me, my quick movements the cause of her incessant moans. She said something, but I wasn't paying attention, my only focus selfishly on what I needed right then.

For as much as I didn't want to, I remembered the countless times I'd buried myself inside Kalista, the soft purrs she'd made making me cherish her that much more. We'd loved each other with a fierceness that scared me at times because I'd believed I'd cease to exist if she ever left me. As it turned out, I was right. I had stopped living the day she took off, and while my heart still beat inside my chest, I wasn't the same person I was back then. I'd closed myself off from the world, plastering on a façade so my family and friends wouldn't worry about me as much as they would've otherwise.

The familiar pull in my balls warned me I was going to explode soon, but because I wasn't done with Beth yet, I pulled out and flipped her on her back, my surprise move evident with the sharp inhale she took. Initially, I didn't want to look at her, but for what I had planned, I needed to see her eyes. To watch her reaction and see that what I wanted to do was okay with her.

Spreading her legs wide, I slammed back inside of her. "Rake your nails down my chest." I needed to feel a bite of pain to spur me on. Without an ounce of hesitation, she glided her long fingernails down my damp flesh, the slight sting enough to do the trick.

My hold on her hips relented when I moved my hand up her

body, twisting her pert nipple between my fingers. She writhed beneath me. I leaned in close, my mouth hovering over her other breast, my tongue flicking out to tease before my teeth captured the pert bud.

"I'm so close." Her pussy clenched me as the air left her lungs. I moved so our bodies were flush to each other and whispered in her ear.

"I want to try some breath play. Are you okay with that?" Beth would agree to anything I wanted, I was sure of it, but I didn't want her to say yes if she was truly terrified. While I enjoyed inflicting a certain amount of pain during sex, I wasn't a sadist. I moved back so I could see her face.

"You want to choke me?" she asked, staring up at me with a touch of uncertainty. As long as she showed no outward signs of real fear, I'd forge ahead.

"Yes."

She didn't hesitate long before she nodded, her tongue sneaking out and wetting her bottom lip. After my hand snaked around her small throat, I applied a small amount of pressure before starting to move inside her again. My assault on her body wasn't as harsh as before because I needed to gauge the correct amount of strength to use to restrict her breathing. That was most important. Only after I determined the force needed to deny her of free-flowing oxygen would I punish her with my cock.

Knowing I had control over how much air filled her lungs was a dangerous drug, but I remained cautious because this was the first time I'd tried this with Beth. Having experience with other lovers, I knew exactly how strong my hold had to be to make it pleasurable for both of us, the woman experiencing a more intense orgasm, while I felt more in control than ever before.

"Is it too much?" I asked, tightening my fingers. She shook

her head slightly, her nostrils flaring, her pink lips parting to inhale as much oxygen as I would allow.

Several more seconds and I'd be a goner, so I constricted her breathing a little more, sinking my teeth into her neck. Her body arched off the bed and I thrust deeper, careful not to break skin as my orgasm ripped through me. The harder I fucked her, the more her body trembled, and while she couldn't scream out that she loved my punishment because of my hold, I saw the thrill in her eyes and felt it in the way her pussy milked every last bit from me, her own pleasure tearing through her at the same time.

Moments afterward, I removed my hand from around her neck and slipped from her body. "Are you okay?" Words seemed to momentarily escape her, a simple nod the confirmation I needed that I hadn't gone too far.

Studying her and determining she truly was all right, I hopped off the bed, rolling off the condom as I disappeared into the bathroom. I washed up, content I'd been able to rid some of my anger, but when I glanced at my reflection in the mirror, the remaining fury I concealed bubbled up, imprisoning me once again with no chance of escape.

Ever since Mike told me Kalista was back, I'd been unable to return to my blissfully numb existence, everything I'd harbored toward her since the day she left coming back full force.

The heartbreak.

The denial.

The confusion.

The undeniable rage that came after I realized she wasn't coming back, that she didn't care enough about me or our relationship to end things in person. Her actions drove home that she never truly loved me; otherwise, she wouldn't have taken off on me like she did.

I questioned every time she professed her love for me. Every time she shared in the dreams we wanted to accomplish. Why had she lied to me all those years? What could she have possibly had to gain?

When I was finished, I reentered the room and came to stand by the edge of the bed, Beth remaining flat on her back. When I reached for my discarded clothes, she finally moved, swinging her legs over the side. She was close enough to run her fingers down my arm.

"That was amazing. I've never come so hard in my life." I smiled at the compliment before leaning down to place a chaste kiss on her lips.

"I had fun, too." Her expectant grin faltered when I threw on my clothes and snatched my keys from my pocket.

"You can't stay?" I had no idea why she continued to try and get me to give her more when I'd been as forthcoming as possible. Just when my aggravation with her increased, I took a slow breath and reminded myself that because I hadn't cut her off completely, I was to blame for her unrealistic fantasy of thinking I'd somehow cave and give her what she wanted. Me.

"You know I can't." My smile never reached my eyes as I said goodnight and walked out of her room.

For as much as I hated to admit it, I was never going to be able to fuck away my rage and sadness. The only thing that would expel the feelings dwelling deep inside me was an up-close-and-personal conversation with Kalista.

The realization hit me hard, but I also felt overwhelming relief that I'd finally get the opportunity to make her answer for what she'd done to me.

$\mathcal{M}$y conversation with Jasmine played over and over in my head. Admittedly, I'd felt much better after I'd told her everything, but disclosing my story meant it was real. A part of me argued that I'd waited this long and had not told Eli, what would a few more days or weeks mean? But the reality was, now that I was back home, I was all out of excuses, knowing damn well he had a right to know about his son, and Holden about his father. I'd most likely done irreparable damage to both, and while fear and uncertainty had been my justification in the past, albeit delusional and ill thought out, I couldn't hide from what needed to be done any longer.

Jasmine gave me his office number and location. She didn't have his personal number, nor was I ballsy enough to call it even if she did. Going back and forth between wanting to call him or simply showing up at his office kept my mind busy for hours—days, even. Every time I worked myself up enough to dial his number, I would only let it ring twice before I hung up, my courage flying right out the window.

Each day, I would tell myself *today is the day*, but every day, the hours passed in silence. I'd done nothing, hiding out in my mother's house as if the bricks and mortar were going to protect me forever. I was being selfish, trying to protect myself as well as Holden for as long as possible.

Would Eli even want to get to know his son? Was he prepared for such life-changing news? Although Jasmine had told me she didn't think he was serious with anyone, I really had no way of knowing if she spoke the truth or not.

There were so many times I'd dreamed I could reverse time and handle my situation differently, but the girl I was made the decision she thought she should at the time. But in turn, I'd robbed myself from the life I'd dreamed of—Holden from being raised by both his parents, and Eli from the future he'd spoken often of.

With age came wisdom, but also remorse.

And I was riddled with the shit.

Tired of dwelling over what should have been or what could be, I snatched my phone from the table and dialed Jasmine's number. Praying she was available to grab something to eat, I crossed my fingers tighter with every ring.

"Hello?"

"Hi. It's me."

A deep rush of gratitude washed over me that she reached out to rekindle our friendship. I didn't deserve it, not after the way I'd left things. If I'd been a better friend, I would have reached out to her long ago, explaining everything then and swearing her to secrecy.

But as the years passed, I knew I was in too deep to ever try and salvage any sort of relationship we'd had.

"Kalista… how are you?" she asked, the sound of surprise evident in her voice, as if she was dumbstruck to hear from me a week after she showed up on the front porch. I couldn't say I blamed her, however.

"I'm good. Listen, I was wondering if you were free for

dinner tonight?" I prayed that by me reaching out to her after her visit, it was the first step in truly rebuilding what we'd once had, wishing to become as close as we were when we were younger.

"Let me check with Steve to make sure he doesn't have any late meetings. I'll call you back in a half hour."

"Okay. Let me know." I probably sounded desperate, but I didn't care, needing my friend more than I realized.

As I busied myself while I waited for her to call back, images of the man I feared seeing again washed over me. Many a night sleep had eluded me, thoughts of Eli and me so much in love, our world suddenly ripped to shreds because of a rash choice I'd made. When I learned he'd fulfilled his dreams of becoming a lawyer and was doing well for himself, I smiled, though I hated I wasn't in his life to celebrate his accomplishment with him. Although, I had no one to blame but myself, a decision I had to learn to live with.

I never loved another man the way I loved Eli. There was someone I thought I could have had a future with, but the relationship turned bad. In fact, it was the main reason I'd decided to move back home.

JASMINE and I agreed to meet at Caluzo, our favorite restaurant growing up. They were famous for their carbonara, the best I'd ever tasted.

Looking around the eatery, I was comforted seeing that nothing had changed, minus a new coat of paint on the walls. My heart swelled from the nostalgia, but a pang of hurt sliced through me at the same time. Because Caluzo had been my favorite place to eat, Eli had indulged me and had brought me here often. My eyes watered from the rush of memories.

"Too painful? We can go somewhere else if you want." Jasmine reached across and covered my hand with hers.

"Yes," I whispered, moving my hands into my lap. Her comfort made my overwhelming sentiment worse, although it wasn't her fault. I was on edge, probably would be until I talked with Eli—whenever that might be. She scooted toward the edge of the booth, but before she stood, I clarified, "We don't have to go. I meant yes, this place brings back a lot of memories, but I want to stay."

"Are you sure?"

"I'm sure." After she resituated herself, our waiter approached, asking for our drink order. While I wanted to tell him to bring me an entire bottle of wine, I settled for a glass, as did Jasmine.

"Are you thinking about him?" The mention of him plucked at the last bit of strength I possessed, and because I didn't want to delve into the topic of Eli Warner so soon, I lied. Sort of.

"I was thinking about all the times you and I came here, stuffing our faces until we had to unbutton our jeans." We both laughed at the recollection. "I'm surprised we both didn't weigh five hundred pounds."

"We certainly ate that much in pasta. That's for sure." Jasmine's easy smile had me breathing a sigh of relief. I loved being around her, always had, but we were grown women now. Before I called her, I had some reservation as to whether we could really pick up where we left off, but sitting across from her, my hopes were coming to fruition. It was as if no time had passed between us at all, like we were still those twenty-year-old hopeful friends, looking forward to our futures together.

Our waiter interrupted our walk down memory lane, placing our drinks in front of us before taking our order. We sat in a comfortable silence after he disappeared, me tapping the silverware with my fingertip while she played with the edge of her cloth napkin.

My eyes raked over the restaurant, watching some of the other patrons, when Jasmine's words brought me back around. "So, have you worked up enough nerve to call him yet?" Arching a brow, she lifted her chin and leaned back in her seat.

"Don't pussyfoot around, woman." I'd certainly missed her straightforwardness, and while slightly taken off guard, I was thankful because I needed to talk some more about the things running around inside my head.

"You'll quickly remember that I'm blunt."

"How can I ever forget?" Brushing back a lock of hair that had fallen over my eye, I looked at my dear friend, preparing myself for this conversation. "The simple answer is no. I haven't contacted him yet." I took a sip of my drink before sighing. "I don't know what to say. How do I even begin to apologize for leaving him, never mind working up the courage to tell him about Holden? He's going to hate me, probably even more than he already does. He'll never forgive me," I said, defeated. "Maybe I'll just stay hidden." I was only half kidding.

"I don't believe he'll hate you, although I'm sure he'll be more than pissed off you never told him he has a son. But from what I remember of Eli, and the way he loved you, I'm hopeful you two will be back on decent terms sooner than you think."

"I hope you're right." Her expression suddenly changed, a concerned look streaking across her face. "Oh God, what?" I had no idea what she was going to say, and that notion made me uneasy. I took two more sips of my wine for courage.

"I'm beyond thrilled you're back, but what made you return after being gone so long?"

I should have ordered the damn bottle.

"It's a long story," I responded.

"Well… we have three hours, so spill it." The edges of her mouth kicked up, even though I was sure she could tell by my darting eyes that the topic was touchy.

Where to begin?

I'd never told anyone the full story—besides the police, of course—about what happened. But I had every confidence Jasmine would lend a sympathetic ear to what I'd endured.

She drummed her nails on the top of our wood table, her eyes wide in anticipation of my answer.

"I came back because I had no other choice." Nervously playing with the strap of my watch, I leaned back in my seat and tried to get comfortable. "His name was John Kellison. He was one of the doctors, a pediatrician, at the hospital I worked for back in Vermont." Shaking my head, I cleared away the sudden urge to withdraw into myself and continued speaking while I was still brave enough to tell her everything. Not even my mom knew all the details, but I trusted my friend wholeheartedly. "We often ran into each other, sharing a lot of the same shifts. Thankfully, I had a wonderful babysitter to help me take care of Holden while I worked, and I was at the hospital quite a bit, doing my best to support both of us. And we were doing just fine until…." I drifted off, averting my eyes from hers for only a moment.

The memories were sometimes too much, so I blocked them out the majority of the time. But with my return home, I realized at some point I'd have to disclose the reason why.

Reaching across the table, her hand gently covered mine once more, showing me with one simple gesture she was there for me. Taking a deep breath, I continued.

"We started dating and everything was fine at first. Until a couple months in when he pushed me to move in with him. Because it was way too soon, I told him no. And while I cared for him, I was still unsure about us. It wasn't any one thing in particular that made me hesitate about him, but there was something I couldn't quite put my finger on. As I later found out, I was right to hold back." Finishing off my glass of wine, I signaled to the waiter for a refill, two glasses being my limit that night because I still had to drive home, although my house wasn't far from Caluzo.

The past flooded in and before the undertow of what happened dragged me under, I spilled the rest of the story in haste, hitting on all the pertinent details.

"I dragged my feet until I felt the time was right, which never came. A year into our relationship, John became more demanding of me and my time. We both worked long hours, and I felt guilty about not being with Holden more, but I had to earn enough money to make sure we were taken care of. Whenever I did have some free time, I often chose to spend it with my son, a decision that didn't sit well with John the further into our relationship we got.

"One night, I decided to take Holden to eat at one of his favorite restaurants. When we were walking back to the car afterward, I spotted John sitting across the street... watching us. The hairs on the back of my neck rose, and although I couldn't see his eyes from that far away, the entire scene disturbed me. As soon as I turned the car on, he called me. I asked him where he was and he lied, telling me he was still at the hospital. He obviously hadn't realized I'd seen him. From that day forward, I was more on guard than ever before, slowly distancing myself from him. Each day that passed brought out more of his aggressive side, until one night everything culminated in a nasty argument."

With my hands slightly trembling, I reached for my drink. Swallowing an extra sip, Jasmine remained patient while I told my story.

"It's okay," she whispered, nodding. "Take your time."

Flashing her a weak smile, I forged ahead. "He'd come to my house late, waking me from a sound sleep. I'd told him earlier that day I couldn't see him, making up some excuse about having plans, and he seemed okay with it, but him showing up proved the exact opposite. He wouldn't stop banging on my door until I opened. At that point in our dwindling relationship, I wasn't scared of him, per se. I wanted to end things between us but just hadn't found the right time to do so, or more specifically, the courage. The break-up was going to be awkward, especially since we'd continue to see each other at work. I just kept putting it off for another day. Anyway, I let him inside my apartment. I ignored that niggling feeling in the pit of my stomach. I should've turned him away, but I didn't. Besides, I didn't want him to wake Holden, or any of my neighbors. He wasn't there two minutes when he started in about never making time for him, ignoring his calls and even accusing me of seeing someone else."

"He cut me off every time I tried to speak and realizing he wasn't going to listen to anything I had to say, I asked him to leave. He refused, and that's when his temper came out full force. He started shouting about knowing I was going to dump him and that he would never allow that to happen. Before I could demand he leave a second time, he shoved me so hard I fell and hit my head on the edge of the coffee table. He continued to yell, telling me that he wasn't going anywhere and that neither was I, that he'd never allow me to leave him. While we'd had our occasional arguments, he'd never acted like that before. I looked for signs that he'd been drinking, but he was stone-cold sober. The only thing I noticed were that his eyes were glazed over, but I didn't know why. I came to find out later he'd been abusing prescription drugs, but I hadn't known that at the time.

"When I'd finally scrambled to my feet, my hand holding the back of my head, I pleaded again for him to leave." I blinked back the tears threatening to fall, remembering what happened next. "Instead of taking off, he... he attacked me."

Jasmine gasped, her hand flying to her mouth to stifle her reaction. "Oh, no, Kalista. I'm so sorry." She leaned in closer. "He didn't ra—"

"No, thank God. He never forced himself on me, although he did hurt me. Every time his fist connected with a part of my body, he'd shout that he'd kill me before he'd give me up."

Watching her reaction hit home how dire my situation had been. I realized it was bad. Hell, I lived it, but seeing the fear and concern written all over her face added to the dynamic of what had happened.

"The absolute worst part was when Holden came out of his room. As soon as he saw John looming over me, he ran at him and tried to tackle him, but he was no match for a grown man. As soon as he was close enough, John whipped around, grabbed him and threw him across the room. I'd never been so scared in my entire life. I no longer cared what happened to me, just as long as Holden was okay."

Countless seconds of silence passed between us, me trying to calm my erratic heart, and Jasmine trying to digest everything I'd just laid at her feet.

Finally, she spoke. "What happened?" Her hands shook, mirroring mine. "Please tell me that bastard was arrested and thrown in jail."

"He was. My neighbor heard the commotion and called the police." My fingers flitted instinctually over my torso in a protective move. "I ended up with two fractured ribs, a split lip, countless bruises, and a concussion. They charged him with domestic battery. I found out later he'd done it to a few women in the past, but the charges never stuck because the others refused to press charges."

"Why?" she asked, just as confused as I was.

"I have no idea." I finished my second drink and pushed the glass to the side. "They sentenced him to two years in jail, and because I didn't want to stick around when he was released, I decided to move. I gave my two weeks' notice, packed up everything and came back home."

A small sense of relief rushed over me being able to confide in Jasmine. Although John would be behind bars for some time, there was a part of me that feared he'd come after me when he was released. Would he forget about me and move on to some other unsuspecting victim, or would the time he spent locked up spur his obsession for me even more? Either way, I was far away from Vermont and hoping to start a new life. Or should I say, start over?

Coming home had been the necessary choice to make, not only for me but more importantly, for Holden. I'd do whatever I needed to in order to keep him safe. He was my whole world. If something ever happened to him, I'd cease to exist.

An hour later and we were both still fully engrossed in conversation, the back and forth flowing just as easily as it had when we were younger and inseparable. Thankfully, we'd switched topics to those of a lighter nature, talking about our jobs, which I still had to secure, and our children.

At some point, I was so focused on what Jasmine was saying I almost missed the sight of someone walking through the front door. And it wasn't just anyone. It was freaking Mike Hawkings. Of all people to saunter into the same restaurant, what the hell were the chances? After our last encounter, running into him again was the last thing I needed. Besides, I was in no mood for another riot act.

I was so shocked at seeing him again it took me a second to realize he held the door open behind him, waiting for someone else to follow him inside.

My heart slammed to a halt and time stood still as I waited for the mystery person to appear. A sheen of sweat coated my palms, my vision blurring the longer I concentrated on him and that damn door.

A tall, blond man suddenly walked in behind Mike.

It wasn't Eli.

"Thank God," I mumbled, a rush of air propelling from my lips as my eyes focused back on my dear friend. I hadn't even realized I was holding my breath until it was pushed from my lungs in relief.

"Are you all right?" she asked, tilting her head to the side.

"Yeah. I'm fine. It's just…."

"Just what?"

"Mike just came in. I'm praying he doesn't notice me, because talking to him again is not high on my list of things to do anytime soon."

Jasmine whipped her head around so fast I thought she was going to break her neck. "Mike Hawkings is here?" She searched the restaurant until she spotted him taking a seat at the bar, then turned back to look at me with wide eyes. "Shit! I haven't seen him since graduation night, when we—" A blush painted her cheeks and I was reminded of the story of their sexual encounter from many years ago.

"Oh, yeah." I laughed, reaching across the table and slapping her hand. "I forgot you got down and dirty with the man-whore of our class." Mike was a very popular guy in high school, no doubt carrying that status into adulthood. He really was very handsome and charming... when he wasn't chastising me, of course.

Jasmine slumped forward and sighed. "He's still hot." Her head swiveled toward him once more, and I swore she appeared as if she was committing him to memory the way she stared at him.

Tapping the table, I asked, "Hey, aren't you married, woman?"

"Yeah, but I'm not dead." She wiggled her eyebrows and we both chuckled, and I had to admit it felt good to find some sort of amusement after what I'd told her earlier.

Glancing back to the bar one final time, she parted her lips to speak but snapped them shut before a single word left her mouth. I turned to look as well, and of course, it was at that exact moment that Mike caught us staring at him.

"He saw us. Shit. Shit. Shit." Fidgeting in my seat, I tried to remain calm and look as much at ease as I could, praying he took pity on me and stayed away.

Fat chance.

With every step he took toward our table, I silently prayed our waiter would bring our check, so we would have a valid excuse for rushing out and not engaging him in conversation. But our waiter was nowhere to be found. *Damn him.*

Jasmine's gaze was glued to Mike, smiling at him as he approached. And thank God, his eyes were pinned to hers and not me. He was dressed in dark jeans and a white button-up, the sleeves rolled up to his elbows. His dark, curly hair was unruly, but in a purposeful way. He looked good, just like the last time I saw him.

Only when he stood next to our table did he decide to pay attention to me, nodding in acknowledgment. He seemed to be in a better mood this time around, so I relaxed some, all while still being on guard. Mike was notorious for saying what he wanted, whenever he wanted. Anything could fly out of his mouth at any time.

"Ladies. How are you?" Leaning down, he pressed a lingering kiss to Jasmine's cheek, brushing a strand of her blonde hair behind her ear as he righted himself. She mumbled something in response, but I was too busy hoping he wouldn't mention a certain someone to pay much attention.

"Kalista, so nice to see you again. And so soon." His lips curved up, his brown eyes glinting mischievously, and I wasn't quite sure why. He silently goaded me, but the last thing I wanted to do was get into an argument with him again.

"Mike," I responded, short and sweet, talking myself out of fleeing the restaurant right then.

Uneasy silence surrounded all three of us, no one knowing quite what to say next. Mike's stare bore holes into me as he waited for me to speak. But I never did. *He's the one who came over here.*

Finally, he took the hint and stepped back from the table. "Well, I'll leave you to it." Looking to Jasmine once more, he said, "So nice to see you again, beautiful." Then he flicked his eyes to me. "Kalista." When he uttered my name, he spoke volumes. I had no doubt he'd told Eli I was back home, and I was sure he was fully aware that I hadn't contacted his friend yet. The only reason he'd come over to us was to intimidate me. He had no intention of sitting down and chatting it up with the two of us, driving down memory lane and all that happy horse shit.

Even through his plastered-on smile, I'd detected an ounce of anger, and there was no mistaking it was directed toward me.

"Oh, my God! He's still gorgeous," she whispered, fanning herself and laughing. When she lowered her hands, she spun her wedding ring, either reminding herself she was married, or wishing she wasn't. If I had to guess, I'd say it wasn't the latter. She caught me watching her and repeated, "Not dead."

I shook my head, thankful Jasmine had been able to keep me in somewhat good spirits. As soon as our waiter came into view, I called him over and asked for the check, telling him we were in a hurry. There was no way I was sticking around for Mike to change his mind and waltz back over to us.

Plus, I didn't want to risk running into Eli, his friend no doubt having called him to tell him where I was.

ELI

"*A*re you still there?"

The phone rested in the crook of my neck, ignoring my friend and lost to regrets of not rushing over to Caluzo's last night when Mike had called to tell me Kalista was there with Jasmine. I battled on whether seeing her again, in a crowded restaurant of all places, was the best decision. I could've avoided a scene in public, but the encounter wouldn't have allowed me to obtain the answers I needed for closure. If there even was such a thing for me. She could've refused to talk to me, then where would that have left me? Strangers sitting there witnessing my flash of anger and despair? No, thank you.

"Hello?" Mike huffed into the phone, finally pulling me back from my bout of what if.

"Yeah, sorry. I'm here."

"You're thinking about her, aren't you?" His teasing tone was quickly abated with my aggravated one. I believed Kalista would always be a sore subject for me.

"Fuck you." It was the only thing I could think of to say. "Why are you calling me, anyway?" I hadn't meant to take out my frustration on him, but Mike's flippant reaction to the debacle I now faced annoyed the hell out of me.

To see her or not to see her.

That was the question.

"Well, Mr. Happy Pants, I'm calling for a favor. I have a friend who needs some legal advice. He's starting up a new business and needs some tax guidance."

"I'm not a tax attorney, Mike. That's not my specialty." Rummaging around on my desk, I found the final page to the contract I'd recently drafted hidden under a pile of papers.

"You know stuff about tax law, though, don't you?"

"Yeah, some."

"Well then, that'll work. I told him to come by your office tomorrow around five. Hope that's okay."

Quickly looking at my calendar, I confirmed the time slot was open. "Fine. But you owe me."

"You know I'm good for it."

"Uh-huh," I mumbled before disconnecting the call.

THE FOLLOWING EVENING, I was lost in the drones of contracts when the buzzer from my secretary interrupted the flow I'd been able to achieve after a few long hours of working on the same damn brief.

"Mr. Warner, your five o'clock is here." What I loved about Barbara was she was blunt and to the point. All business. All the time.

"Show him in, please."

No response needed on her part.

Moments later, the handle of my office door turned and in walked Barbara, dressed impeccably, as usual, wearing a plain black dress with a black and gray sheer scarf tied loosely around her neck. Her shoulder-length black hair was twisted into a bun, showcasing her mature yet soft features. If I had to guess, I'd put her in her late fifties, although she could be older.

I stood and rounded the edge of my desk, walking toward Barbara and the mystery man Mike had insisted I meet with. He was standing behind her, and although he towered over her, I only caught a glimpse of his face. When I looked back at my secretary, her brown eyes flashed with fear, although she gave me a reserved smile before disappearing from my office before I could dissect her expression.

Once she was gone, I turned my attention toward the guy standing in the middle of my office and extended my hand in greeting.

"Hi," I said. "I'm Eli Warner. And you are?"

My five o'clock appointment stepped forward, his eyes roving over me, from top to bottom, assessing me. Studying me. The muscles in his jaw twitched as he stood taller, the intensity in his eyes challenging me as he extended his palm.

"I'm Marek. Mike said you were a busy guy, so thanks for seeing me on such short notice." I had a gut feeling this guy found being polite an unnecessary burden. He stepped back, glancing around my office quickly before heading toward the couch. Normally, new clients sat in one of the chairs in front of my desk, but not him. He made himself right at home.

"Got anything to drink?" he asked, jerking his chin toward the small liquor cabinet in the corner of the room.

"Sure. What's your poison?"

"Whatever you got is fine."

With my back turned, I heard Marek situate himself on my sofa, the leather of his cut blending with the leather of the couch, the ominous sound not lost on me at all.

His presence put me on alert. Yes, he was a friend of Mike's, and while I didn't think my good buddy would send a dangerous man to see me, there was no denying who'd walked into my office.

The man sitting ten feet from me was none other than the President of the Knight's Corruption motorcycle club. Their main "headquarters" was right here in California, the patch on the front of his cut proving as much. His club was infamous, the crimes unspeakable to most, although tales spread far and wide to everyone in the surrounding areas.

I handed him his drink before walking back toward my chair, a slight nod from him showing his appreciation. "What is it I can do for you?" My breathing slowed the same time my heart thrashed inside my chest. Waiting for him to speak, all sorts of thoughts ran through my head.

What if he came here to threaten me to get into bed with the club?

What if he threatens me or my family if I refuse?

What if I stop making assumptions and hear what he has to say?

Instead of answering my question, though, he asked one of his own. "You know who I am, don't you?" He leaned forward and locked eyes on me, a slight smirk kicking up the corners of his mouth as he bathed in my uneasiness.

Even if he wasn't wearing that menacing leather vest, which told the world what club he belonged to, Marek still looked like someone not to mess with. It wasn't his appearance that made me think such a thing. He wasn't burly and bald with a handlebar mustache. He had short dark hair and a well-groomed beard. Instead, there was something about the way he carried himself and the way he scrutinized me with those eyes of his, watching my every move as a predator would its prey, daring me with a simple glance to step out of line, that made my anxiety top off.

I remained silent while I contemplated how to answer his question. If I said yes, that I knew exactly who he was, would that put me in more danger, basically confessing I knew he was a criminal? And if I answered no, would I inadvertently offend him, telling him his reputation, as well as that of his club, was in fact nothing to pay attention to?

"It's not a hard question, Eli," he said, laughing at my uncertainty.

So, what answer did I give him?

"Kind of."

I fidgeted with a few of the papers still strewn on top of my desk, the only sign I was indeed uncomfortable. Before he walked into my office, there wasn't a single person on the face of this earth I was afraid of. But I wasn't dumb enough to think the man sitting in front of me couldn't bring a world of hurt on me and everyone I loved if he felt I was a threat. From what I understood, the reach he had spread wide across the country, chapters formed in all different states.

I'm going to kill Mike.

Before I could elaborate on my response, he placed his drink on a nearby table, stood from the sofa and walked toward me, stopping when he reached one of the two chairs on the opposite side of my desk. He sat, leaned back and folded his arms across his chest, his long sleeve white shirt making his cut look even more intimidating up close.

"I can see I make you nervous. Don't be. You're doing me a huge favor here, and the last thing I want to do is make you uncomfortable." His tone was light, but the crease between his eyes and defensive body language screamed the opposite. In order for me to get through our meeting unscathed, and for me not to appear weak in front of him, something I most certainly was not, my brain scrambled his words as the truth. "You said you kind of know who I am. I call bullshit." He smirked that time, calling me out on my half lie. "I think you know exactly who I am and what I'm a part of. And that's okay. It makes me happy people such as yourself have heard of me and my club." I'd be lying if I said his expression softened and he put me at ease, because he sure as hell didn't. But when his grin widened, although slightly, I tamped down the wave of apprehension traveling through me.

There was more to Marek than met the eye, but I didn't wish to unravel the various other parts of his personality. Relaxing a little, I leaned back further into my chair and released a slow and steady breath. It was subtle, but he noticed.

"Good," he said, nodding as if an unspoken conflict had just been resolved.

Tapping my fingers on the surface of my desk, I asked a simple question, one which had plagued me since he'd walked in. "So, how do you know Mike?"

"I've been fixing up a '71 Super Glide FX for the past few months, a surprise for one of the guys at the club, and I was out taking it for a ride." He stopped speaking abruptly. "You have no idea what I'm talking about, do you?" he asked, an amused look on his face.

"Sorry, I don't. I assume you're talking about a bike?"

"Yeah... a Harley. While I was out for a ride, I came across Mike's garage, and since the bike was bucking and giving me some issues, I stopped in and asked if I could use some of his equipment. I was too far from the club and didn't want to test it in case I broke down on the side of the road. Turns out, one of the plugs was a wrong fit, and thankfully, he had what I needed. I'm still in the process of learning how to fix up older bikes. We have our seasoned mechanics, but I wanted to handle this one myself. My next venture is building one from scratch." He grinned, putting me a bit more at ease.

"Anyway, Mike and I got to talking about all sorts of things, my club's new business ventures being one of the topics of discussions. It was then he told me he had a friend who was a lawyer." Marek leaned closer. "And it just so happens I'm in need of some legal advice."

"I'm sure you know plenty of lawyers," I blurted before I could stop myself. Internally, I flinched, but I schooled my expression because I didn't want him to see me falter in any way.

He rose from his seat, and for a moment, I had no idea what he was going to do. Would he lunge over the desk at me for my flagrant comment? I was sure his reputation had been carefully constructed, and for a stranger to be so brazen surely would have some sort of consequence.

Instead of retaliating, however, he just laughed and walked back to the table by the couch to grab his drink. After he'd returned, he took his seat again, this time, crossing his ankle over his jean-clad opposing leg, looking as casual as could be.

"True. But no one I trust to give it to me straight. I'm trying my best to do things the right way." He tilted his head. "At least when it comes to some things." He winked, seconds before he downed the last of his scotch, placing the glass on my desk and pushing it forward, indicating he wanted another.

I gave him a refill before we settled into our conversation, learning he was in the process of setting up a few new businesses. Bars and strip clubs, pretty much what I expected from someone like him, even if that was me thinking stereotypically.

"All the brothers are looking forward to free booze and pussy, leaving it up to me to take care of everything behind the scenes," he said, the corners of his mouth curving at the mere mention of his club.

I provided him a list of things he would need to do, from obtaining a liquor license for each bar, to setting up an LLC to protect personal assets, to learning about employee laws. Although I doubted they'd have issues with their employees where they would have to consult outside of their club. Call it a hunch.

An hour later, our meeting came to an end. I had to admit, while I was cautious in what I chose to say to him, knowing damn well he could make my life miserable, or even cease to exist, my impression of him had changed over the course of our time together. Not to get me wrong; one look at him and the way he carried himself, there was no doubt he'd kill you as soon as welcome you with a hug. But there was something shrouded underneath it all, which told me he wanted something better for him and the very dangerous club he was the leader of.

Handing him a piece of paper with some of the places he would need to visit, I walked him out, stopping by Barbara's desk to make sure she was all right. She hadn't heard from me for some time, and although that wasn't odd while I was engrossed in a meeting, I'd never met with the president of a notorious MC before.

ELI

*A*fter a very long day at the office, my meeting with the president of the Knights Corruption MC still rattling around in my brain, I drove down a street I hadn't visited in years.

Swirls of oranges and red lit up the sky and I couldn't stop some of the memories from seeping in. Kalista and I used to lay in her mother's backyard and gaze at the world around us right before the night crept in. It was then, while watching the different colors the sky would turn, that we'd delve into all the things we wanted to accomplish together, all the places we longed to visit. There was something about this time of day that made us think anything was possible and I didn't know if it was because the world slowed down briefly before the blackness of the night invaded or what, but I remembered being so happy planning our future while we rested on our backs and looked upward.

A car pulled into the driveway of Kalista's mother's home. I was parked down the street, contemplating what I would say if and when I saw her again, the appearance of the vehicle telling me I might just have to make that decision in the next several moments. My eyes were glued to the automobile, my heartbeat increasing as I sat there waiting to see who would emerge. For all I knew, it could be her mother, although instinct warned me otherwise.

Finally, the driver side door opened, and a woman emerged. My lungs seized up when I saw the one person who was responsible for turning me into the man I was—broken. Her dark hair was longer than I remembered, a sudden breeze playing with a few of her strands and blowing them into her face and shielding her from me, if only for a few agonizing seconds. Swiping the hair from her face, she walked toward the rear of the car and opened the back door.

As she leaned inside, I couldn't help but stare at her. I was far enough away to remain undetected, but close enough to see her sexy curves. Her ass was still as delectable, especially encased in those damn jeans, the back of her shirt riding up so I could see a hint of skin.

My brain instantly flooded with the images of her completely bare, all the times we'd had sex, showered together, or just lazily walked around the apartment naked. We never were able to keep our hands off each other, so putting on clothes just seemed like a waste of time most days.

Before I lost myself any further into the past, someone walked out of the house and approached her.

A young kid.

A boy.

Twenty minutes prior to her arrival, I'd rolled down my window and killed the engine. Even though nighttime was rolling in, the California heat was still prevalent, although not as warm as it was earlier that day.

As the boy drew closer to her, his voice drifted in the breeze, his words causing me to stop breathing altogether.

"Mom, why didn't you call me to come out?" he asked, taking some of the bags from her hands.

Mom?

So, she did have kids, or at least one.

"Holden, I *can* carry a few bags in the house." Her tone teased but was also assertive. It was then I remembered she hated when I'd carried her bags or opened the door for her, throwing it in my face that she wasn't some weak female who couldn't do anything for herself. But I couldn't help it; my mother raised a gentleman. Although the way I was feeling right then was anything but.

I was so focused on the scene unfolding in front of me, I almost missed the name she called him.

Holden was my middle name.

It can't be.

There's no way.

It's just a huge coincidence.

Leaning forward, I squinted, trying to get a better look at the young man. His hair was the same dark shade as mine, but that didn't prove anything. He looked to be anywhere between thirteen or fourteen, putting him at the right age from when she'd left. But because he was turned to the side, I couldn't get a good look at him.

Until he turned around and faced the street.

Then I saw it.

And it was like looking in a mirror.

If I didn't know any better, I would've thought I was all twisted up in some sort of nightmare. But I wasn't. I was looking at the woman who tore my heart into a million pieces and a boy who looked too much like me to ignore the conclusion I'd come to.

He took two steps forward and locked eyes on me. If he was indeed my son, which I couldn't see how he wasn't, had she told him about me? All sorts of crazy-ass questions rattled around inside my head, but before I gave them life, Kalista turned to see what or who had grabbed her son's attention, and as soon as her eyes landed on me, they widened in fear. The quickness of her breaths gave away everything I'd suspected.

Countless seconds passed before anyone made any movements.

It's now or never.

I probably wouldn't have approached her tonight, being satisfied with just seeing her for myself, but now that I'd seen Holden, I was forced to make a move.

I exited my car and slammed the door, my determined steps causing Kalista to reach for the boy's arm and quickly usher him toward their house, disappearing inside before I made it across the street.

There's no more escaping the past now, sweetheart.

KALISTA

J practically shoved Holden into the house and told him that he needed to go to his room and do his homework while I made dinner. When he opened his mouth to argue, I put my hands on his shoulders, turned him around and gently pushed him toward the stairs, the look on my face telling him not to argue.

Thankfully, he listened.

Even though I was aware this day was coming, I'd still been shocked to see Eli sitting down the road from our house. I wanted to meet with him on my terms, and certainly not when Holden was around. But I supposed that's what I got for putting off our encounter.

Holden had just cleared the top step when a heavy knock sounded at the front door. I stood in the kitchen debating on whether to answer, delusionally hoping maybe he would just go away. But if I remembered anything about Eli Warner, it was that he was a stubborn man.

He knocked again, then a third time, that one more angry than the first two poundings. I hurried toward the door, not because I wanted to answer but because if Holden came downstairs, I'd have more of a headache to deal with.

Eli had seen my son, but did he realize he was his as well? Had he put two and two together that quickly. Shaking my head at the ludicrous thought, my guilt fueling my paranoia, I stood tall and turned the handle of the door.

My heart slammed against my chest the second the barrier between us was no more. I kept my head down, looking at his shiny, black dress shoes, hoping and praying he'd walk away without saying a word. But the thought was ridiculous, assuming Eli had waited years to finally confront me for what I'd done to him.

If my mom had been home, I could've sent her to answer the door as a diversionary tactic, but then that wouldn't have worked out for long because she'd been telling me for years I needed to tell Eli the truth. All of it.

The air between us had become stagnant, my eyes still focusing on his shoes. I needed a few more precious seconds before I faced my past.

And my future.

"Look at me," he growled.

I suppose my time's up.

Pulling a breath, I lifted my head until my eyes landed on his. For the briefest of moments, I was bombarded with a rush of images of the two of us together all those years ago. Panic and fear had taken a backseat for the time being.

The man standing before me was not the same guy I'd left behind. Eli was obviously older, and if it was even possible, he was more breathtaking than he was in his youth. Sexy scruff hid his strong jaw while highlighting his full and tempting lips. Now wasn't the time to become enthralled with his looks, but I couldn't help myself, my body reacting to him as it always did. He was broader than I remembered—hell, he even looked taller. From the expensive-looking suit he wore and the way his hair was styled in that perfect coif, mixed with a hint of messiness, it was apparent he had done very well for himself. Never mind the hunk of steel he drove here in which probably cost more than my mother's house.

My lustful thoughts kept me frozen in the entryway, and while his eyes raked over me from head to toe, I doubted he was lost to his own lust for me. Rage flashed behind his stare. Clearly, he hated me. And I didn't blame him. Not at all. I'd left him, only a note telling of my abandonment.

The most uncomfortable stillness swirled between us, his lip curling up in disgust as he pushed past me and into the foyer.

"Where is he?" he shouted, loud enough to scare me but not loud enough to draw Holden's attention from his room upstairs.

"Who?" I played dumb. Probably not the best choice. Eli stalked toward me until he'd backed me against the nearest wall, his nostrils flaring while his eyes bore holes into me, intimidating me in ways I'd never even realized he was capable of.

I was trapped.

Nowhere to go. Nowhere to look except deep into his fury-filled blue eyes.

"Holden."

It took me a precious second to realize he'd spoken, and when it finally registered exactly what he'd said, my mouth dropped open in utter surprise.

"How do you know his name?" Had he run into Jasmine? Had she spilled her guts to him, forgetting to tell me she betrayed my trust?

"I heard you say it. When he came outside to help you." I hadn't even realized I'd said Holden's name out loud, but then again, I had no idea Eli was watching us, either. "How old is he?"

"Please."

"How old?"

I bit my lip as a distraction before answering, "Fourteen."

"Fuck," he grumbled, pulling a large breath through his nose.

"Leave him out of this, Eli. This is between you and me." Without thinking, I placed my hands on his chest, the rapid thumping of his heart telling me he was more than amped up. I wanted more than anything to shove him away, to cry and beg for him to leave before anything escalated, but my body betrayed me. A sharp jolt sliced through me, my own muscled organ quickly matching his rhythm. And I wasn't the only one affected. As soon as he'd felt my touch, he physically jerked, but not enough to dislodge my hands from him.

Glancing down at my fingers, he stilled a minute before his eyes met mine again. For a momentary flash in time, his features softened, like he was in the midst of a beautiful memory of us.

A memory of two very different people.

Finally, he backed up while still managing to crowd my personal space. "He's my son. He has everything to do with this. Does he even know? Or did you keep me a secret from him just as you kept him from me?" He started to pace, his hands tugging at his hair in frustration. I feared him right then. Not that he would physically hurt me, but that he would do something drastic to tear my carefully orchestrated life of lies apart at the seams.

I was wrong for keeping Holden from his father, and vice versa, but I'd made enough excuses over the years to justify my actions. Or at least enough to allow me to sleep at night.

Well… some nights.

When I remained silent, Eli stopped moving, cocked his head and not so patiently waited for me to answer. He was beyond angered, his rage shrouding him like the heaviest of fogs. He clenched his teeth, his jaw pulsating under the weight of his annoyance. I'd only seen him react this way a handful of instances during our time together, and only once was it ever directed at me, when he'd mistakenly thought I encouraged another guy to grope me at a bar.

"He doesn't know about you," I confessed, tears welling in my eyes as I spoke. "The decision I made was for the best back then. Please understand." I took a single step toward him.

"Understand?" he shouted. "Understand what? That you left me a note telling me you no longer wanted to be with me? Understand you never even thought to call me, not once in the following years after your disappearance to tell me what I'd done to make you leave? Understand you had my son," he gritted. "My fucking son, but decided it best... for you... to keep him a secret from me. For. Fourteen. Years!" He crushed whatever distance remained between us and grabbed hold of my arms. "What exactly do you want me to understand?" he asked me once more.

I heard footsteps above our heads, no doubt indicating Holden was going to make an unwanted appearance very soon. Eli had shouted several times, and there was no doubt in my mind that Holden had heard. My son was protective over me, and in most cases, I thought it was sweet. But not this time. All I prayed for was for him to remain in his room and allow me the necessary time to convince Eli to leave.

But his bedroom door opened, the creak of the hinge alerting me he was on his way down.

Eli heard my son... *our* son... bouncing down the steps, and his head whipped in the direction of the noise. Before I could say anything, Holden walked around the corner, stopping dead in his tracks when his eyes landed on the both of us. Thankfully, Eli had released me seconds before and had taken a step back.

"Mom?" Holden was in front of me soon after he appeared, glancing from me to Eli and back again.

He really was the mirror image of his father.

"Are you all right? I thought I heard shouting." He instinctively huddled closer, standing between me and Eli. Holden was respectful toward his elders, but when it came to me, he made sure I was taken care of before his manners to others. I couldn't have asked for a better child.

Pushing his hair back from his forehead, I answered, "I'm fine, honey. No shouting. Just excitement." I flashed him a smile, although I was a nervous wreck on the inside. I had no idea where I was going with this tale, but my mouth spewed the words my brain concocted.

When Holden looked back at Eli, he stepped forward and extended his hand, his manners back in full effect.

"Hi. I'm Holden Ellington," he greeted, waiting for Eli to reciprocate his welcoming. Although my son was only fourteen, he was very mature for his age. I forever joked he was an old soul.

Eli ignored me and focused on our son, his bottom lip disappearing between his teeth, an old habit he did whenever he thought heavily about something. He composed himself before extending his hand forward to meet Holden's. Eli's bottom lip popped free and his mouth curved in the all-too-familiar smile I'd long since forgotten.

He was breathtaking.

My heart skipped a beat as I watched them both, their smiles the exact same, just decades apart.

"Eli Warner. It's a pleasure to meet you, son." The implication of his words were not lost on me. I pleaded with my eyes for him to not say anything right then, and thankfully, he didn't.

"My middle name is Eli," Holden said. My breath caught in my throat while I waited for some kind of eruption or revelation from either one of them, but nothing happened.

After countless seconds of them staring at each other, I broke the unnerving silence by clearing my throat. "Honey, Eli is an old friend who heard I was back in town and stopped by to say hello." Moving behind my son, I placed my hands on his shoulders and ushered him from the room. "Let me say goodnight to him and I'll start dinner." My actions were rude, but I had to do something before it all became too much and Eli changed his mind and blurted out just what *son* really meant. Calling over his shoulder, he said, "Nice to meet you, Mr. Warner." *Ever the polite kid.*

"My pleasure. I'll see you again soon, I'm sure." As I walked back toward the first and only love of my life, every muscle in his body tensed. Eli was livid, and there was no way he was going to leave quietly. "I have every right to march up those stairs and tell that boy I'm his father." His hands clenched at his sides, the flesh of his skin losing all color in his anger.

"I know, but please don't. Just give me some time to think of what to say to him."

"You've had fourteen years to tell him." He glared at me, struggling to rein in his temper so he didn't lose control and start yelling again. Explaining the noise as excitement a second time wouldn't fly. "You tell him tonight, Kalista. I mean it. I'll be back tomorrow evening. I'm not letting one more day go by without getting to know him."

Before I could beg for more time, or apologize again, or ask for forgiveness, or a thousand other things streaming on a loop through my head, things I'd wanted to purge for a long time, the front door slammed shut, and I was left standing there trying to figure out what the hell I was going to tell Holden.

ELI

hat the hell just happened?

When I'd driven down that damn street, the only thing I'd been hoping for was to catch a glimpse of Kalista. Nothing more, realizing when and if I saw her, I would decide then how I wanted to proceed.

Never in a million years did I ever imagine I would have walked out of her house a father, my world flipping on its goddamn ass without so much as a warning. I thought her leaving me all those years back was the worst thing that ever happened to me.

Boy, was I wrong.

I have a son. A fourteen-year-old son, for Christ's sake. It was both the worst and best news I had ever received. Every part of me wanted to rip into her for being selfish all these years, keeping father and son apart from each other, denying us both the truth while shielding herself from the inconvenience of having to deal with me after she left. There was no excuse good enough that could warrant such an action. None. But I had to admit, I couldn't wait to hear what lies she was going to tell me when I stopped by their house again the following evening.

Holden. She named the boy after me. Sort of. That had to mean something, even though she gave him her last name. I'd rectify that issue soon enough. My son is a Warner, through and through, and there's no more denying it.

My head was messed up. I had no idea how to handle my situation, and I desperately needed to talk to someone. My first thought was to stop by Mike's house, but then I thought better of it. I still owed him for setting me up by meeting with Marek, never giving me any warning whatsoever. *Dick.* Plus, besides the unexpected drama of his sister Sierra being pregnant, he didn't know anything about dealing with something of this magnitude. *All the man does is work and have sex.*

As the scenery whizzed by, the road seeming as if it would never end, I found myself pulling into Dray's driveway. It was dark out now, but it wasn't too late, although since my brother was in full domestication mode, he might consider it rude to stop by at this hour. Once he learned the reason for my visit, though, I was sure my interruption would be forgiven.

Out of everyone I knew, *he* would understand what it was like to suddenly become a father. No planning. No expectations.

The history between him and Essie was still very much a mystery to us. She had become pregnant very early on in their relationship, but tragically, she had lost the baby, their son Ethan, which was a devastating time for not only them but for the rest of our family, as well.

Ringing the doorbell, I prayed I didn't wake my beautiful nieces; if I did, I was sure both of their parents were going to give me hell. As my finger covered the button again, the door opened and, in the entryway, stood my lovely sister-in-law.

"Eli," she greeted. "What are you doing here?" She looked beautiful as ever, wearing jeans and a plain T-shirt. Her dark blonde hair was pulled back into a messy bun and I didn't believe she had a stitch of makeup on, but her radiance shone through all the same. She smiled but her expression faltered when she took a good look at me. Pulling me inside, she closed the door behind us and immediately hauled me into her warm embrace. I gave Dray shit, always teasing him when it came to Essie, but that time I really needed her affections. I was so fucked-up. All I wanted to do was close my eyes and be comforted. "What's wrong? You can tell me."

Silence.

I had no idea what to say. I was tongue-tied because everything I wanted to tell her was going to come out wrong and mean, although I had every right to react in such a manner.

"Really?" I heard a gruff voice asking from a few feet away. "You show up at all hours of the night and instantly accost my wife?"

"It's eight o'clock, you ass."

"Whatever." Dray strode toward us, looking irritated and tired, and I wasn't sure his mood was entirely because I'd shown up unannounced. Strands of his dark hair stuck up in the back and he looked frazzled.

Essie released me and I stepped back. "I'll leave you two alone. But if you need me, Eli," she said, patting my arm, "you be sure to come and get me." She leaned into her husband. "I mean it. Dray, don't mess around tonight. Something is wrong." While she whispered her parting sentiment to my brother, I heard them loud and clear.

Something is wrong. They have no idea.

As I heard Essie's retreating footsteps, Dray threw his arm over my shoulder and pulled me into his den, releasing me before walking toward the liquor cabinet.

Plopping down on the couch, I slouched forward and cradled my head in my hands. *Where do I even start?*

I never asked for a drink, but my brother knew whatever was going on with me required a little help, of the scotch persuasion. Bumping my shoulder, he shoved the glass into my hand before taking a seat at the opposite end of the couch.

"What's going on, big brother?" His tone was light, cautionary.

Taking a healthy sip, I raised my head and found his worried stare. Normally, my family referred to me as the carefree one, the jovial one, and the smartass. Usually, I would agree. But right then, I felt like a stranger, even to myself.

"I'm a father."

Three little words, yet they held such a profound impact. I felt as if the life I'd been living up until then had been a lie. My existence for the past fifteen years had been a series of meaningless encounters with women, all the while doing my best to mask the pain and hurt which swirled around inside me, destroying any chance I had at another relationship with the opposite sex.

All because of her.

And she'd managed to do something even worse. She'd kept my son hidden from me for close to a decade and a half, depriving me of the opportunity to help raise, teach and love my child.

Dray choked on his drink, having been in midswallow when I blurted that out.

"What do you mean? You're going to *be* a father, or you already *are* one? Who is the woman? Is it someone you messed around with briefly? What am I saying...? Of course it is. You don't stay with anyone longer than, what is it, three months? Not since *her*, at least."

I was shocked that he rambled so much. Then again, I hardly ever talked to him about my personal life. He seemed to be out of his element with the topic as much as I was.

"What's with the twenty questions, man?"

"You can't drop a bomb like that on me and expect nothing. So, spill it." He knocked back the rest of his drink, reached for mine, finished it as well then walked toward the decanter and poured us both some more before rejoining me.

"I'm not sure if you know this or not, but Kalista's moved back. She's staying with her mom." His raised brows had me filling him in with what I knew. "Mike told me he ran into her a couple of weeks ago at a coffee shop. But it took me that long to gather the courage to try to see her." I ran my hands up and down my thighs, praying the back-and-forth motion would calm me.

"I totally understand. She did a number on you when she took off."

"Yeah," I mumbled. "She did." Clutching my chest, I asked, "Do you know what it's like to have someone betray you like this?"

He nodded and relaxed in his seat. "Yeah, I do," he confessed. "Although yours is a different scenario by far, I can relate to the onslaught of emotions you're probably feeling right now."

Shit! I forgot about the situation between him and Essie in the beginning of their relationship. He'd made reference to her betrayal only once in my presence, after we'd argued about the way he'd been treating her, but he never revealed the full story. And never would. Whatever transpired between the two of them would stay hidden from everyone else.

Deciding it was best to blurt out the rest of my story, I dove right in. "I finally drove to her mom's house and parked down the street until I decided on a game plan. I had no idea what I was going to do or say when I finally saw her. I was going over all different scenarios in my head when I saw a car pull into the driveway. Then I saw her. It was as if no time had passed, and I was looking at the love of my life as if I was twenty again."

Shaking away the distant memories didn't make anything I was going to say any better... or worse. "She was unloading the groceries from the trunk when a young boy came outside to help her." Gripping the back of my neck to try and assuage my knotted muscles, I grunted, "Fuck, Dray. He looks just like me, minus the fact he has her green eyes. She even named him after me. His name is Holden Eli."

I stopped talking, the image of Holden flashing through my head at warp speed. He'd gone his whole life probably thinking his father didn't want to have anything to do with him. And I… I didn't even know he existed. Anger and sadness battled together, destroying me even more than I already was.

Seeing my brother's wide eyes only drove home how astonishing my new situation really was. To be able to shock Dray was certainly a feat.

"What did you do?" he asked, leaning closer.

"Once she saw me, she practically ran in the house with him. I didn't think, I just reacted. There was no way I was leaving without getting the answers I deserved. She let me in, I confronted her, and she admitted the boy is mine. She asked for time to tell him and I told her I would be back tomorrow night. She has until then. That's the long and short of it," I finished saying, praying talking about it would help to relieve some of the emotional trauma.

Blowing out my frustration, my hands found my head again, my fingers raking through my disheveled hair in helplessness. I had no idea what was going to happen next, besides Holden finding out the man he met briefly was in fact his father.

I could see my brother trying to compute something, his lips moving in silence as his eyes furrowed in concentration. I knew what he was trying to figure out.

"Fourteen, Dray. Holden's fourteen." Standing, I walked toward the large bay window. Looking out into the silence of the night, my mind was blank. Too much information had been discovered that night, and my brain was in the process of trying to sort through it all.

Well, I had twenty-four hours to figure out my next move.

As for now, another drink is definitely in order.

KALISTA

*S*itting by Holden's bedside, gently brushing his hair away from his eyes, I wondered exactly what I should tell him about Eli. Or more to the point, why I'd kept his father from him.

Eli was a good man. Even encased in all his hatred and anger toward me, I saw the man underneath I knew all those years before. He would have been a wonderful father, and I'd stolen that away from him. No matter how much I thought I was making the right decision walking away from him back then, there was no reason I should have kept him—kept them both—in the dark for so long. But the more the years snuck by, the harder it was to go back on my initial choice.

Until I was forced back home.

I shuddered to think what decisions I would've made or not made had I not left Vermont.

I saw the look in Jasmine's eyes when I'd told her my reason for leaving when I was all of twenty years old. It made sense to me back then, but I agreed that if someone laid that same excuse at my feet today, I'd look at them like they were only operating with half a deck.

Eli's strict plan for our future was all he ever talked about. Us going to college and fulfilling our dreams, getting married *then* having children. He would whisper to me at night, *'We have a plan, and nothing will steer us from our path.'* As soon as I found out I was pregnant, I tried to tell him, but my roundabout way was too subtle, to which he repeated his mantra. I chose right then and there to free him from the burden of having to raise a baby before he was even legal to drink. I thought my actions were selfless, but I came to discover they were the exact opposite.

"HOLDEN, sweetheart, we have to talk when you get home today." I scooped a healthy serving of eggs onto his plate, buttered his toast then poured him a glass of orange juice. Doting on my son was not a duty but a pleasure, his grateful smile showing me how much he appreciated the simplest of gestures from me. While I'd woken him in plenty of time, tiredness latched on to him and wouldn't let go; otherwise, I was sure he would have asked me fifty million questions about our upcoming talk.

He was a smart, curious young man by nature and usually could pick up on the subtlest of hints when I was overwhelmed with something. His concern for me was sweet, but sometimes I wished he'd enjoy his childhood instead of worrying about me.

"Honey? Did you hear me? Please come right home after school."

"Where else am I gonna go?" he sleepily joked, propping his head in the palm of his hand while he took a bite of toast. "I haven't really made too many friends." His lips turned up in a very familiar smile, but his sad eyes tugged at my heart. Pulling him away from his friends was difficult, but the move was necessary.

"Yet. You haven't made many friends yet. But you will, I promise." Kissing the top of his head, I cleared the table once he'd finished, handed him his backpack, and grabbed my keys.

After my return home, I placed a call to the few hospitals I applied at and asked if they had made any decisions about filling the position for the radiologist tech. Each one of them gave me similar answers. They should know in the next couple weeks and they'd be in touch either way.

Shoving aside my slight wave of desperation, I set about cleaning the house before checking in with my mother. After I'd told her about what happened with Eli, she decided to spend the week with her boyfriend, giving the three of us some privacy. While I appreciated her gesture, I wished she was there with me. I needed someone in my corner, because once I told my son everything, there was no doubt father and son would join sides against me. Or maybe that was my paranoia getting the better of me.

The hours ticked by way too fast, and before I knew it, I was back home after having picked up Holden. He sauntered through the front door, flinging his backpack to the floor before heading toward the kitchen to choose a snack. His daily routine.

He sat at the kitchen island, his nectarine already half eaten when he said, "You were right." He swallowed before continuing. "I made a new buddy today. His name is Josh. We're gonna hang out later this week."

"I have to meet his parents before you go and make any plans."

"Mom," he groaned. "I'm not a baby anymore. You don't have to meet my friends' parents." Tossing the pit of the fruit in the garbage, he stared at me, silently trying to dissuade me from embarrassing him.

"No can do. You know the rules." I turned my back on him because he was going to give me those pleading eyes of his, the look that sometimes made me cave and give him what he wanted. He left the kitchen and I finished washing the scattered dishes in the sink, dreading the conversation I needed to have with him, worry causing me to chew the inside of my cheek.

Once the last plate was rinsed, I dried off my hands and slowly walked toward the living room, my heart threatening to burst out of my chest with every step I took toward the truth. Holden had been watching some comedy show and groaned when I shut the television off, but his annoyance quickly dissipated when he looked at me, my expression alone telling him whatever I wished to discuss with him was serious.

"Honey, I have something I need to talk to you about." My mouth had suddenly become dry, but my hands compensated with moisture. "I don't know how else to tell you this... but..." I faltered. *God give me strength.* "I want to talk about your father."

His eyes widened at the topic which had always been a sore subject. It had been a selfish act on my part, but I could never find the strength I needed to talk about Eli or the decision I'd made that affected all our lives. Anytime he mentioned him, I would choke up, tears threatening to break free and give away all the anguish I held close.

Only when Eli had given me no choice but to deal with it, did I realize the full impact of keeping father and son apart all these years. What a heartless disservice I'd done to them both.

Self-pity aside, I had to tell Holden everything and hope he could forgive me someday.

My son remained quiet, eager to hear whatever I was going to tell him about the one man he'd been curious about his entire life.

"Do you remember the man who came over to visit last night?"

He nodded, his bottom lip disappearing between his teeth in nervousness, a trait he apparently shared with both his parents.

"Is he... my... dad?" he asked, his voice cracking with overwhelming emotion. Holden shifted in his seat while he kept his eyes trained on me.

"Yes, sweetheart, he is. Eli Warner is your father."

He tried to remain strong and brave, but my revelation was too much for him to contain, his tears breaking free and coating his handsome cheeks, his emotions pouring forth only to break my heart. All he'd ever wanted was to be like his friends. All of them fortunately had a father figure in their lives, even if their parents were divorced. The fact I denied my son that part of his life was gut-wrenching, more so since I was able to see just what the news meant to him.

All of a sudden, he looked nervous. "He was yelling at you last night, wasn't he?" His chest shook with choppy breaths. "Does he want to take me away from you?"

Gathering him in my arms, I tried my best to calm him. It was rare Holden showed his vulnerability. He was always my strong, brave boy. It tore my heart out he was hurting, worried we were going to be ripped apart.

"No. He doesn't want to take you away. He just wants the opportunity to get to know you. That's all."

"Then why now? I thought he didn't want me," he whispered. Pulling out of my embrace, he wiped his tears before finding my eyes again. "Why now?" he repeated.

I was already twisted up, thinking there was no way our night could become any more sorrowful, and then he dropped that bomb on me. Thinking his own father never wanted anything to do with him was beyond awful, and in my quest to keep Eli a secret, I'd never once considered Holden would have thought such a thing. I was too wrapped up in keeping my past where I wanted it... in the past. And as the years ticked by, I lied to myself, believing keeping up the façade was what was best for Holden when really it was what was best for me.

I pulled him to me once more, hugging him tight and wishing my hug could erase all his hurt and pain.

"Oh, honey, I'm so sorry." I sobbed, unable to remain strong, weeping harder because my son had felt he wasn't worth his father's love and attention. And I should have known better, because I often experienced many of those same thoughts, growing up myself without knowing who my father was. Wishing one day he would show up on our doorstep and tell me what an awful mistake he'd made, and that he loved me and would be the dad I'd always wanted. To be the father I'd always needed.

When I was finally able to catch my breath, I told him the worst of it. "Your father didn't know you existed before last night. And yes, he was yelling at me, but only because he was so upset with me that I kept you from him." While it was extremely difficult to say those things to my son, it was also a relief to finally tell him the truth.

"He didn't know about me?" He sniffed, his red nose and watery eyes gutting me, but his tensed muscles relaxed in my hold.

"No, he didn't. I'm so sorry" was all I kept repeating. After more time had passed, and we were both no longer crying, I decided it was a good time to tell him Eli was coming over for a visit. I left out the part about his father giving me no choice in the matter. When it was all said and done, I couldn't deny I was relieved I'd been forced to reveal the truth after so many years of guilt and remorse.

"Eli... your dad... will be here in a few hours. Do you want to finish your homework and help me make dinner before he shows up?"

For the first time in a long time, pure happiness flashed in Holden's eyes, making my heart soar from the shallows of regret.

ELI

*A*fter my long talk with Dray last night, I realized how happy I was to be a father. I'd watched all my siblings with their children, and deep down, there was a part of me that envied them all. I loved all my nieces and nephews, and the fact I had a son of my own almost made me feel complete.

Almost.

There was still one piece of the puzzle missing, and her name was Kalista. Being with her again was surreal. Although I wanted nothing more than to wring her gorgeous neck for keeping my son from me, I couldn't help but miss her, even as I expelled my anger onto her.

Mike was right about one thing. She did look even better than she had when we were younger. Her body had morphed into a woman's, curves in all the right places—no doubt my son the cause for some of them. Her face, though, that hadn't changed except for a few small lines around her mouth and eyes, making her look even more beautiful.

I had no idea what our future held, or if there even was one, but I was willing to hear her out, listen as best I could to why she left me all those years back and why she hid my boy from me.

Snatching my phone from my dresser at the exact time it started ringing, I never looked at the screen before answering, lost in thought of my upcoming evening.

"Hello?"

"Hi, Eli. How are you?" I'd forgotten all about ending things with Beth, my mind wrapped up in more pressing matters. Apprehension riddled her voice and I was sure it had everything to do with my ignoring her calls.

"Sorry I haven't returned your calls," I said. "I've been busy." Slipping on my shoes, I walked toward the steps, my thoughts on Kalista and Holden and not on the woman on the other end of this call. "Listen, I'm on my way out for the evening. Can I stop by afterward?" I wanted to at least be respectful enough to end things face to face. Only an asshole does that shit over the phone. *Or in a note.*

"Yes, of course. I'll be waiting." She sounded happy. Too bad that feeling wouldn't last long.

The car ride to their house was short, only twenty-five minutes separating us. I kept reminding myself that I wasn't going there to interrogate Kalista. That would happen soon. Tonight was all about Holden.

Standing on the doorstep, my nerves suddenly decided to wreak havoc on me. What if my son didn't want to have anything to do with me? What if he thought I'd abandoned him his whole life? Shit, maybe I wasn't as prepared as I thought I was.

Pulling in several deep breaths, I attempted to calm myself after I rang the doorbell, the moments that followed seemingly the longest of my life. I heard movement on the inside and just before the door swung open, I released the air from my lungs. Standing before me was the person I'd come to see, the one person who'd put me on edge yet filled my heart with hope.

Holden blocked the entryway, a big smile spread across his handsome face as soon as he saw me. It really was like looking in a mirror. His dark hair was the exact shade of mine, although his was much wavier. And other than inheriting his mother's green eyes, his nose, eye shape, and mouth were intrinsically mine.

"Hello." He extended his hand as he did the previous night. I had to give it to Kalista; she certainly raised a well-mannered boy.

"Hi, Holden." I reciprocated his greeting. "How are you?"

Stepping aside, he allowed me to enter their home. "I'm good. Great, in fact." The excitement in his tone mirrored his grin.

I followed him into the kitchen, the aroma of something delicious wafting through the air and making my stomach growl. It'd been too many hours since I'd last eaten and I was crazy-famished.

"Mom!" he shouted. "He's here!" Holden turned back around and said, "You can have a seat here if you want." He pointed to a stool by the island.

"Thank you."

"I'll go get her. She's still getting ready. Girls." He smirked, which made me laugh. Whatever notion I had about how Holden would act toward me disappeared with his jest. I thought he'd be reserved and moody, but instead, he seemed comfortable and happy to see me. I had no idea what Kalista had told him about me, but whatever it was, I was truly grateful.

Before he left the room, he turned his head around, held my gaze and said, "Please don't yell at her tonight. She's really nervous." He exhaled an uneasy breath and added, "She's really sorry, too."

How old is this kid?

Fourteen or forty?

He wasn't going anywhere until I acknowledged what he'd

said, needing reassurance that I wouldn't take out my anger on his mother. I nodded.

"I'll be on my best behavior, Holden. You have my word."

My promise seemed to do the trick, his captivating smile brightening his face once again. He disappeared and ran up the stairs, calling for his mother the entire time.

Five minutes later, they both joined me in the kitchen. I'd helped myself to some water and sat at the kitchen table to wait for them. I would have loved something to take the edge off, but I also didn't want to drink in front of my son, not when he didn't know me.

I stood as Kalista made an appearance, my manners kicking in full force, even if residual fury bubbled beneath the surface. Her lips turned up nervously as she rounded the island to check on whatever was cooking in the oven.

"I hope you still like lasagna," she said, shifting her weight from one foot to the other. The simple gesture reminded me of the times she would try a new recipe, anxious I wouldn't like it. But I did. Every time.

"Yes, I do. One of my favorites."

I chastised myself for being entranced with the way she moved, silently cursing when she bent over in front of the oven to check on the meal, her jeans forming around her ass like a sexy glove. Her hair was down, large curls cascading down her back as she swayed from side to side, preparing to set the table. When she reached up on her tippy-toes to grab a dish, her body elongated from the simple movement, I almost rushed forward to press myself against her. She was oblivious to the way I lusted after her, but if she abruptly turned around, my desire would be plastered all over my face.

Damn it! I wanted to hate her. I wanted to yell and scream at her, demand answers, but it was difficult to feel any of the emotions that had plagued me since the day she'd left. I wasn't ready to let her off the hook for what she'd done, but for once, I pictured my future not enveloped in hurt and anger.

The two emotions which depicted the outcome of all my relationships with women.

Until now.

DINNER WAS DELICIOUS, and the conversation flowed between the three of us. Holden recapped his days at his new school, even going so far as spilling the beans about a girl he thought was cute. My boy wasn't shy. Not at all.

Kalista and I exchanged pleasantries but nothing more. She was nervous, just as Holden had mentioned when I first arrived, but I didn't let her mood dissuade me from the goal of the evening. Which was to get to know Holden Eli Ellington. Soon to be Warner.

I offered to help clean up after we finished eating, a gesture Kalista readily accepted. Holden had some homework to finish up, so he took off to his room while his mother and I cleared the table. Promising to come by for dinner again in a couple days made him happy, and in turn, myself.

Kalista handed me a dish to dry. "Thank you, Eli."

"What for?"

"For not making this any more difficult than it needed to be. For not calling me out in front of Holden or yelling at me, demanding answers."

And just like that, my mood changed. Gone was my laidback approach. "I'm not the same man you remember, Kalista. Not by far. But I'm not an asshole, either. My intention this evening was to start my relationship with my son. That's it. But make no mistake… you and I have a lot to talk about. I want answers, and you *will* give them to me." There was a bite to my tone. I didn't want her to think she was getting one over on me, figuring if I didn't bring up the past that she was off the hook, because that was the furthest thing from the truth. I was simply prioritizing the way everything was going to play out. First and foremost was my son... then her and me.

Placing the towel on the countertop, I backed up a step. My stare locked on hers, and for a moment, it was as if time stood still. Roving eyes were the only movements either one of us made.

When I'd gathered my senses, I said goodnight and told her I would call her the next day to make arrangements for me to see Holden again, as well as setting up time for the two of us to have our long-awaited talk.

Before I'd fallen into bed later that night, I'd sent Beth a text letting her know I had to cancel. I was exhausted, both physically and emotionally. While I'd had a great night, I prepared myself for the ones to come, and the discussions which could either help heal or destroy Kalista and me both.

ELI

*F*ive to nine in the morning, and already I was wishing I could chuck it all and leave for the day. But I had too much work to do, too many deadlines pressing down on me to take the rest of the day as a personal one.

My heavy head reclined against my chair, my lids closing for a moment when I heard my office door open. Someone had stepped inside, and at first, I assumed it was Barbara, but then I quickly realized she would never enter unannounced.

Curiosity mixed with a bit of uneasiness had me opening my eyes and as soon as I focused my attention on the man standing in front of me, I jumped up from my chair and angrily stalked in his direction. My glare warned him to keep quiet until I had my say.

His all-too-familiar cocky smile spurred me further, the small flicker of rage burning inside me turning into a full-on inferno with every step closer I took. When I was within two feet of him, his expression finally changed. Gone was the smug grin, his posture locking up right before he retreated a few paces, realizing full well he was about to experience the side of me he didn't like.

Shoving him backward, I hollered, "What the hell where you thinking giving Marek my goddamn name?" It'd been days, but seeing Mike again brought all my fury rushing back to the surface. I'd been on a slow simmer, other pressing issues taking precedence. Otherwise, I would have marched right on over to his place and punched him in his face as soon as he answered the door.

"What the hell is wrong with you?" He righted himself and took a step closer, challenging me.

"I have every right to knock you on your ass right now," I growled, my teeth grinding so hard I thought they were going to shatter. "Why, in that crazy-ass head of yours, did you think it would be okay to give my name to the leader of the most notorious motorcycle gang around?"

His cheeks puffed out with a breath before taking a seat on the couch. "I'm sorry. I wasn't looking at it like that. He'd seemed pretty cool when I met him." He leaned back and jerked his chin toward me. "Why? Did he threaten you?"

"No. But that doesn't matter. I don't want to be associated with those types of people." Mike shrugged, the simple gesture irritating me. "He's dangerous. Everyone he surrounds himself with is dangerous, and I don't need that in my life. Especially now."

"Whatever do you mean?" He chuckled. "Did you reconnect with Kalista? And of course, by reconnect, I mean have sex with her."

"You can be such an ass sometimes, you know that, right?"

"Yeah. No surprise there, my good fellow." He laughed that time, his easiness taking my mind off Marek and his club.

Shaking my head in both annoyance and disbelief, I walked back toward my seat and took a load off. I needed to prepare myself for the many questions he'd have for me once I clarified my statement.

"First of all, no, I haven't slept with Kalista. So, get that out of your head. And second, I was referring to my son."

I stopped talking and allowed my words to hit their target, making the necessary impact.

His eyes widened while his brows shot upward. "Holy shit! Are you serious?" He stopped speaking and tipped his head to the side. "Wait, what bitch has your kid?"

"It really is a wonder you're single," I grumbled.

"Whatever, man. You're just jealous I can have sex with anyone I want."

"So can I." I was about to say something else when I realized it was pointless. He was doing his best to bait me for his own amusement, and I wasn't falling for it.

He proved my point when he slapped his leg and laughed. "I love to get you going."

"I know you do." My anger had almost fully dissipated. I'd said what I needed to about the meeting with Marek, and I was willing to move on. Mike was one of my oldest friends, and while I wanted to punch him most of the time, I loved him like a brother.

He rose from the sofa and poured himself a drink.

"Don't you think it's a bit early for that?"

"Or is it a bit late? That's the real question." He raised the decanter in the air. "Want one?"

"You make no sense. And no, I don't. Unlike you, I have to work."

"Hey, I work plenty."

"Tinkering around on other people's cars doesn't count." I busted his balls. Mike was one of the best mechanics I knew. He'd owned his own garage since he was twenty-two years old, quite a feat for someone so young.

"Fuck you."

"Oh, don't get your panties in a bunch."

He flipped me the middle finger, took another sip of his

drink and retook his seat. "So, tell me all about this kid of yours." Mike was a flippant guy at best, but every so often, he came through and was the friend I needed him to be.

As he settled into the couch, I started from the beginning. I ran through the entire story about first seeing Kalista, then Holden, confronting her then our dinner together. The more I talked about my son, the happier I became, realizing that although I was still angry with her for not telling me about our child, I was blessed to have the opportunity to get to know him now. He really was a great kid, and I looked forward to our relationship.

But Kalista, on the other hand... that was a completely different story.

KALISTA

*O*nly a half hour had passed since Eli left my house and already I missed him. Over the past two weeks, he'd come over for dinner at least six times, and on the occasions he wasn't able to make it, he'd been sure to call Holden. They would talk for an hour about God knew what. Whenever I questioned my son, all he would say was, "It's guy talk, Mom." I never pushed, respecting their private time. Not once did I think that Eli would ever talk badly about me to or in front of Holden. For as angry as he was with me, he wasn't that type of person. And even though he'd proclaimed to have changed over the years, a notion I understood well, he was still a good man.

I was thrilled the two of them were bonding so well. It helped to ease some of the guilt which plagued me on a daily basis.

Speaking of which, Eli had still not demanded any answers from me. With each sunrise, I envisioned that day would be the day he demanded I tell him everything, but the questions never came. Maybe he didn't want to know after all. Maybe after connecting with his son, their love for each other growing every single day, the past was inconsequential.

Maybe I should stop dreaming and prepare myself for the day he will finally call upon me to fess up.

The more I talked about the past with Jasmine or my mom, the more I realized how much of a fool I'd been. I was young, yes, but I should have had more faith in Eli, and in us. I stole his future from him and never gave him a choice, never even gave him a fighting chance.

Lying in bed, entranced in a mystery novel, I was startled when my phone rang. Being at a crucial point in the book, I jumped when the vibrations thumped against my bedside table. "Jesus!" I exclaimed, reaching to grab my cell. Not paying attention, my eyes still raking over every sentence of my story, I hit Answer without checking who was calling.

"Hello?"

"Kalista?"

His gravelly voice broke the intense connection to my book. There was no way I would be able to concentrate with him speaking on the other end of the line. But it shouldn't be for long. The only time he called was to tell me he was on his way over or to talk to Holden. He hardly ever engaged me in conversation, and I didn't blame him. I didn't wish to push him beyond what he was comfortable handling, and if keeping his distance from me made things easier, then I owed that to him. I'd already been selfish once in my life, and I didn't want to be that way again.

"Kalista?" he repeated. "Are you still there?" *Damn, his voice is sexy.*

"Sorry… yes, I'm here." Flipping my book over, I hopped off my bed and walked toward my son's room, preparing to hand him the phone. "Hold on one sec and I'll give the phone to Holden."

"I'm calling to talk to you." My steps faltered. A rush of air almost choked me as I stood in the middle of my hallway, my body tense as I prepared to hear what he was going to say next.

Doing my best to sound calm, I said, "Okay."

"Are you free tomorrow evening?" he asked, the rasp in his voice sending bolts of lust spiraling through me the more he spoke. I would be lying if I said I didn't think about Eli, about us being *us* again. But being delusional was the only thing that saved my sanity. If that made any sense.

We'd spent a lot of time together. Yes, all our conversations and interactions dealt with our son, but we'd still shared the same physical space many times over the past couple of weeks. The initial tension which threatened to strangle both of us seemed to lessen the more we interacted, all while a sliver of allure remained between us.

"Yes, I am." In my nervousness, I never asked why.

"I'd like for you to come to my house so we can talk. Can your mom watch Holden?" He sounded calm, but the nature of what he wanted to discuss instantly put me on edge. I knew it was coming, so I wasn't quite sure why his request surprised me.

"Yes." It appeared I was a woman of few words.

"Okay. I'll see you at seven." Silence. "I'll text you the address."

After we hung up, I numbly walked back into my bedroom and stood in the middle of the large space. So many thoughts flitted through my head, and I couldn't decide which one to focus on. Would our upcoming meeting unravel the small amount of progress we seemed to have made? Would he forgive me for past decisions? Would he hold them against me for the rest of my life? Could I forgive myself if he took the first step, absolving me of all my sins where he was concerned?

He deserved to have some sort of closure after the way I'd left things back then, but would my answers give him what he was looking for?

I'll find out soon enough.

PULLING INTO HIS DRIVEWAY, I unclipped my seat belt, checking myself one more time in the visor mirror before exiting the vehicle. Wanting more than anything for the evening to go well, I whispered a silent prayer before taking a single step forward.

I rang the doorbell and I swore only a heartbeat passed before he appeared. As soon as my eyes connected with his, a strange feeling of lust and anxiety jolted me. I still desired Eli, more after each encounter with him, but I tamped down the feeling because it was inappropriate. Besides, I was just kidding myself by thinking anything could ever happen between us. There was simply no way he'd ever trust me not to hurt him again.

Eli's dark hair was perfectly styled, his three-day-old scruff making him look sexier than should be legal. He wore dark-washed jeans and a black T-shirt. Looking down at his feet, I noticed he was barefoot. His casual attire drove home even more that I was on *his* turf, entering *his* house, ready to have the conversation *he* wanted to have.

A bout of helplessness enveloped me.

"Thank you for coming." Stepping aside, he stretched his arm to the side, gesturing for me to enter. The sound of the large door locking behind me made me jump, an action that instantly embarrassed me.

Maybe because you're guilty, knowing whatever sad excuses you give him won't take away the hurt you've caused.

Quieting my conscience, I walked into the nearest room, a library of sorts. His home was beautiful. Rich colors of creams and blues decorated the walls in paintings, the glow of the fireplace illuminating their every stroke and glide. Rich leather invited me to sit, patterned pillows placed upon the couches for more of a homey feel. Glancing around, I wondered if he had a woman help him decorate. Before I could stop myself, thoughts of him with someone else crept in and I became jealous. A feeling I had no right to have, but it was there all the same.

In all the time we'd been in each other's company, we'd never discussed our personal lives. I had no idea if he was involved with anyone, or God forbid, living with someone. For some reason, I'd naturally assumed since he didn't mention anyone, he was single. But then again, maybe he didn't want to discuss his personal affairs with the one person he could no longer trust.

He directed me toward his couch. "Would you like something to drink?"

Knowing I would either overindulge if I accepted alcohol or throw up because of nerves, I decided water was the safest option.

"Just water, please."

Eli disappeared from the room, which gave me a moment to breathe and collect my thoughts, but it wasn't long enough. He was back in no time, walking straight for me, a glass of water held in his right hand.

We settled on the couch and sat in silence, both of us waiting for the other to start speaking first. My guilt riddled me, and while I didn't want to be the one to lead our conversation, I finally broke after another minute of quiet. I owed it to him to ease the tension I'd created with simply being in his presence.

"Eli," I whispered, deciding enough time had passed and I needed to give him the answers he deserved.

"Don't. I don't know if I'm ready to hear what you have to say." Shifting, he lowered his head and ran his palms down his thighs. "I'd envisioned this moment between us for so long, I don't know what to do now that it's a reality." The slight tremor in his voice couldn't shield the anger in his tone.

Blowing out a breath, he rose from his seat and walked to the other side of the room, lowering his head once again while he stood in silence.

More moments passed and still we were bathed in stillness. Deciding I needed to do something, I approached him. His body tensed as soon as he sensed I was near, and I almost stepped back, but then thought better of it. Having a decision to make, I rolled the dice and gently placed my hand on his shoulder, a move that turned out to be a mistake.

He whipped around so fast, I stumbled backward. He gripped my arms to keep me from falling, but instead of releasing me after I regained my bearings, he pulled me in to him, his warm breath cascading over my face as he held me close. Surprised by his intensity, my lips parted in a gasp, but no words escaped. His eyes seared into mine, silently trying to tell me his innermost thoughts, but I couldn't hear them.

The sharp cut of his jaw, the flare of his nostrils and the intensity in his eyes confused me. Did he desire me or was he enraged? The look on his face battled to land on either side. Trying to shove my bewilderment away, I needed to focus on why I was there... to explain myself in hopes he'd find it in his heart to forgive me.

But before I could say a word... everything changed.

Without warning.

He pulled me closer, the slightest arch of his brow telling me his battle had been won, any trace of anger quickly disappearing.

Breathing in his scent forced my thoughts back to a time when we loved each other, when we would do anything and everything just to hold the other and... just exist.

A grunt erupted from his throat, his full lips parting in anticipation.

What I'd been fantasizing about since the day he stormed into my home and demanded answers about our son was on the verge of ripping my new reality to shreds.

His tongue played over his bottom lip, the action unraveling my hunger for him.

He studied me with such intensity, heat swirled through me and trampled all reasonable thoughts that still remained.

"Fuck it," he growled, and at first, I thought he had reverted back to anger, and that he was going to ask me to leave his house, deciding against having our talk. But the way his fingers dug into my arm before pulling me even closer shot that theory down. "I can't." Again, with the riddles.

I opened my mouth to speak but then slammed it shut just as quickly, having no idea what to say. Part of me wanted to revel in his touch, but another part, the more sensible part, wanted him to free me so I could regain some semblance of thought. Before I mustered the courage to say a word, though, he moved one hand to cradle the back of my head and the other to my waist, his grip punishing.

His eyes fluttered closed seconds before he drew me in the rest of the way.

He slammed his mouth down on mine, his lips unforgiving.

His kiss was fierce.

It was angry.

It was unrelenting.

The surprise of his boldness made me freeze, but only for a moment. Once his tongue begged for entrance, I opened for him, inviting him inside with the headiest need.

Then I remembered what he'd told me. He wasn't the same man I knew.

The Eli I'd known in my youth was gentle and loving.

The man in front of me was aggressive, rough even.

His hold on me intensified the more his tongue dueled with mine, his teeth sinking into the swollen curve of my lip before soothing the bite with soft flicks of his tongue. When I groaned, he pulled back and disconnected our quick lapse in judgment.

Our gazes held each other until he pushed me away, a flicker of regret dancing over his handsome face before he gave me his back again. While a wall of contempt washed over him, I was left panting like a bitch in heat. Bathing in his fierceness hampered any attempt I'd made to regain my composure.

I need to get away from him before something unravels between us we can't take back.

Even as those thoughts filtered through my brain, I had no idea what they meant. His unfettered attack shocked me. Any other time we'd shared the same space, he never bothered to pay me much attention, his focus solely on Holden. Yes, he'd been polite, complimenting my cooking and occasionally helping me clean up, but that was as far as it went.

I had no idea he harbored any kind of affections for me still. Most of the time when he looked at me, it was accompanied with a far-off stare, like he was doing his best to remain detached from me.

But everything was different now.

ELI

hat the hell am I thinking?
That was the problem, though, I wasn't. Conflictive emotions strangled me, none of which I could grab hold of and run with. I was so angry at her all I wanted to do was ice her out with silence. But I also couldn't stop myself from picturing us writhing around together, limbs entwined so tightly I would have no idea where she ended and I began.

Then she'd touched me.

My first instinct was to disengage and shrug away from her, but the heat of her palm eradicated my initial reaction, so I chose instead to give in to what my body wanted.

Or was it my heart?

A noise behind me brought me back around. I was still turned away from her, but I could hear the shuffle of her feet, her apprehension wafting off her in waves.

How was I going to handle us going forward? Without a clear-cut plan, I needed a few moments without the threat of her saying anything to me… or touching me again.

"I'll be right back," I mumbled, disappearing from the room before she could utter a response.

I took to pacing in the kitchen, my fingers twisting and pulling my hair, hoping the sting of pain would bring about some sort of clarity. But the more time I spent alone, the worse my thoughts muddled together. My need to eliminate my demons was so overwhelming, I didn't know how to proceed.

My life was manageable before she showed back up. I tamped down that thought right away because if Kalista hadn't returned home, I would've never found out about Holden. My heart splintered a little at the realization. Slamming my fist on the counter, anger coiled itself around every cell in my body, boiling my blood and making me realize that it was going to take a long time for me to forgive her betrayal. Hard and choppy breaths worked my lungs while I attempted to regain some impression of control. If I walked back out there in this state, she'd shut down and I would be no closer to the truth.

I focused on not only my son but the fact that Kalista had never once pushed me toward him. She'd given me ample time to adjust to fatherhood, allowing me to spend as much time with Holden as I wanted, whether in person on just chatting on the phone. She didn't give excuses to cut our time short, like he had homework, or it was too late. And she'd always been pleasant during our encounters. Hell, she'd even cooked my favorite dishes whenever I stopped by her house for dinner. She was making an effort, but I wasn't completely convinced her motives weren't driven from guilt. I supposed it shouldn't matter, though. Holden was in my life now and that was all I should be focusing on.

Then why did I kiss her? What had I hoped to accomplish by doing that? I could stand there all night and try to justify my actions, but the truth was the moment she touched me, all rational thought flew right out the window.

I craned my neck from side to side and blew out a hesitant breath before steeling myself to finally hear her excuses. Nothing she would tell me would satiate my need for the truth, but I needed to hear her reasoning all the same. Pushing off the counter, I walked down the hall and toward the den.

The closer I got, the faster my heart slammed against my ribcage. The only thing I knew for sure was that Holden meant the world to me, even though he hadn't been in my life for long. We'd bonded quickly and I had the rest of my life to get to know him, to make up for the years she'd stolen from us both.

As far as Kalista and me? I had no idea. Oftentimes, I pictured us as a happy, loving family, but then other times, when reality slapped me in the face, I viewed her as simply the mother of my child. Maybe someone I could call a friend in the far-off future. Nothing more.

But that was the thing about life—it had a way of punching you in the gut. And just when you were doubled over in excruciating pain, it lent you a healing hand. Helping you to stand on your own two feet, with a smile on your face and a lightness around your heart you never knew you would feel again.

No matter how much I planned my future, fate was going to interject. I just had to come to terms with that.

Just as I was about to rejoin her, the chime from my doorbell stopped me. Kalista poked her head out of the room, looking from me to the door and back again. She tucked her hair behind her ear and glanced down at her feet before making eye contact with me once more.

"I'll be a minute."

She nodded before disappearing back into the den. Grumbling to myself because I'd been interrupted, I yanked the front door open and expected to see one of my brothers or even my mother.

Instead, Beth was the one who'd rang the bell. The woman I'd been sleeping with was the one who had interrupted my evening. She brazenly showed up at my house when she never had before. I'd always gone to her, for specific reasons... to avoid shit like this happening. I wasn't naïve enough to think she'd never find out where I lived, but it was an unwritten rule of sorts that she wasn't allowed here.

"Hi," she said, wobbling on her feet as she looked me over. She wore a tight blue dress, her tits propped high and on display. While I guessed she'd worn the outfit to entice me, bending her over was the last thing I wanted to do.

I stepped onto the porch and closed the door behind me, my closeness causing her to step back.

"What are you doing here?" My solemn expression was a dead giveaway I was more than annoyed. Never mind the fact I was frustrated with myself for not biting the bullet and ending it with her weeks before like I'd initially planned.

She couldn't have picked a worse night to intrude.

"Is this a bad time?" She grabbed for the railing to steady herself, and it was then I realized the full gravity of her condition. She was drunk. In all the time I'd known Beth, I'd only seen her tipsy one time. The night we'd run into each other at the bar when Mike had spilled the beans about his sister being pregnant.

"Yes." I should've explained, but my patience had evaporated.

She averted her eyes and at least had the decency to realize maybe this wasn't her best move.

"I needed to see you," she slurred.

Not wanting to get into this with Kalista waiting for me inside, I averted the discussion to one of a more serious nature.

"Did you drive here?" Right after the question left my mouth, I looked over her shoulder and saw her white Audi parked in the driveway. Even though I was pissed she was here and didn't wish to see her any longer, I didn't want her to harm herself, or God forbid someone else, by driving drunk. She was lucky she hadn't crashed on the way here.

"How else was I going to get here, silly?" Her lopsided smile fell when she let go of the railing and grabbed my shirt. She stumbled closer, the smell of alcohol strong on her breath.

Sensing the situation was going to become more awkward, I bit the bullet and invited her inside.

Standing in my foyer, I contemplated several scenarios, but before I landed on any one of them, movement in my peripheral vision jerked my attention away from Beth. Kalista's gaze raked over the intruder, most likely trying to make heads or tails of the drunk blonde woman and her role in my life. Neither of us had ever discussed whether we were in a relationship, so as far as Kalista knew, Beth could've been my girlfriend, showing up at my house like she'd done dozens of times before.

I'd suddenly become conflicted between explaining myself to the woman I needed answers from and letting her think I'd moved on just fine without her.

Constantly questioning myself where she was concerned slowly drove me insane. Nothing had been the same since I found out she'd moved back home. The hurt and anger I'd felt before her return had exploded the second I saw her. Then my rage had doubled when I found out about Holden.

Anarchy plagued my entire life, my emotional state all over the goddamn place these past weeks. I felt like I had to work even harder at displaying my "everything's fine" face to everyone around me, including Kalista. Well, when I wasn't giving her my "you'll answer for your betrayal one day" face.

Minus my break in judgment earlier when I kissed her, I'd been successful in portraying aloofness.

Until Beth showed up.

Drunk and pulling my focus.

Tripping over her own two feet, Beth staggered forward. I reached out to catch her, and that was when she saw Kalista. The two women stared at each other, both trying to figure out who the other was to me.

Kalista was reserved and quiet, her eyes and quickened breaths the only signs she struggled with blurting out fifty questions.

Beth, on the other hand, wasn't so discreet.

Looking back and forth between me and the mystery woman standing in my house, Beth asked, "Who is *she?*" Eyes unfocused and faltered movements proved she was even more intoxicated than I'd originally thought.

"It's complicated," I answered. I had no idea what to say or how much to reveal. Not knowing what role Kalista played in my life, other than being Holden's mother, made me not want to expand on my answer.

"Are you sleeping with her, too?" Beth whispered, but it was loud enough for Kalista to hear. Turning my head in her direction, I saw her step back inside the den, her eyes flying to mine before she turned around. It was quick, but I'd seen the pain on her face before she walked away, leaving me to deal with Beth in private.

Refusing to answer her, I pulled her back toward the front door. "Stay here." With a stern look, I waited for her to agree. Instead she wanted to ask more questions.

"Who is she, Eli? I have a right to know." Tears welled in her eyes, and while a small amount of guilt rose up inside me, I didn't have time to deal with a drunk and emotional woman. Although, wasn't the sentiment redundant?

"Just wait here."

Beth looked away from me and I took that as her acknowledgment that she'd comply.

When I walked into the den, I found Kalista pacing. "I'll be back in a half hour." She flinched. "Don't go anywhere." She gave me a curt nod before I disappeared again.

Grabbing my keys from a nearby table, I headed out the door, holding onto Beth so she didn't trip down the steps. Once I buckled her into the passenger seat of her car, I called Mike, asking him to meet me at her house so he could give me a ride back home. It appeared as if Beth had finally given me the push to end things with her once and for all.

KALISTA

"I'll be later than I thought."

"Really?" From the tone of my mom's voice, it seemed like she thought my delay was a good sign, as if Eli and I were becoming closer and were well on our way to working things out. That was how I interpreted her one-word question, at least. But things between us were complicated, and that was downplaying the situation.

I had no idea who the woman was who showed up, drunk and asking if Eli was sleeping with me too. Was she his girl-friend? If so, I would've thought she'd have been angrier if she really believed he was having sex with me. But I didn't know what sort of relationship they were involved in. One thing was apparent, though. Eli was having sex with her, and the conjured images of them together upset me.

I had no right to feel that way. I had no claim to Eli whatso-ever. But it didn't stop my heart from aching or from the unfortunate feelings of jealousy to appear.

"It's not like that, Mom," I mumbled.

"Not yet, but it will be. I've seen the way he looks at you when you're not paying attention. He still loves you, honey.

Have no doubt about that." She'd been present at a few of the dinners Eli, Holden, and I shared. Eli had been pleasant as could be toward her each time, but that wasn't shocking. He held no ill will toward her, even though she'd never disclosed my whereabouts or told him about me being pregnant when I left. No, he placed all that blame on me, as he had every right to do.

"I think you're seeing something that just isn't there, Mom. You're having delusions of grandeur again." I tried to make light of her statement because I couldn't afford to possess even the slightest bit of hope that what she said had any merit. I never mentioned the kiss from earlier because that would only fuel her sentiment and I didn't have the strength to reason with her or argue for that matter.

"A mother knows." She chuckled. "And even more so, a woman knows." I heard the smile in her voice, and before I felt the need to argue her point, I heard the gravel of the driveway kick up, signaling Eli had returned.

"Mom, I have to go. He's back, and we still have a lot of stuff to talk about." I took a deep breath. "Are you sure you're okay with canceling your plans tonight to watch Holden?" Her grandson was the apple of her eye, but I wanted to be sure I wasn't inconveniencing her all the same. She'd already been so generous letting us take over her house, depriving her of privacy for who knew how much longer.

"Don't be silly," she said. "And Kalista? Be smart if you have sex. You don't need another baby right now. Maybe after you've worked everything through and are back on your feet."

What the hell?

"Mom!" Eli had chosen that exact moment to enter the room. Our eyes locked, and I must've looked like a deer in headlights, although there was no way he could've known what my mom was babbling about.

"Oh, shush. Go and have fun."

She hung up before I could say anything else.

"Is everything all right?" Eli walked toward the edge of the couch. I'd been pacing while talking on the phone, my nerves evident from my conversation, but focusing back on Eli, a rush of a different kind came over me.

Heat flushed my cheeks, and my heart beat so fast it almost scared me. He wasn't helping any, either. While he looked tired and disheveled, he was sexy as hell. My attraction toward him had only intensified since he started showing up, but looking at him standing before me, hands shoved deep in his pockets, his shirt rumpled and sections of his hair sticking up, I couldn't help but think of him naked.

Then a thought crashed over me, dousing my excitement.

"Did you have sex with her?" I blurted, clamping my mouth shut so I wouldn't say ask another stupid question.

A smug look settled over his face right before he sat on the couch. "Why do you care?"

Good question.

"I don't. I was just curious." I lied, of course. "Is she your girl-friend?" His casualness stressed the limit of my nerves, and the cockier he acted, the more on edge I became.

"I don't do the girlfriend thing. Not since—" He glared at me, challenging me, making me squirm where I stood.

"So, she's just someone you're sleeping with then?" I pushed my luck, but I couldn't help myself. The need to know what she meant to him ate at me until I couldn't do anything but think of them together. I needed for him to clarify the role of that woman in his life if I was going to properly focus on anything else.

"Not anymore."

"Oh," I whispered, taking a seat at the far end of the sofa. I didn't think it wise to sit close to him, especially when our back and forth was going to turn into the conversation I'd been dreading since I moved back home.

Long ago, there was a time when we could exist in comfortable silence. But not tonight, and probably never again. The tension lingering in the air was palpable, part of it sexual while the remaining majority was a mixture of hurt and anger.

Fidgeting in my seat, I tried to give off the air of calm but failed miserably. "Why did you ask me to come over tonight?" I damn well knew the reason but needed him to start talking because I was going insane with all the possibilities of where our evening could head.

The expression on his face hardened, preparing for battle, no doubt. And I was kidding myself if I thought I'd walk away unscathed.

He cleared his throat before leaning forward, the thick rasp of his voice hypnotizing.

"You know why. I want answers as to why you left me all those years ago. Why you never thought to call me afterward, even years later. And why in the hell didn't you tell me you had a child? *My* child?" He grunted before shifting in his seat, waiting for me to answer all his questions. "Let's start with those, shall we?" The more he spoke, the more his demeanor changed. He was angry, yes, but it was more than that.

Pain danced beneath his façade. He tried to hide those emotions from me, but I saw them.

"Can I have that drink now?" I asked, hitting the point where I needed something to take the edge off.

He disappeared from the room, returning two minutes later. I needed more time to gather my thoughts, but I couldn't very well ask him for it. He'd tell me I'd had enough time already, and I wouldn't be able to argue with him because I'd had fifteen years' worth of the precious commodity.

Eli handed me a glass of red wine, but instead of returning to his end of the couch, he sat right next to me, his thigh touching mine and sending a jolted tingle through me.

Was it lust or anxiety? Or a bit of both?

After taking a small sip, being conscious not to gulp down

the entire glass, I placed my drink on the side table and turned back in his direction. *It's now or never.* Giving him my full attention, I answered his first question.

"Why I left you all those years ago is complicated, Eli." His lips parted to interrupt, but I held my hand up, halting the words building in his throat. "Please. I need to get through this." He closed his mouth. "Looking back on the thought process of a twenty-year-old is frustrating because I would handle things very differently now. You have to believe me. But I was scared and confused, and I thought I was doing what was best. For you. And for me, because I didn't want you to resent me... had I stayed."

"What the hell are you going on about? That's not an answer. You're skirting around my question." His temper rose, but he held on tightly to the reins. Barely.

With heavy trepidation, I attempted to clarify my response. "I found out I was pregnant and decided it was best for me to leave." Then I hurriedly added, "The baby would have ruined your well-planned-out future for us. The surprise of a life-altering circumstance would have stopped you from following your dreams, and in turn, you would have resented me in the process. Maybe not at first, but over time you would have." Breaking eye contact, I hung my head in sorrow. "I left because I wanted you to be happy, Eli." He shifted in his seat, each creak of the leather more ominous than the last. "Back then, I thought I was doing the right thing. Why should both of us have to give up our dreams?" Tears broke free and coursed down my cheeks. As quickly as I wiped one away, another followed, until finally, I gave up. I was upset, not only with myself but with the selfish decisions I'd made back then. There was nothing I could say to him except, "I'm sorry."

Countless seconds of silence followed my confession. Finally, when I couldn't take the torture any longer, I glanced up only to find him staring at me.

146 | S. NELSON

Expressionless.

What the hell is running through his head?

Does he understand why I left?

Does he hate me more now that he finally got his answer?

Does my excuse make it worse or better?

"Eli?" My voice sounded foreign to me. "What are you thinking?"

Blowing out an exasperated breath, he leaned forward and rested his elbows on his knees. He shook his head before saying, "You want to know what I'm thinking? I'm thinking that's the stupidest fucking answer you could have given me." The corner of his lip turned up in a snarl right before his leg started to bounce up and down, his telltale sign he was ready to explode. Thankfully, in the past, I'd only seen it a few times. His head jerked in my direction. "Are you seriously asking me to believe that... that pitiful excuse as to why you ripped my goddamn heart from my chest?"

The muscle in his jaw ticked, the light scruff he kept on his face doing nothing to hide his physical reaction. I parted my lips to say something, anything, but he jumped up from the couch and paced in front of me, a barrage of expletives flowing freely into the air between us.

"Please, tell me you're kidding right now, Kalista," he growled. "Tell me you left me for another guy. That I'd believe." We waved his arm around in the air. "Not this shit." I remained quiet because what I'd told him was the absolute truth. "No way you threw away our future just because you didn't want to 'hold me back.'" It wasn't a question.

My reasoning wasn't logical now, but it was to me back then. Maybe I let the fear of becoming a young mother drive my irrationality. Whatever the reason, I couldn't go back in time to change it. I would if I could.

"Tell me the real reason!" he shouted. "I've waited fifteen years to find out why." He stopped pacing, stalked toward me and stopped when his feet touched mine. He was physically close, but emotionally so far away. "Tell me right now before I really lose my shit." The sad part was for as angry as Eli was right now, his temper could and most likely would reach another level.

"I told you the real answer," I whispered.

"What?"

Doing my best to control my trembling lip, I repeated, "I told you the truth. I swear." Craning my neck, I looked up at him as he towered over me. "I know it doesn't make sense to you, Eli, but it made sense to me back then. I'm so sorry. I don't know what else to say."

I couldn't look away, even though the muscles in my neck started to ache because of the position of my head.

"Fuck!" he roared, stepping back and swiping the lamp from the table. The crash made me jump, but I never said a word. I'd apologized, but it didn't mean anything to him.

Tugging on his hair, he demanded again, this time in a gruffer voice, "Tell me the real reason. I have to know." His words were more rhetorical than anything. He was in such a state of disbelief his brain wouldn't let him compute my answer as the truth.

"I'm sorry," I repeated for the third time that evening.

Moments later, after he seemed to calm down a little, albeit only slightly, he took to pacing again. He caught my eye, looking at me like I was a stranger, and I supposed to a point, I was.

"I'm going to ask you one more time to make sure I have this right." He inhaled a deep breath. "You left me, hid my son from me his whole life, and never looked back because you thought one of us should be happy? One of us should follow the dreams we'd talked about? Do I have that right?" If he could have killed me with a simple glare, he would have.

"Yes."

"You need to leave! Now!" he abruptly shouted, his anger

returning full force. Because I'd never seen him this furious, having no idea what he was capable of in this current state, I didn't argue. I kept my mouth shut, grabbed my purse and walked toward the front door. Not once did I glance behind me for fear of what I would see.

Sobbing the entire way home, I had no idea how we were going to move forward. It was obvious from his reaction he would have accepted any other reason than the one I gave him.

But I couldn't lie.

Not anymore.

ELI

"*B*ut you don't understand, Mom," I argued, defending my stance on the debacle that was my life. "Her reason for leaving is utter bullshit." Kicking the chair next to me, I repeated, "Just bullshit."

Vivian Warner wasn't a woman who tolerated a raised voice for very long, but the compassion in her eyes told me she felt my pain. She'd seen me spiral into depression for months after Kalista left, barely leaving my room but for something to eat and to shower. When her sympathy for me had crossed over to concern, she gave me a good talking to, reminding me my life had to go on, that I would be happy again one day. I hadn't wanted to hear anything she had to say, but the woman was relentless.

Eventually, the hurt that suffocated me loosened its grip little by little until I was able to push her from my mind, only thinking about her every couple days until it was every couple months, then eventually… every couple of years.

After enough time had passed, I was able to open myself up enough to engage in controlled relationships with women.

"Controlled" being the operative word. I said who, I said when, and I said for how long.

Lately, I felt as if my life was spiraling away from me. I'd ended things with Beth and was consumed with thoughts of Kalista, hoping for our relationship to return to what it was all those years back.

But I knew it could never be.

I didn't trust her, but worse than that, I didn't trust myself when I was around her. She didn't know it, but a simple glance in my direction and I was fighting myself from dropping to my knees and begging her to love me again.

Pathetic, I know.

Never before had a woman fucked me over so much that I didn't know which way was up. I'd worked hard over the years to detach myself emotionally, even from my family to a point, because I never wanted to experience her level of betrayal ever again.

Placing a cup of coffee on the table for me, my mother sat in the other empty chair. Raising her own mug to her lips, she took a sip before speaking. "Honey, I know you're hurt. And because I know how vulnerable you are right now, I won't give you a hard time for not telling me sooner about my newest grandson, but you have to find a way to move past this. You can't go back to the way you were before." She blew on the hot liquid before taking another sip. "I simply won't allow it." She half smiled before pushing a plate of fresh-baked muffins toward me, but food was the last thing on my mind.

My mother looked slightly pensive before she spoke again, and I couldn't understand why. At least not until she uttered the words which stabbed me in the heart. "While I will never condone the decision Kalista made back then, I can see why she feared your reaction... had you found out about the pregnancy."

Her words rendered me speechless for an entire minute,

during which I tried to understand what she could have possibly meant, but there was only one explanation. "I would have never been upset with her for being pregnant. How could you even think that?" The fact my own mother was taking her side was extremely hurtful, calling all my insecurities and emotional trauma back to the forefront, when I'd been somewhat successful in pushing everything away for so damn long.

"No, honey, that's not what I meant. I know you would have been happy with the news, but I can understand her reservation in telling you. All you ever talked about was how much planning out your entire life made things so much easier. When I tried to tell you that life is messy and unpredictable, that sometimes fate steps in to force people to take a different path, you'd laugh and dismiss me like I had no idea what I was talking about."

I slammed my fist against the top of the table in frustration, but then quickly reeled my fury back in. "So, you're saying it's my fault then?"

"No, of course not, sweetheart. I'm just saying maybe you should take a look at what part you may have had to play in the way things turned out." Sensing I was about to yell again, she cut me off before a single word left my mouth. "Again, I don't condone what she did to you, Eli. Not one bit." She gave me a reserved smile. "Just think about what I said."

Silence stretched between us, and after several deep breaths and internally battling with myself to calm down, I gave in to my mother's love and understanding. No matter what, she always had my back.

Maybe I should give Kalista's words some thought. The stubborn part of me wanted to refuse, but I didn't want to continue holding on to such anger anymore. I was exhausted.

"When was the last time you saw her?"

Dropping my head, I answered, "Two weeks ago, when I demanded she leave my house." I'd refused to lay eyes on her until I could control my rage enough not to fly off the handle again. Talking to her on the phone was another issue, but I had to do it in order to get in touch with Holden. But any conversation we had was curt and brief. She'd tried several times to apologize again, but my response was cold silence. A few times, I thought she had been crying, the rasp in her voice indicating she struggled with our situation, as well. Even though I wanted nothing more than to take her into my arms and soothe her, I couldn't bring myself to move past her deception. Not yet. And the fact I battled both lines of anger and compassion confused me even more. I found it hard to pick a lane and stay within the lines.

Reaching across the table to take my hand in hers, my mom's next words threw my world into a tailspin.

"Don't be upset, but they're coming here to our family dinner tomorrow."

"Who?" I pulled my hand away from hers, already knowing the answer.

"Kalista and Holden. And before you even attempt to make up an excuse to try and get out of it, don't. You will be here. In fact, I told her that you'll be picking them up so you can ride over here together. Like the family you are." Astonishment knocked me from side to side before I could see straight again, let alone voice my objection.

I stood up so fast I kicked the chair behind me with enough force that it skidded across the kitchen tile. "There is no way in hell she's coming here, around our entire family!" An instant headache had me rubbing my temples. "It's not happening. I'll bring Holden, something I should have done weeks ago, but she is not stepping foot in this house. She's not coming near me until I decide it's time." My heart pounded so fast I was positive my blood pressure rose to an unhealthy level.

Walking around the table, my mother came to stand in front

of me, placing her hands lovingly on my stubbled cheeks. "Honey, look at me." My attention roved everywhere else but on her. I knew as soon as I made eye contact, she was going to work her mother voodoo and make me concede. "Eli," she said more sternly. I finally looked at her, the pulse in my throat beating rapidly. "I know you're all messed up inside that handsome head of yours but trust me. Everything will work out as it should." Lowering her right hand, she placed it over my heart. "You need to let this heal, sweetheart."

"I don't know if I can, Mom. I've tried to over the years... but I'm stuck." I was mentally drained. It'd been a hell of a two weeks, and I was surprised I was still functional.

"But you have answers now, honey. Answers you've been waiting years to hear." I tried to interject, but she shut me down with an arch of her beautifully manicured brow. "It may not have been the answer you wanted, but it was an answer, nonetheless. She was young, Eli. And young people often do things they later regret, their way of thinking completely different to the older versions of themselves." She threw me a sympathetic look, patting my arm before taking a step back. "Just give her a chance. For Holden's sake." *And there's the clincher.*

Leaning down, I placed a kiss on her cheek. I needed to leave, to go home and sort out my overactive brain, and apparently prepare for dinner the following evening.

Before I left, however, I asked a question I should have earlier. "Why are we not having dinner at Dray and Essie's like usual?" My brother and his wife had been hosting dinners every week for the past three and a half years, so for the plans to be changed shocked me.

"Because I thought it would be better if we were on neutral ground." I didn't bother to ask what she meant by that, because I knew all too well that if Kalista entered my brother's house, there was no doubt in my mind, he'd let her have it as soon as he saw her. This way, the dinner being held at our mother's house, he'd hold his tongue. At least, I thought he would.

"And do I even want to know how you got Kalista's number to tell her about the dinner?" She glanced at my phone before pursing her lips. "Unbelievable," I muttered, shaking my head but not surprised she'd taken matters into her own hands.

ELI

*A*s I rapped on Kalista's front door, I contemplated canceling the entire evening, but I knew my mother would kill me, and more than anything I didn't want to disappoint her. She'd done so much for me over the years. I tried my best to make her proud and chickening out of family dinner simply because I was still conflicted about Kalista wouldn't be right.

Realizing I was going to lay eyes on her soon had my heart twisted up, but at the same time, my brain screamed at me to keep my distance, to dispel whatever hold she had over me. It was impossible for a sensible man to love *and* hate one woman simultaneously. Therefore, I believed that madness pressed the edges of my sanity, threatening to destroy me before I decided which emotion to claim.

The one thing I did know for sure was that I was still furious with her, which was why I hadn't seen her in two weeks.

Two weeks of utter confusion.

Two weeks of trying to figure out if she'd really told me the truth when I'd confronted her and demanded answers.

I'd swung by several times to pick Holden up and talked to

him every day on the phone. No matter how I felt about his mother, I would never take it out on my son.

Holden flung open the door, wearing dark blue pants and a white button up shirt. I thought he was dressed more formal than necessary just to have dinner with my family, but it was his first time meeting everyone so I had no doubt Kalista wanted to ensure he made a good impression.

"Hey, buddy." I ruffled his hair when I walked past him.

"Hi, Dad," he said, closing the door behind us. He'd asked me a week after he'd found out I was his father if he could call me Dad, and I confessed nothing would make me happier. I thought the muscles in his young face were going to freeze he smiled so big.

"Is your mom almost ready?" I asked, circling the kitchen island to grab a drink from the fridge.

"I'll go check." He disappeared and raced up the staircase.

Not two minutes later, he ran back into the kitchen, skidding to a halt before running into me. "Someone's excited, I see." I laughed, pulling him into a quick hug.

"Yeah, I am. I've never had any family before, other than Mom and Grandma." He dipped his head in sudden shyness, a trait that didn't fit him in the least. "Do you think they'll like me?" he whispered, his body language telling me he was worried about the upcoming introductions.

I lifted his chin. He needed to see the sincerity in my eyes while I abated his sudden fears. "Are you kidding me? They're going to be fighting over who is going to spend more time with you. You'll beg me to leave, you'll be getting so much damn attention." My words seemed to hit the intended mark.

"I'll wait outside for you guys!" he shouted, vanishing out the door before I could stop him.

I was midswallow when Kalista finally walked into the room. Lowering my drink, I devoured the sight of her. Every time she was near, the air bristled with an electric current, and it took everything in me to ignore it as it threatened to zap any restraint I'd been holding onto.

A simple but beautiful black dress hugged her in all the right places, accentuating her curves to a point I'd almost forgot all about being angry with her. Her rich, dark hair was styled in large waves splayed down her back, tempting me to capture the strands and twist them around my fingers. As she walked toward me, I focused on her toned, tanned legs, which seemed to go on for miles. She wore a pair of red heels, putting her at the perfect height for me to peer into her eyes without leaning down too far.

She was utterly dangerous in every way possible.

Pure and simple... she was a knockout. She was going to pull my focus all night, my anger receding a notch as I imagined all the things I would do to her if given the opportunity. Once my eyes reached her face again, she blushed, biting her lip in nervousness.

"You look nice," I said curtly, refusing to babble on about how gorgeous she looked and how much I wanted to rip her dress off her body. Yeah, that wouldn't be the best thing to say, especially when I was trying to appear indifferent, resentment still niggling away at my heart.

"Thank you," she replied. "So do you."

I was still dressed in my work suit. I didn't have time to go home and change because my afternoon meeting ran later than I'd hoped. Nodding in acknowledgment, I walked in front of her out of the house, allowing her to lock up before we set off to my mother's for dinner.

The only chatter during the entire ride was between me and my son. "I got an A on my science test today, Dad," he exclaimed, bopping his head to the song on the radio. *This kid is too much.* He was so full of life; it almost had me seeing red again that she'd kept him from me. I'd missed so much. But I didn't want to ruin the evening, so I bit my tongue and gave him the congratulations he deserved.

"That's awesome, Holden. I'm very proud of you." I caught his eye in the rearview mirror, to which he beamed back at me.

"So, how far is it to your mom's house... I mean Grandma's house?" Before I could answer, he fired more questions at me. "Wait. Is that what I call her? Grandma? Or should I call her nana? Or something else?"

I laughed. "You can call her whatever you want. But all the other kids call her grandma."

"Okay." My answer seemed to satisfy him.

Fifteen minutes later and we were heading up the driveway. I was sure my mom told my entire family we were coming. Dray was aware of the situation with Kalista and Holden because I'd barged in on him when I needed someone to talk to. Then I'd spoken to both Dex and Cal a couple days later, telling them all about the new addition to my life. They were extremely supportive and excited to meet their new nephew.

But seeing Kalista again? Not so much. I was sure my mother told them to be on their best behavior, but I had no doubt any one of my brothers would tell her exactly what they thought of what she did to me, if ever they found the opportunity to be alone with her. Hell, they would probably do it right in front of me, figuring I would chime in and band together with them against her. And they would be half right.

The front door opened wide before I even had an opportunity to turn the handle. On the threshold stood my mother, beaming from ear to ear once she laid eyes on her guests. Giving me a quick hug and kiss, she ushered me into the foyer, turning her attention on her newest grandchild and his mother.

Pulling Kalista into an awkward but loving hug, she kissed her cheek and declared, "Finally. You've come back home where you belong." My mother was upset with her, but she didn't show it. It wasn't the time or place, but I was sure she would give her a stern talking to when the opportunity arose. The two women had always gotten along very well in the past, but Kalista's abrupt departure obviously strained their relationship.

"And this handsome young man must be Holden," she gushed, stepping closer to get a better look.

"Yes, ma'am," he answered. *So much for calling her grandma.* His wide eyes took her in, a bout of nerves taking hold of him until my mom pulled him into her embrace.

"You call me grandma, honey. Okay?"

"Yes... Grandma." She kissed the top of his head before directing us further into her house. A delicious aroma wafted through the rooms, making my stomach grumble loudly. It was then I remembered the last thing I scarfed down was a bagel, and that had been ten hours ago.

"Damn, Mom, that smells good."

"I know." She laughed, walking past the three of us toward the kitchen.

We were the first to arrive, which I had planned on purpose. I figured it would be easier if we weren't bombarded with my entire family. Holden wasn't typically shy but meeting an entire brood of Warners was intimidating for the best of them, let alone a fourteen-year-old boy. Then there was Kalista. I shouldn't care about her being uncomfortable, but I was. To a certain degree. Holden was very protective of his mom, and if she was out of sorts, he would be, as well. And I wanted him to enjoy the evening.

"Can I help you with anything, Mrs. Warner?" Kalista asked, fiddling with the material of her dress.

"You can call me Vivian, Kalista. No need for formalities. It's not like we've just met for the first time. I've known you since you were Holden's age, for goodness' sake." My mother smiled, but there was a seriousness laced in her tone, which almost went undetected. "Just because you've been gone for years doesn't mean I've forgotten all about you."

And there it is. My mother's dig about her abandonment.

My mother held her smile so Holden never caught on she was inadvertently scolding his mother. Kalista lowered her head and took a seat at the kitchen table. The look on her face told me she knew it was coming, and the tensing of her muscles told me she was going to take it.

But nothing further fell from my mother's lips. I was sure they would have an extensive talk soon, but not right then.

"Do you want anything to drink?" I asked my son before turning to look at Kalista.

"Water, please," they both answered in unison.

"Water it is." After handing them a glass, I chose to sit between them, looking at my watch and taking notice it was about time for everyone to start arriving. *Then the real fun begins.*

"I see you still refuse to shave your beard, sweetheart," my mom jibed. I parted my lips to speak, but she cut me off. "I know, I know. The ladies love it." She turned to Kalista and asked, "Is that true? Do the ladies love the scruffy look? Don't you think Eli is handsome enough not to have to cover his face with a five-day-old beard?"

Oh, Lord Jesus! I knew what she was doing. She was trying to make Kalista admit she was still attracted to me, pushing the envelope and making us all uncomfortable in the process.

"You don't have to answer her." I gave Kalista an awkward grin.

"No, that's okay." Turning her attention back to my mother, she took the opportunity to engage her in conversation. "Ladies do love the scruffy look as of late. So, he looks very handsome like that, but I do agree he is handsome without it, as well." A pink flush crept over her cheeks. "He's even more handsome than he was before." Her last words were more of a whisper, but we all heard them.

So as not to keep the awkward tension building, my mother saved the moment. "And because my boy is so darn good-looking, that means so are you, Holden. I bet you have all the girls chasing you."

"There are a couple of them who won't leave me alone," he said in all seriousness. He had no idea what he was in for. Being my mirror image at that age, I remembered girls chasing me down the hallways in school just to get my attention. I was shyer than my son was, so their constant attentions made me uneasy, but the older I became, the more I liked it. But I never had much use for anyone other than the woman sitting next to me. It was always her I wanted. She was the only girl for me back then.

Question is... is she still? After all these years, is Kalista Ellington the only woman I'm meant to be with? Has fate dropped her back into my world for a reason?

Bumping his shoulder with mine, I said, "You'll like the attention when you get older. Trust me."

He shrugged. "If you say so." He took a sip of his drink and looked to his mother.

I was about to ask where everyone else was when I heard the front door open, two little girls squealing as soon as they entered the house. My nieces. Isla and Emma. Which obviously meant Dray and Essie were here.

Dray was the one I confided in the most back when Kalista had left me, so he'd been the one who witnessed most of the hurt and destruction she'd caused. And out of everyone, he was going to have the biggest issue with seeing her again, even though he had a heads-up she was coming.

Pushing my chair away from the table, I prepared myself when both of my nieces rushed toward me, flinging themselves into my arms at the same time. "Umcle Ebvis!" they yelled, giving me a kiss on each of my cheeks. Their affections were returned tenfold when I gathered them in my arms, stood up and twirled them around and around. I loved these little princesses as if they were my own, and my brother knew it. He smiled big, watching our display of affections and silliness. He was still laughing when he laid eyes on Kalista. Then his entire demeanor changed, his body bristling with an undertone of anger and mistrust.

I sensed the abrupt tension in the air circling around all of us, threatening to do some serious damage unless someone took action.

And that someone had to be me.

Looking around at my family, I felt a bit overdressed. Dray wore dark jeans and a cream sweater while Essie wore the same shade jeans as her husband but with a black and white striped top. My mom was even wearing jeans, but she dressed them up with a teal silk blouse and a strand of pearls. She was a class act, always, through and through.

Placing the girls back on the ground, I removed my suit jacket and hung it on the back of my chair before heading toward my brother and Essie. I knew what I had to do to turn his attention away from Kalista. He was shooting her daggers, but thankfully she'd kept her head down as soon as I left her side. For as upset as I still was with her, I couldn't help but feel bad for her being pushed into the lion's den.

"Essie, don't you look ravishing." I pulled her close, whispering, "Please keep him in check tonight," before I released her. The sight of us hugging drew Dray's focus and he stepped closer.

"Every freaking time, Eli? Don't you ever get tired of it?" He smirked, punching me on the arm.

"Get tired of what? Groping your beautiful wife? Or of seeing your reaction... every freaking time?" I mimicked him, goading him so he'd keep his attentions on me and his wife and not Kalista.

"Whatever." He looked over my shoulder. "Where is this nephew of mine?"

Once Holden realized Dray was talking about him, he rose

from his seat and came to stand next to me. I pushed him in front, my hands resting on his shoulders as I introduced him to his aunt and uncle. He was tall for his age, and I had no doubt he'd reach my height of six one before the age of eighteen.

"Dray, this is my son, Holden. Holden, this is my younger, pain-in-the-ass brother Dray, and his beautiful wife, Essie. Your aunt and uncle."

Holden being the polite, well-mannered boy his mother raised him to be, extended his hand to one after the other. "It's nice to meet you," he said.

My brother shook his hand, his eyes crinkling at the corners while he greeted his nephew. "Welcome to the family. Don't go screaming for the hills too soon, though," he joked. Once he stepped back, Essie drew Holden into her embrace.

"It's such a pleasure to meet you, sweetheart. And if anyone gives you a problem, you come and see me. Okay?" She kissed his cheek and my son blushed, turning to look at me with wide eyes. Essie had that effect on people. I clapped my hand on his shoulder and winked. Essie soon left the room in search of her daughters, returning a minute later. She had Isla and Emma by the hands, pulling them next to her as she introduced them to my son. "This is your cousin Holden. Say hi."

"Hi," they whispered in unison. They were shy when it came to strangers, but once they felt comfortable, forget about it. They craved attention, Emma more than Isla, and it was easy to give it to them. Precious beyond measure, they stole everyone's heart.

"Holden, these are your cousins, Isla and Emma."

"Hi," he replied, stepping back and glancing up at me, his lips pursed in concentration. "Do twins run in our family?" *What an unexpected question.*

"Well, I think so. Right, Mom?"

"Yes, they do. Your great aunts, Betty and Althea, were twins.

And I believe there was another set of twins a few generations before them. Twin boys, I believe."

My son smiled before blurting, "So if Mom gets pregnant, there's a chance she could have twins?"

What the hell?

Everyone in the room fell silent, glimpsing back and forth between me and Kalista, their eyes questioning why our son would have asked such a thing.

I had no idea where his head was at. He had never seen any kind of affection between his mother and me. We were cordial to each other but nothing to indicate we were going to get back together. Maybe it was simply wishful thinking on his part. I mean, what kid didn't want his parents to be together?

"Dinner is almost ready," my mother announced, taking the focus off me. She removed the casserole from the oven and set it on top of the stove. "Go wash up."

"Do you want to come with me, honey?" Essie asked Holden, each of her daughter's hands in hers.

"Thank you." All four of them disappeared from the kitchen, leaving no barrier between Dray and Kalista. Thankfully he didn't seize the opportunity to chastise her, instead walking up behind me and mumbling, "This should be fun."

KALISTA

"**W**here's Dex and Cal?" Eli asked, spooning a healthy heaping of food onto Holden's plate. Without asking, and without looking at me sitting beside him, he snatched mine from in front of me and fixed me a plate before serving himself. "I thought for sure they were both going to bring their brood of offspring tonight." He chuckled as his mother laughed, taking a small sip of her wine.

"Dex had to go out of town, something about a project delay, so Dela has the kids. She sounded exhausted, so I told her not to bother coming tonight, that she should get some much-needed rest. And there is something running through Cal and Bridgett's family because they all sound awful. Which reminds me, honey, can you stop by their house to drop off some of my homemade chicken soup?" Vivian stared at Eli, but he was too consumed with his mother's cooking to realize she was speaking directly to him.

"Eli, I think your mother is talking to you," I whispered, leaning closer and catching a whiff of his scent. A subtle hint of cologne mixed with a woodsy smell sent my hormones into overdrive. Tamping down my inappropriate and ridiculous reaction, I straightened myself in my seat.

"What?" he muffled, placing a hand in front of his face so as not to talk with his mouth full. After swallowing, he asked more clearly, "What?"

"Can you please drop by Cal and Bridgette's after dinner and bring them some soup?"

"You want me to walk into that cesspool of germs?" he asked. I believed he was only partly serious. "Why can't Dray drop it off on his way home? He lives closer to them."

"Oh, don't be a baby," his mother chastised, a small smile upturning her rose-colored lips. She loved her children immensely, the same way I loved my son, but I couldn't imagine having to share my heart with four boys, then eight grandchildren to boot.

"Fine," he gave in. "I'll do it, but if I catch whatever they have, you're taking care of me, and I want my very own special batch of your soup." It was nice to see Eli smiling and laughing, appearing somewhat relaxed, especially after our encounter two weeks ago. But I quickly remembered how loving his family was. They'd always made me feel as if I was one of them. It had been like Dray, Cal, and Dex were my own brothers, their protectiveness over me when Eli wasn't around both annoying and thoughtful.

I'm sure they feel differently about me now.

For the next twenty minutes, idle chit-chat and laughter filled the air. The meal was beyond delicious, and the wine went down a little too easy. I made sure to have only one glass, needing to be prepared in case someone asked some hard questions during dinner. I prayed they wouldn't, but it was the first time they'd seen me since I abandoned a member of their family.

While I had been the one to leave, that didn't mean I hadn't been torn up about my decision. I'd cried myself to sleep many a night, wondering if what I'd done was for the best. Then on top of my broken heart, I had a child to raise, all on my own. Again, my decision, but it didn't make the pain go away any faster.

In fact, I still felt the gutting loss of the love of my life. It was only eased a fraction because I now had Holden.

Essie tended to her young daughters, bringing Holden into their conversation every now and then. Everything was going well until I felt someone's eyes on me. When I dared to look in his direction, I was bombarded with Dray's fiery stare. He looked much like he had years ago, only his dark hair was a bit longer, and he had a few extra lines around his eyes. He was a very handsome man, the resemblance to Eli uncanny, but the contempt in his eyes made him look dangerous.

His clenched jaw told me something was about to happen, something I wasn't going to like. For as much as I tried to prepare myself for such an encounter, I simply had no idea what to expect in the way of questions or chastisement. My main concern was that I didn't want my son to witness me being upset, which in turn would trouble him. And he didn't deserve that.

"So, Kalista." Dray leaned back in his seat and folded his arms over his chest, causing his wife's eyes to dart from him to me then back again. She'd picked up on his demeanor much like I had seconds ago. "Where have you been all these years? And why did you decide to move back home now?" His words were harmless enough, but his tone wavered between irritation and anger.

"Honey," Essie whispered. "You said you weren't going to do this." She glanced across the table at me, compassion laced in her amber-colored eyes as she shrugged ever so slightly, apologizing for what she couldn't stop.

"What?" He smirked. "I asked her a simple question. Am I not supposed to wonder where she's been, only to return years later with a son? Eli's son? My nephew?" Unfolding his arms, he rested them on the edge of the table, never taking his eyes off me.

To my surprise, Eli tensed in his seat beside me, an action I found comforting, even though the simple gesture wouldn't shut down the conversation. Dray had always been stubborn, a trait I doubted changed over the years.

My heart threatened to beat right out of my chest, I was so anxious. "I've been in Vermont for the past fifteen years."

"Yeah, we all know how long you've been gone." His tone had changed slightly, and it was enough to make Holden take notice. My son glanced up at me with a questioning look on his precious face. I subtly shook my head, gesturing everything was okay. If Dray wanted to do this, I would, but not while the children remained at the table. I needed to protect Holden in case things got heated.

Dray and I had always gotten along famously in the past, and I prayed he would take mercy on me and not embarrass me in front of everyone. But his loyalty to Eli outweighed anything we'd ever shared, so I prepared myself.

"Do you want to have this conversation in private?" I asked, hopeful he would drop it.

"Nope."

Eli spoke up before I could respond, leaning across the table as he addressed his younger brother. "This isn't the place, man," he scolded.

"No? Well, I'm not afraid to pussyfoot around her like you are."

Their mother pushed away from the table, the squeak of the chair legs causing a quick distraction. "Holden, can you help me bring Isla and Emma into the other room? We can put on a DVD for them while the adults catch up."

He looked unsure at first, knowing something wasn't right. But when he received the reassurance not only from me but from his father as well, he followed his grandmother into the adjoining room.

Once they were all out of sight, Eli let loose on his brother, his voice careful not to rise above a certain level so as not to frighten the kids in case they could still hear.

"I don't pussyfoot around her. You have no idea what Kalista and I have discussed, nor is it any of your business. Let it go," he barked, slapping the table to emphasize how serious he was.

"Not my business? Did you just say that to me?" Dray gripped the table in frustration. "Was it my business when you broke down after she left, driving yourself crazy because you thought it was something you did? Was it my business when you wouldn't come out of your room for months on end? Was it my business when I had to drag you out into the land of the living a year... a goddamn *year* after she abandoned you with nothing but a fucking note? Huh?" he yelled, rising from his seat. "Tell me, brother. Tell me again it's not my business."

Was all of what he'd just said true? Unshed tears blurred my vision at the realization that I'd done more damage to Eli than I'd ever thought possible. I swore my guilt would be my demise one day, and after hearing everything Dray just said, I deserved every bit of retribution. Whether by Eli, his family or fate itself.

"Say another word, and I'm coming over this table after you." Eli's panting quickened, and I was positive if I laid a hand over his heart, I would feel its erratic pounding.

Taking his focus from Eli, Dray pointed a finger at me and menacingly said, "You're not welcome here, Kalista. Holden is, but you are not."

Before I could part my lips to say anything in response, although I had no defense to retort, Eli made good on his threat. Thankfully, Essie had risen from her chair the same time her husband had and was standing between both men. Placing a hand on each of their pumped-up chests, their demeanor changed slightly.

"You both need to calm down." Pulling her hand away from Eli, she turned all her attention onto her husband, taking his face in her hands and saying, "Baby, it's not your place. You have to ease up. This is Eli's issue."

Being referred to as someone's *issue* hurt, even though I knew she hadn't meant it the way I took it.

After several intense seconds, he nodded and backed up a step. Essie then turned toward the other man bristling beside her, reaching forward to take his hand in hers. "You have to know your brother is only worried about you. This is all coming from a place of love." Squeezing his hand, she added, "You know that, Eli."

I held my breath as I waited to see what would happen. Finally, Eli backed up as well, never saying another word as he disappeared into the other room, leaving me all alone with the angry lion.

Essie sensed my extreme uneasiness and walked toward me, placing her arm over my shoulder as she escorted me from the room. "Don't worry about him, Kalista. Although I don't know you, I know enough of the story to know you did a number on Eli years back. Now again with your return." My steps faltered the more she spoke. "I'm not judging, but you have to understand where Dray is coming from. He's protective to a fault, and it comes across as harsh sometimes."

"I remember," I admitted.

"Good. So, you know." She flashed me a genuine smile, helping to slow the quick beat of my pulse. "Just give him time. Everything will be fine." I wanted to ask who *he* was but didn't have the strength to continue with the conversation. All I wanted to do was take my son home and forget the evening ever happened.

Even though the night hadn't turned out to be the most pleasant of experiences, I focused on the positives that happened.

Holden finally met some of his father's family.

Minus the small dig from Vivian, she seemed to welcome me back.

What Dray had said to me was probably going to be the harshest thing he would utter. He'd always been good for telling someone how he felt, then moving on and letting it go.

I believed I found a new ally in Essie.

And finally, Eli had defended me to his brother.

That had to mean something.

ELI

I had a feeling something was going to happen, knowing full well Dray had to purge himself of the vile feelings he held toward Kalista. He *was* there for me back then, dragging me from my bed when all I'd wanted to do was wallow in self-pity and sleep my life away. I understood his anger toward her, but he also had to realize that it was my life, and I had to deal with the events which had unexpectedly unraveled from her return home. Thankfully, Essie had been there to save us from beating the shit out of each other. I didn't need my son witnessing something so violent, even though both of us were entitled to the way we'd reacted.

My need to defend Kalista from my brother's fury was inexplicable to me, but I'd felt it just the same. My innate need to protect her didn't make any sense, but then again, neither did any of the other feelings I'd been experiencing as of late.

We'd left the house so quickly I completely forgot to take the soup I was supposed to drop off at Cal's house. I was sure my mother understood my need to get the hell out of there as quickly as possible.

The road ahead was dark, my thoughts so consumed with

replaying the scene over and over in my head, I almost forgot I wasn't alone in the car.

It wasn't until my son spoke that I realized I wasn't the only one who was upset over the night's debacle.

"Dad? What happened between you and your brother? Why were you yelling at each other?" I had no idea how much he had heard, other than the rise of our voices, so I wasn't about to divulge what our argument entailed. The good thing with kids was you could always play things off as *adult issues*. Although, Holden wasn't far off from being a legal adult himself.

"Brothers fight sometimes, son. It happens. Doesn't mean we don't love each other." I didn't have a clue what else to say.

"I wish I had a brother to fight with," he mumbled. His mother didn't hear him, but I did. A sudden rush of sadness filled my heart imagining how lonely he must be sometimes. Sure, he had friends, but there was nothing like the unconditional love of a brother. Even through all the disagreements and heated, testosterone-fueled wrestling sessions, love bloomed underneath, a special kind of bond which lasted forever. For the lucky ones, at least. I enlisted myself in that category because I had Dray, Dex, and Cal. And Mike, who was also like a brother to me.

For some unfathomable reason, a strange thought passed through my head, one which baffled and confused me even more than I already was.

I'll see what I can do about getting you a brother.

I damn near swerved off the road. Where the hell did that come from?

Steadying my nervous hands, I stole a hurried glance at Kalista. She was peering out the window and watching the world pass us by. Her body language indicated she was fine, possibly simply processing the night's events, but then one of her hands swept across her cheek and quickly wiped away a fallen tear.

The night had been too much for her. She'd been brave, probably expecting something was going to happen, and in turn, she handled it like a champ. But there was a crack in her façade of strength, and once I'd witnessed it, I felt awful for being the one who had subjected her to my brother's anger.

I knew right then we had to talk about so many things. Finish our conversation from a couple weeks before. Neither one of us was going to be able to move forward until we did.

I WALKED in behind them both and threw my keys on the table by the door. The clanking sound caught Kalista's attention immediately.

"Are you not leaving?" she asked her eyes red and puffy, her lower lip trembling slightly.

"We need to talk," I said determinedly before moving past her to catch up with Holden.

I left her in confusion. Again. I wouldn't be surprised if, at some point during the evening, she snapped and threw me out of her house. I'd been pushing her limits for weeks, just waiting for her to finally have had enough.

The person I'd known years before would have never put up with my shit, forever telling me to go to hell at the first sign I was acting like an ass. She was strong, independent, and fierce.

But this version of her was different. She was meek, timid even. She never raised her voice, always just taking anything I dished out, whether it was yelling at her or simply ignoring her. I didn't know how much more she was capable of absorbing without splintering apart.

I'd been a dick since I'd discovered she'd returned home. First, I believed I'd been justified because she'd hid my son from me. But as time passed, I should have talked to her, heard her out and tried my best to move on to become the parents

Holden needed and deserved. But what did I do instead? I threw her out of my house once she'd given me the answers I'd been desperate for. Then I ignored her for two weeks as if she was insignificant, merely a problem to tolerate for the sake of my son.

Wanting to finally forge ahead and create a civilized relationship between the two of us, I followed Holden up the stairs, talking about what we were going to do for the upcoming weekend. There was a movie he wanted to see, and I told him I'd take him, as long as it was okay with his mom. It had an adult rating, so I wanted to check with her first.

Closing his bedroom door, I backed into the hallway without looking and smacked right into Kalista as she rounded the corner. She laid her hand on my back to stop me and unlike the time she'd touched me at my house, a warm feeling encased me. It was familiar. I stole a few precious moments before I turned around to face her. She dropped her hand and retreated until her back was flush against the wall.

I stepped closer.

"We have to talk," I said, studying every tiny nuance of her beautiful face.

"I know," she replied, fidgeting with her hands, her eyes still red but now anxious. Her attention flitted between me and the ground, coming to rest downward when all was said and done.

"Look at me." The urgency in my voice betrayed the stoic man I tried to portray. If at any point she sensed an inkling of what I felt, then she'd have the upper hand. And I'd fought for years to make sure that never happened again. Not with any woman.

Slowly tilting her head up, she locked those beautiful green eyes on me, and a sudden heat pinged between us. Refusing to overthink the energy swirling through the air, I swallowed hard, realizing my mouth had become parched.

Kalista parted her lips to speak but instead inhaled a ragged breath. Her shoulders tensed, and it was only when she exhaled that she relaxed a little. "Where would you like to talk?"

My pulse kicked up a notch realizing we were finally going to hash out what needed to be said.

Maybe we could find a place where both of us could peacefully exist, instead of always being on opposing sides, guilt, mistrust, regret, and anger hiding in the shadows ready to snatch away whatever tranquility was present.

While I was nervous, I was also relieved because the longer we waited to have this talk, the more I felt my life would be on hold. And I was tired of living in limbo.

Since we were already upstairs, I walked toward her bedroom, never looking behind me to see if she followed. Seconds later, I heard her heels tapping on the hallway floor, and then suddenly become quiet as the carpet from her room swallowed the noise.

There was a chair in the corner, but it was covered with her scattered clothes. I could have cleaned it off and given us space while we chatted, but instead, I chose to sit on the edge of her bed. She looked to the chair then to the space next to me. She ended up choosing to stand, harassing her bottom lip between her teeth.

I shrugged off my suit jacket and loosened my tie, wanting nothing more than to disrobe altogether, take a hot shower then crawl into bed. But I wasn't home. I was in Kalista's bedroom. It'd been the first time I ventured inside, only having seen it during a quick tour Holden gave me once of their house.

"You can come closer. I won't bite." I should've smiled after saying what I had, but the only thing I did was lick my lips and continue to stare at her.

"Eli, wh-what did you want to t-talk about?" she stuttered. Years back, whenever she was nervous, she'd trip over her words. I found it adorable then... nothing had changed.

After the way I'd treated her, I should've apologized then

moved on, but something ate away at me, a desperate need to find some sort of resolution in order for us to move forward together. In what sense, I had no idea, but talking more about what we expected from the other would be a good place to start. Besides, there was one topic in particular I needed answered, one I should've broached the night she came to my house to explain what happened all those years ago. But I'd become so incensed, I'd thrown her out, fearing what I'd say if she stayed.

I patted the seat next to me, and while she looked reluctant at first, she complied. Even in the dimness of her room, I saw a light blush cover her cheeks.

Internally fumbling over my words, I counted to three then asked the one question I should have two weeks ago. "Why did you decide to come back after all this time?" Whatever her answer was, I vowed not to judge, overreact or yell at her. There could be a thousand reasons why, and even if it didn't make sense to me, much like why she'd left, I'd keep a cool head. I would take her answer as the truth and devise some sort of plan for both of us to move on.

A lock of hair fell over her eye when she turned to face me. Before I realized what I was doing, my fingers trailed along her temple and rested on the side of her face before tucking the errant strand behind her ear.

Soft breath kissed my palm before I moved my hand away, silence circling us and threatening to tear apart whatever progress we'd made, which hadn't been much.

When I'd agreed to pick up Kalista and Holden earlier tonight, I envisioned a tense dinner, followed by a silent car ride back to their house afterward. The possibility always existed that one of my brothers, or mother, for that fact, would make some sort of comment to Kalista, but I never thought the situation would become as heated as it did, Dray spewing all that shit at me. At her.

To say the night hadn't gone as planned was an understatement. And there I was, still with her, sitting next to her on the bed and waiting for her to answer my question.

Her silence allowed my brain to conjure all sorts of memories of the two of us, even fantasizing about making some new ones.

My urge to bury myself inside her overwhelmed me, thoughts of ravaging her until the sun came up most certainly weighing heavy on my mind. *That damn dress is partly to blame.* The possessiveness I'd felt earlier when protecting her from my brother still raged on, tamped down only to allow me the cognizance to deal with one thing at a time.

Instead of looking away, Kalista kept her lovely eyes focused on mine, her teeth doing a number on her plump lower lip.

"It's a long story." My shoulders deflated a fraction when she spoke. "But you deserve to know everything." On a sharp inhale, I settled in for her explanation, half expecting she'd breeze over her reasoning, giving me some sort of generic answer. *Just listen,* I silently repeated, recognizing this entire situation was difficult for her, if her chewed lip and fidgeting hands were any indication.

Keeping my distance while still sitting close, my eyes followed her every subtle movement. Hesitation bled from her fingertips, making the air in the room more intense as the seconds ticked by.

"I ran away from someone." Immediately after she spoke, she hopped off the bed and hurried across the room, turning her back on me before hanging her head.

Out of all the reasons she could've given me, did it have to be another man? I realized the prospect was within the realm of possibilities but hearing her refer to one hurt more than I wanted to admit.

"Did you promise to love him forever, too?" I hated every word that left my mouth, not only because I didn't want to picture Kalista in the arms of another man, but they reminded me of what she'd done to me, as if I could ever forget. My words were thoughtless, but the pain I felt rose up inside me and forced its way from my throat. "Shit!" I punched the mattress beside me before standing, staring at Kalista and willing her to look at me. But she kept her head down. Then a sob escaped, and her shoulders shook, and I felt like an asshole.

The longest minute of my life passed before she finally calmed. Or so I thought. As soon as she sensed I was close, she whipped around and glared at me. Even though her tears continued to fall, she was pissed, and oddly enough, I'd been waiting for her anger to make an appearance.

She took a single step toward me and pointed in my face. "You never stalked me, *Eli*. You never attacked me. You never beat me so bad I ended up in the hospital. You never shoved our son so hard he flew across the room." Her voice rose with each devastating statement. Swiping away more tears, she moved even closer. "So no, to answer your question, I didn't profess my love to him for eternity. I had him arrested, left the life I'd known for years and moved back home." Reaching out to touch her arm proved to be volatile. "Don't touch me," she shouted. "Are you happy now?" Her breaths were choppy, her chest moving in quick succession as she tried to control herself. "Kalista, the heartless bitch, got what she deserved." She tried to run past me, but I blocked her escape, the look in her eyes morphing from anger to fear, reminding me of some sort of dangerous and frightened caged animal. I moved my hand toward her once more. "Don't touch me," she repeated, her voice barely audible. She kept her eyes pinned to mine and I wanted nothing more than to take away her pain, but I couldn't. I'd only added to it.

"I'm sorry." Every part of me wanted to tackle her just so she'd allow me to hold her. But I restrained myself and approached with caution. Her posture locked up when I moved into her, and before she could attempt to flee once more, I pulled her into me. She fought me, shoved at me to try to push me away, but soon gave up the fight, retching sobs dispelling her anguish.

"Forgive me." I rubbed her back to soothe her, my touch seeming to quiet her soulful cries, all while she kept her hands locked at her sides. "I had no idea." There were still questions that needed to be answered, but there was time for that later. Right now, all I wanted to do was comfort her, her distress rocking the both of us to our core.

Soon afterward, she wrapped her arms around my waist and stepped into me, hugging me tighter than I believe she ever had before. More of her tears fell and I held her as she released the torments that had weighed her down for God knew how long.

When she finally calmed, I pulled back and caressed her cheeks, wiping away the last of her sadness. "I'm so sorry. For everything. I should've been more open that night instead of blowing up at you and kicking you out of my house. I should've given you a chance to explain without shutting you out. I was so angry." I lowered my lips to hover over hers.

"I'm the one who's sorry. I never should have left you back then without talking to you." She closed her eyes briefly. "I never should have kept Holden from you." A lone tear escaped, but I caught it with my thumb.

Our mouths were so close we shared the same breath. I didn't want to overstep and take advantage while she was vulnerable, but I wanted nothing more than to taste her again. I'd kissed her once since her return, but it was done in anger and frustration.

Now our circumstances had changed.

KALISTA

*S*o much had happened in the span of not only the past couple of hours but in the last twenty minutes, my emotions doing a great job of rendering me utterly useless because they were all over the damn place.

When we'd entered my bedroom, I had no idea what to expect, dashing all my lingering and inappropriate thoughts when I saw Eli sitting on my bed. At first, I was confused, then I was nervous. Then in the flick of an instant, I'd flown straight through to anger before catapulting into sadness.

Now here we are, our mouths so close his lips tickled mine. We'd both apologized for our part in everything that had transpired in the past and most recently. So then why was he still here? Tormenting me with the idea he wanted more, if only for tonight?

He looked at me like he used to when we were younger, before I broke his heart. Could it be possible for him to completely forgive me? To even go so far as to picture a life with me moving forward? Or did he only have one goal right now, to get me into bed? Because if that was it, he didn't have far to go to achieve such a feat. My defenses were weakened so if Eli attempted to seduce me, I'd cave.

Neither one of us made the first move, still entranced with the intimacy we shared. Was he waiting for me to initiate, not wanting to exploit my vulnerability? Did I want him to be the aggressor, stealing my indecision and persuading me to take the leap?

Our new dance was torture.

Deciding to make the decision for us both, I erased the millimeter of distance and pressed my lips to his, reveling in the feel of his delectable mouth, my mind running rampant trying to guess at what he would do.

Would he pull away?

Would he lean in?

Were we moving too fast?

Four heartbeats later, he finally gave in.

To me.

To us.

He opened his mouth, his tongue flicking out and gliding over my bottom lip in the sweetest seduction. "I need you so bad," he growled, moving his hands from my face to grip my arms, pulling me impossibly close. What were we doing? I wanted to delve into the ramifications of allowing myself to be swallowed up by Eli, but my need to be consumed by him trampled the consequences. So, I let go. With my mouth slightly agape, I gave him the permission he sought and welcomed his desire for me, our tongues dueling as he walked me backward toward my bed.

The back of my legs soon hit the edge of the mattress, Eli holding on to me as if he feared I'd somehow disappear. His kiss became more aggressive, baring his teeth to nip the tip of my tongue before sinking those pearly whites into the plumpness of my bottom lip. Before I could reciprocate, though, he abruptly released me and stepped back, wariness pulling his brows tightly together.

"What's wrong?" I asked, reaching to touch him, but my arm fell to my side when he retreated another step.

His chest inflated before he released a strained breath. "I'm different now, Kalista. I'm not the same man you once knew."

"What do you mean?" Instead of answering, he just stared at me, and I could only imagine what was going through his head. "Tell me what you mean."

"I'm different now," he repeated, hanging his head and finally breaking eye contact.

"Yeah, you mentioned that, but you still haven't clarified anything." My imagination ran wild, yet I had no clue what he meant.

His head shot up when I reached for him once more. "I need to fuck... hard. Rough. I can't do loving and tender. I haven't been that way since—"

"Since I left," I finished.

A simple nod confirmed what I'd said was right.

Instead of allowing his words to sink in, my curiosity took over and I fired question after question at him. "Are you into BDSM? Do you need to hurt women to get off? Do you need them to hurt you back? Why do you need to have rough sex?" I felt like I was talking to a stranger, and I supposed to a point... I was. Eli had been a twenty-year-old guy when I'd left. But standing in front of me was a thirty-five-year-old man, the harsh years of my abandonment seemingly taking their toll on him, hardening him in ways I could never fathom.

I straightened my posture and stepped into his space, and that time he didn't pull back when I reached out to touch him. I placed my hand on his chest, the thrum of his heartbeat pounding against my fingertips. My gut told me I'd been the one who turned him into someone who could only enjoy sex if it was rough, so I decided right then and there that I wanted to be the one who would bring him back. Back to the Eli who would look deep into my eyes while his body stoked mine, slow and steady. Back to the Eli who used to cradle me from behind and play with my breasts, whispering sweet things in my ear before he nudged my leg forward so he could push inside me.

I was willing to sacrifice tenderness in order to give him what he needed. I owed him as much.

He moved around me to sit at the bottom of the bed, leaning forward to rest his arms on the tops of his thighs, staring into the open space in front of him instead of looking at me. I swore he stayed frozen like that for the longest time before finally lifting his head.

"I'm not into BDSM, although I tried it for a stint." He hesitated before adding, "And yes, I need to hurt the woman, and she me. But the pain always leads to pleasure, Kalista. I'm not a pure sadist." He stood before edging closer, all while still giving me the space I needed to compute his words, to devour them fully. "I wouldn't do anything you couldn't handle, so please stop looking at me like that. I can't take it when you look at me like that," he whispered before dropping his head again. I had no idea I gave him any sort of expression, but apparently, I had, one harsh enough for him to pull his eyes from mine.

It took me some time to find my words, but once I did, I dove in headfirst, my need to connect with Eli outweighing any hesitation I held close. "What do you need to do?"

A simple question, but there didn't seem to be a simple answer. He'd admitted he hadn't been gentle and tender with a woman since me, which told me he needed the pain to numb the hurt and anger I'd left him with. By no means was I a psych major, but anyone with a brain could understand the reasoning behind his new proclivity. A small wave of hesitancy had me fearing that once he got his hands on me, he wouldn't be able to control himself. After all, *I* was the woman who had initially fed his urge to be rough.

Completely lost to my inner ramblings, his words startled

me when he spoke. "I need to be in control, manhandling the woman any way I see fit. Spanking is a big part, as well as hair-pulling and biting." He grimaced before adding another tidbit of information. "I've dabbled in breath control, as well."

"You mean choking?" My raised voice was quickly lowered.

"Yes."

Once he'd finished explaining himself, a wariness seemed to drift over his handsome face. A reluctance that wasn't there seconds ago. Gliding the back of his hand along my jaw, he shook his head, opening and closing his mouth several times but never saying anything.

"What?" I asked, not sure I wanted to know the answer.

"I'm not sure if I can do any of those things to you. There was a time I desperately wanted to but now... I don't think it's possible."

"Why?" I asked, curious about what made me so special. Or not so special, depending on how I looked at it.

"Because I don't want to taint my memory of us together. Back then. My life since you has been nothing but a string of women, women I've had brief relationships with, if you can even call them that. I've never brought any of them home to meet my family. Not a single one." He turned his back to me, his hand massaging the tight muscles of his neck. "I closed myself off, only taking what I needed, when I needed it, and how I needed it. They complied because they wanted to be with me." He sounded conflicted. I doubted he wanted to face me while he recanted his long list of sexual encounters, but I needed to see his face. His eyes were expressive, and it was rare he could hide something from me while I was locked on to them.

Moving in front of him, grabbing his arm when he tried to turn to the side, I halted him with a shake of my head. Like me, he did what he needed to in order to get through the day, and while his confession saddened me, I needed to tell him something sincere yet painful.

"I know what I did to you is unforgivable, but please don't let me be the reason you go through the rest of your life never experiencing love." My heart broke saying those words to him, because all I wanted was for him to take me in his arms and profess his undying love to *me*. To tell me he never stopped loving me, even when he was angry with me.

Even when he hated me.

I laced my fingers with his, staring at our joined hands while I contemplated what I'd say next, if anything. The love I felt for the man standing in front of me had never diminished over the time we'd been apart. It had only been put on the back burner while I existed in a world without him. I lived simply to exist, Holden being the one bright shining star in my otherwise dark life.

And since I still loved Eli, I wanted more than anything for him to be happy. Even if it wasn't with me.

When I returned my eyes to his, I exhaled, freeing the weight of some of my guilt with my admission. "I want you to love again, Eli. We were over-the-moon happy back then, and I want that for you again." Each word was like a tiny razor blade slicing me to pieces. I didn't know how I would react to seeing him with someone else, even if it was five years in the future. Hell, I was jealous and heartbroken when that woman had shown up at his house, and that was before we'd crossed over to the place we were now, wherever that may be. Our relationship was still fragile, the slightest kink threatening to unravel everything once and for all.

Tightening his fingers around mine, he surprised me when he asked, "Is that what you want to do? Find someone else to love?" His look was both desperate and angry. I didn't know how to answer him. I didn't wish to be alone for the rest of my life, but I also wasn't ready to delve back into the dating world either. My last go at a relationship landed me in the hospital. Then there was the fact that I'd never truly given myself to another man either because half of me was missing the day I'd left the love of my life.

The man standing in front of me.

The father of my son.

"I don't want to find someone else. But the sad truth is our history, while wonderful before I left, is now tainted with disappointment, distrust, and uncertainty. All on my part, I'm aware, but it's there nonetheless."

He chewed at his bottom lip, his expression guarded as if he was afraid I would read his thoughts and reject whatever he was going to say before he voiced it. "What if we work on it?"

I tried to pull my hand away, but he restrained me, his furrowed brows doing nothing to hide the hope in his gaze.

He guided me back toward my bed, forcing me to sit while he loomed over me, trapping me until I answered. What did I want to say? What did I *need* to say? Of course, I would have loved nothing more than to try *us* again, but was it futile? Would he ever find it in his heart to truly forgive me? To trust me again?

At first, his proposal seemed to come out of thin air, but if I was honest with myself, something had been building between us ever since we'd seen each other again. Whatever that was derailed a bit after I explained why I'd left all those years ago. But now, the spark of intensity had been fueled and the fire raged once more.

My love for him never waned; it was simply put high up on the shelf, taken down to look at and ponder over when I was sad and lonely. Regret eating me up inside until I decided enough was enough and put it away for another day.

Leaning down, he placed his hands on my thighs, bringing his face so close to mine that if I inhaled quickly enough, our lips would graze over each other. "So, what do you say?"

I moistened my bottom lip, biding me some time before I

answered. I wanted to consider his offer, but I wasn't sure if it was some sort of test. *Yeah, that's where my head went.*

"Are you really saying you want to be with me? To start over?" My heart kicked up a notch as I waited for his answer.

He responded by pressing his lips to mine, forcing me down until I was flat on my back.

"Yes. I want to give us another shot. I want us to try and be a real family." He hovered above me, looking into my eyes and revering me as only he could. Words eluded me, my brain battling with my body the longer he lingered over me.

Entwining my fingers at the nape of his neck, I tugged on his hair and raised my head at the same time I pulled him close. I parted my lips and he responded, his tongue sweeping through my mouth to taste me, to drive me insane.

He was gentle, slow, loving. Everything he claimed he couldn't be. *I knew he was still in there, even if he didn't want to believe it.*

In a few simple movements, he repositioned us so we were near the headboard, my legs falling open so he could settle between then. He lifted the hem of my dress and tucked his thumb into the waistband of my lace panties, toying with the material but not removing them. His fingers skimmed over my skin before digging in, his kiss setting me on fire. I'd kissed other men before, but the connection I shared with Eli was on a whole other realm.

He knew how to touch me, tease me, worship me in ways that made me yearn for more.

"Eli... please," I panted, begging for everything he was willing to give me.

"Fuck, Kalista. You have no idea how much I want this." Instead of ridding me of my dress, he hopped off the bed and tore at his clothes, removing every shred of fabric in record time. I laughed when he tripped over his foot, but he righted himself before falling. He returned my grin, but his laughter was soon replaced with longing, his piercing stare focused only on me. One step toward the bed and I held up my hand to stop him. "Let me look at you." I scrambled to sit upright, devouring the sight of him and committing him to memory in case he changed his mind about us afterward. He was glorious, every crease, every hard-sinewy muscle begged to be stroked. It'd been a long time since I'd laid eyes on his body, and while he'd been a rare specimen back then, he was even more beautiful to me now.

"Do you like what you see?" he asked, seduction laced around the edge of each word. He reached for my leg, but I moved to the middle of the bed. While I wanted to prolong the anticipation, I also needed some time to be sure I could do this. I needed to be ready to give him what he needed. He told me earlier he couldn't do any of those things to me, but I didn't believe him. There was no way he could change overnight, even if he wanted to. "What's the matter?" With one knee on the mattress, he leaned over and grabbed my hip, holding me still. "How is it possible that I haven't ripped off this dress yet?" The smug grin on his face told me he'd correct that mistake. And sure enough, he lifted the hem of my dress up my body until the fabric cleared my head, pulling the cups of my bra down until my breasts spilled over, taking one into his mouth then the other before sitting upright once more.

He pushed me to lay on my back, his hands traveling over my flushed skin. He gripped the lace fabric of my panties with both hands, and instead of fiddling with them like he'd done before, he ripped them. Then he set about doing the same thing on the other side until I was freed for him to feast on.

His eyes trailed over my body right before he pinched my nipples. I gasped and writhed beneath him, but he paid me no mind, feeling his way down further until he came upon the scar on my lower abdomen. "What happened?" A deep crease appeared on his forehead as he studied the faint mark.

"It's a cesarean scar." I placed my finger alongside his. "Holden didn't want to come out otherwise." I smiled at the memory, although I'd been scared out of my mind when the doctor had told me my baby was in distress and they had to wheel me into surgery.

"I'm so sorry I wasn't there with you," he said, caressing my cheek before tilting his head slightly to the side. I didn't know what to say to that. He hadn't known about Holden, and his apology ricocheted through me, the guilt I still held close rising up to strangle me.

Sensing my twinge of awkwardness, Eli pressed his chest to mine, nestling in the space between my jaw and shoulder, his warm breath tickling my skin. Instead of enjoying the closeness, I envisioned all the ways our encounter could go wrong. I swore my mind was my worst enemy sometimes. Reservation took hold and I stiffened beneath him.

"What's wrong?" he asked, pulling back to look at me. I wanted nothing more than to lose myself to the sight of him, to the feel of his hands roaming my heated skin, but I was frightened. Not because I was necessarily afraid he'd hurt me, not completely, but because I feared I wasn't good enough for him any longer, in any way that counted.

"I don't know if I can give you what you need." Rising up on my elbows, I whispered, "What if I can't please you now?"

"Why would you think that?" He shook his head. "Never mind, don't answer." He pursed his lips and squinted his eyes, an expression I remembered finding quiet endearing when we were younger.

"What is running through that head of yours?"

"I'm trying to think of a way to convince you that you're all I want. Any way I can get you." His chest deflated before he moved down the bed, leaving every bit of me completely exposed. I attempted to close my legs, but he stopped me with a firm hold on my knees, parting my thighs even wider. "Don't ever hide from me." His voice had deepened, became raspier. When he licked his lips, my hips rolled, and from the way he looked at me... there... I realized we both wanted the same thing. "I just want you to feel." He positioned himself until his breath rushed over me, his fingers opening me so there was nothing left to hide from him. "Don't think," he said, right before his lips closed over my clit, the tip of his tongue flicking over the sensitive bundle of nerves.

I gasped right before quick breaths were pushed from my mouth. I gripped his hair and pulled him closer, the stubble of his short beard tickling me, the friction from his mouth driving me insane. Without a word spoken, he pushed two fingers inside me, pumping them while he ate my pussy. I enjoyed his torment, his mouth and hand working me toward bliss when I almost shot off the bed. He touched something inside me that sent a jolt through my entire body, and I couldn't determine if I liked it or not. I tried to push him away in my confusion, but he threw his arm over my belly to keep me still.

"What's wrong?" He didn't wait for me to answer before he continued his sweet torture. I relaxed, albeit briefly, before he touched the spot once more.

"Eli," I cried, trying to move up the bed.

"Did I hurt you?" he mumbled, holding me firmly in place between flicks of his tongue.

"No," I replied, still confused why I suddenly felt like I had to pee yet wanted him to do it again. "It's a strange feel—" I moaned when he bit my clit, careful to only apply the slightest of pressure. He'd never touched me this way when we were younger, but I refused to chase the thought of how he'd gained his experience since me. Instead, I gave in to his touch, an electric buzzing starting at the base of my spine and shooting everywhere. He hit the spot again and my release was imminent. I couldn't catch my breath, so I held it until my lungs burned. He hit it again and sucked on my clit at the same time, my looming orgasm just within reach, but before I could give in to the wave threatening to crash over me, he pushed my knees toward my chest.

"I'm so close." I bunched the sheets in my fists.

"I know, but trust me, you'll like this position better." His confidence mixed with the smug gleam in his eyes made me believe him. Again, thoughts of how he knew so much threatened to wreck my heart, but I chased away the dreadful thoughts and images and focused on the way he made me feel. His reverence for my body soothed my soul and had my heart melting. My impending orgasm was brought back to life within seconds of him getting his mouth on me and his fingers inside me, crooking them and stroking me into oblivion.

"I can't," I cried, wriggling to get away from him, yet pulling him closer at the same time, my hands gripping his shoulders.

Eli said nothing, his tongue lavishing me quicker than before, his teeth bared to elicit a sting of pain before assuaging the ache with his skillful mouth.

I tried to straighten my legs, the intensity of what I felt borderline too much, but he held me in place with ease. The only sound he made was a growl when I shifted to the side, but he righted me into place just as my body locked up and I came harder than I ever had before. I swore when I closed my eyes, spots of flashing lights lit up the darkness, the air catapulted from my lungs over and over. Thrashing my head from side to side, I reached for the top of Eli's head, and just when I thought I wanted to push him away from me, allowing me to ride out the last of my orgasm, I thrust upward as I yanked him closer. I swore I could feel him smiling against me but gave up caring as the last of my tingling jolts slowed.

My heart pumped so fast I became dizzy but thankfully, the feeling didn't last long. Eli had disappeared from between my legs and was now sitting back on his haunches, his eyes roving over me with a sense of accomplishment.

Moments later, I finally found my voice, my breaths regulating back to normal. "That was amazing. How did you—"

He shook his head. "Don't." He looked to the side before back to me. His brief look of hesitation was gone, replaced with a hunger I remembered from long ago. "You're so beautiful." My legs straightened out but fell open when they hit the mattress. Eli was on me in seconds, finally unhooking my bra and tossing it to the floor before spreading me wide again with the nudge of his knee. He positioned himself on top of me, his hips pinning mine to the bed. "I've missed you so much, baby."

I wanted to tell him the same, to tell him how sorry I was for the hundredth time, but his lips stole my words before I could form them.

ELI

*A*t the beginning of the evening, I had no idea whatsoever we were going to end up in her bedroom, me pinning her down with my head buried between her gorgeous thighs.

How quickly things changed when the possibility of something more presented itself. But it wasn't merely a yearning to be with Kalista that had me rethinking our entire situation, but a need. One so fierce it drove me insane, desperate at the thought of us connecting like we once had.

I loved Kalista. I'd never stopped, even after years of absence. I tried to seem unaffected by her, but I'd crumbled during dinner. Coming to her defense was the first brick to fall from the wall I'd built around myself since she'd left me.

From the first time I'd laid eyes on her again, even while I'd been furious with her, I'd pictured us just like we were, her beneath me and begging for me to please her. Before tonight, while I wanted to consume her, I also wanted to keep her at a distance emotionally. I wanted to torture her yet show her I'd moved on without her.

But the love we'd once shared continued to burn underneath, just waiting for gasoline to be poured on the fire, threatening to erupt at any moment. And that accelerant was my brother humiliating her, spurring my incessant need to protect what was mine. To come to her defense and show her I was the man who would take care of her.

Delusional?

Maybe.

Caveman-like?

Sure.

But I didn't care.

Pinning her hands above her head, capturing both in one of mine, I trailed the other down her cheek, then her neck, moving until I reached her breast. My swollen cock pressed against her opening, and when she twitched and thrust her pelvis upward, the tip entered her.

I had to have her.

I had to ravage her and show her how much I'd missed her.

I had to bury myself so deep inside she would feel me for days.

But I stopped moving, needing to get something out of the way before we continued. "Are you on the pill?" It wasn't sexy talk, but it was necessary. I needed to know if I should be wearing a condom, even though I hated the idea. Since her, I'd always been careful, wearing protection no matter who I was with. But with her, it was different. I didn't want there to be any kind of barrier between us when I finally sank inside her. I was in good health, but I hesitated briefly when I had to ask her about hers. "Are you good? You know…" I fumbled over my words, stealing my eyes from hers in quick desperation. Asking her if she was on birth control was completely different than asking her if she had an STD.

Thankfully, she put me out of my misery, chuckling at my apparent embarrassment. "Look at me, Eli." She brushed her mouth against mine before laying her head back onto the pillow. When I complied, she said, "I started taking the pill a year after Holden was born. And I haven't had sex with anyone without a condom. Not since you. But I do get tested regardless, every year at my annual exam. So, I'm good to go." The faintest smile curved the corners of her lips. Her affirmation was all I needed before my need to claim her reared to life once more.

With the flex of my hips, I pushed in further, roughly pinching her nipple until it puckered. Kalista gasped, but I never allowed her to say a word, my tongue sweeping through her mouth and swallowing her screams.

She devoured my need for her as I did hers, our kiss intensifying, my need to dominate her dueling with hers to touch me. She wriggled her hands, but I kept them in place, wanting to show her what I could do to her, to show her she didn't need to be fearful of the way I was now. Although there was no doubt in my mind that I wouldn't treat her like I had the others, I couldn't tamp down every point of the roughness I enjoyed.

My hunger drove me to obliterate her, and without a second of hesitation, I thrust until I was seated to the hilt. She sucked in a gulp of air before throwing her head back and closing her eyes. I swore every muscle in my body tightened. I pulled back to start moving, but her clenched face made me stop.

"Give me a second." Her plea sounded pained, and I internally cursed myself. I'd hurt her without meaning to, or had I? I was well endowed, and I should've remembered what it was like for her to take me in one swift motion. And whether it was my need to be rough or my need to be deep inside her that fueled my actions, I couldn't say for sure. Possibly a mixture of both, although deep down I didn't wish to harm her in any way. Not anymore. Soon after, she lowered her eyes to mine and said, "I trust you." She'd given me everything when she uttered those three words.

"Wrap your legs around my waist." She did as she was told, linking her ankles and squeezing me tight. As I moved inside her, I was hit with all sorts of random thoughts and images. Of her with other men, faceless men. Of her screaming out from someone else's touch. Before I lost myself to deep in the concoctions of my imagination, I reminded myself that no matter who she'd been with while we were apart, no one could please her like I could. No one, past or future, would be on the receiving end of the love that was laced in her eyes, other than me. Possessiveness shuddered through me, pulsing through my veins and threatening to wreck every inch of me.

Pushing everything aside, I focused on the feel of her body wrapped around me. On the way her pussy milked my pleasure from me, threatening to be my undoing if I didn't slow down. I'd waited so long for this moment; I didn't want it to end before I'd had my fill. But that was the thing, I didn't believe I'd ever get enough to satisfy me. I'd want more, then even more still.

Would she?

Kalista twisted her hands in my hold. "I need to touch you. Please," she said when I didn't make a move to release her.

"If you touch me, I fear I'll lose it." Even as I heard the words, I didn't understand the severity of my confession, but I realized what I spoke was the truth. Her legs wrapped around me was one thing, but if she ran her hands over me, if she scratched me, if she inflicted any amount of pain, I feared the beast inside would rise up and take control, hurting her when all I wanted to do was protect her, to ease her into my tendency.

"I trust you," she repeated, looking at me with such reverence I wanted to worship her until the end of time. Then she raised her head and captured my mouth, baring her teeth right before she nipped my lip. When her head rested back on the pillow, she smiled. "I think I'll like it a bit rough." Her smile disappeared when an animalistic growl erupted from my throat.

"Don't say those things to me," I warned, my reserve splintering apart with each heartbeat. I warred with the ways in which to take her that would satisfy the fiend inside me and that would also satiate her curiosity, all without going overboard. Back and forth, my uncertainty was going to give me a splitting headache if I didn't land on a decision in the next couple of seconds.

"Show me what you like." She wasn't going to give up, pulling her arms in a downward jerk in an attempt to break free from my grip… and that time I let her. She latched on to my hair with both hands, yanking the strands until a wave of pain made me shudder in excitement. I had a sinking feeling neither of us would walk away unscathed.

Resting on my forearms so as not to crush her with my weight, I reached behind me and unhooked her legs, throwing one of them over the crook of my arm and pushing toward her chest like I'd done earlier. I swiveled my hips before withdrawing until only the tip remained, leaning down to take her nipple into my mouth before surging forward, biting down as soon as I'd hit her womb.

Kalista screamed and I immediately covered her mouth. "Quiet." I winked to soften my harsh demand. "You don't want our son to hear you getting fucked, do you?" She rested her hands on my shoulders and at first, I thought she was going to shove me back, but she latched on with her nails and dug in.

"More," she cried, keeping her voice low, bucking up, her body begging for what she asked for. I tormented her other nipple the next time I thrust deep and I swore I almost came from the way her body stole everything from me. Her pussy coaxed my pleasure, her nails giving me the bite of pain I required. And her pants and moans gave me the acceptance I needed.

I took a breath to calm the incessant desire to punish her with my cock. If I abandoned all rationale and warning my brain shouted at me, I'd scare her for sure.

Withdrawing, I flipped her onto her stomach before she

could stop me, pulling her hips back and positioning her on all fours. I reentered her on a shout, smacking her ass right before I twisted her long hair around my fist and yanked her head back. She couldn't see me, but she sure as hell felt every inch slamming into her over and over.

I rutted inside her like a wild animal, cursing each time she demanded more, wishing like hell she'd come back to me years ago. My body was on the brink of explosion, and because I didn't want our tryst to end just yet, I tugged her upright until her back rested against my chest.

With her hair still in my grasp, I tugged her head to the side and captured her earlobe between my teeth. I bit down enough to make her gasp but not enough to break skin. "Do you like that?" My free hand snaked down her body, pinching her clit before she had a chance to answer. She tried to nod, but she couldn't move because I had her pinned to me.

I started to move again, slowly at first while I stroked between her legs, smacking her clit while simultaneously biting her shoulder, leaving behind a small indentation.

She moaned and again, I placed my hand over her mouth before whispering in her ear, "If you make another sound, I'm going to spank your ass so hard you won't be able to sit for two days." When her breath hitched, my thumb slipped between her lips and she nipped me, hard enough for me to jerk my hand away. My smirk fell as I surged into her, over and over. She never made another sound, not one above a whisper, at least.

I gave her a taste of the sex I enjoyed, all while not pushing her beyond what I believed her limits might be. Although, I supposed only time would tell what those would be.

Right before the first wave of my release hit, I pulled out on a regretful groan, pushed Kalista onto her back and thrust inside her. I enjoyed various positions, but missionary had always been one of my favorites with her, especially when we were about to come. The way she looked right before she exploded drove my own release, and right then wasn't any different.

"Eli... I... don't stop... I'm gonna—" She babbled incoherently, her body convulsing as her orgasm shuddered through her. My lips covered hers, pouring every bit of myself into our kiss, bottoming out inside her seconds later.

Afterward, nestled into the crook of her neck, I expelled my first real breath since the day she left me.

KALISTA

With my head resting on Eli's chest and listening to his heartbeat slow with each breath, I smiled, for so many reasons. He wanted to work on us again, giving me what I'd wanted since the day I found out I was pregnant... the opportunity for the three of us to be a real family, something I didn't think was possible when I'd first returned home. A surge of guilt would forever exist with the knowledge that I stole the first fourteen years of their relationship, but I hoped to make amends each and every day going forward.

Another reason for my elation was simply the man lying beneath me, and the gift he'd given me that I didn't realize I needed, which was him in all his glory. After Eli told me he needed to inflict a level of pain during sex, as well as receive it, I'd been nervous, uncertain I could handle what he liked. I'd also been wary because I didn't believe I could give him what he needed. And if Eli, especially after confessing he wanted to work on *us*, didn't find fulfillment in our sex life, my wariness could destroy everything. All hope that we could forge ahead and be a couple again could be lost.

Thinking about the way Eli and I were together years back, I wouldn't classify our sex life as having been boring or even strictly vanilla for that matter. We'd tried light bondage and some role play. But the way he treated me tonight was on a whole other spectrum than what we'd ever experienced together. His aggression and dominance turned me on. Every sting of pain turned into pleasure, an occurrence I hadn't been aware of being possible before him. While I believed he'd downplayed his inclinations, I looked forward to exploring his tendencies each time in the future.

Running the pads of my fingertips over his chest, delighting in the feel of his sculpted muscles, I tipped my head upward. "Can I ask you something?"

He looked down at me before kissing my temple. "Anything."

"When you threatened to spank me so hard that I wouldn't be able to sit for two days...."

"Yeah?" His top lip twitched with hesitation, his eyes narrowing and burrowing into mine.

"Is it wrong that the thought of you doing that excites me?" A rush of air left his lungs right before the corners of his mouth curved up. His relief fueled my curiosity, and I suddenly craved more of his aggressive side.

My hand lingered on his chest before moving south, tickling the spot above his hipbone I'd known well before venturing toward his cock. One touch and he was already springing back to life. I watched in amazement as he thickened, then wrapped my fingers around him, squeezing, relishing in his reaction to me. An entire eight minutes had passed, and I was ready for another round.

Eli groaned before thrusting further into my hand. "Already?"

"If you're up for it." I didn't wait for his response before straddling his waist, gliding him through my folds and coating him with my excitement. "Show me more," I said, positioning the tip of him at my entrance. "I think I need it." I ducked my head, heat rising through me at my admission.

"You need it?" His question rattled me, and when I looked at him, I saw the crease between his brows, yet he smiled at me. A salacious, smug, intoxicating smile.

"Yes."

A heartbeat later, he flipped me on my back and pinned me to the bed with his body, his expression deadpanning and heightening the flicker of reservation that burned beneath the surface. Perhaps my admission tore away the last shred of his restraint. "Are you sure you want this, Kalista? Because once you open this door, I won't be able to shut it."

My internal warring sprung to life because I didn't know exactly what he was going to unleash on me. So far, he'd bitten me, pulled my hair and fucked me hard, throwing in a single slap to my bottom for good measure. Although he'd threatened to redden my ass, a sentiment that still excited me. But what if he tried to choke me or hit me? Would that be something I could handle?

"I'd never push you too far," he said before hopping off the bed and disappearing into my closet. I was going to ask what he was doing, but he reappeared in front of the bed, holding the ties to two of my robes, one in each hand, looking devastatingly sexy in all his nakedness, his cock throbbing between his legs. He was next to me in seconds, looping a knot around each wrist before securing my arms to the headboard. "Wiggle around and see if you can get free." I did, but nothing happened. I wasn't going anywhere, even if I wanted to, which I most certainly didn't. "If anything I do is too much, or scares you in any way, just tell me to stop and I will." Nervousness raced through me, but before I delved too deep, he stroked my cheek with the back of his hand. "Trust me." I nodded, chewing on my bottom lip because my words had escaped me.

Once he was satisfied with his handiwork of restraining me

to the bed, he nudged my legs apart and laid between them, his arousal pressing against me, eliciting my need for him to claim me again. His lips skated from my jaw to my ear, then below, sucking the sensitive skin into his mouth to mark me.

"I'm conflicted," he said, running his tongue up the shell of my ear.

"About what? I trust you, Eli. If I thought —"

"Be quiet," he said, the low and dominant way he spoke feeding my arousal. "You'll only speak if you need to tell me to stop. Do you understand?" I parted my lips and inhaled. He grabbed my face, his fingers flexing against my jaw. "Not a word otherwise." I nodded, and he turned my head to the side and whispered back into my ear. "I can feel the heat of your cunt. You want me to fuck you, don't you?" In all the time I'd known Eli, I'd never heard him use the word cunt, and while I typically found the word crude and offensive, there was something about the way he said it, mixed with the restraints and his hard body pushing me into the bed that wanted him to say it again. But I didn't dare utter a word. "But first, back to my confliction." He jolted back until he was on his knees, then he flipped me on to my stomach, my arms forming an X over my head. "While I want to slam inside you and not stop till you scream, I want to revere you, as well."

"You can do whate—"

A rush of air sounded right before the sting of his slap against my ass cheek registered. I groaned and tried to move up the bed, but it was futile. With just that one hit, my strength had been stolen. The radiating pain morphed into something indescribable, but before my brain could decipher what that was, Eli spanked me again. Then a third time. Then a fourth.

A yelp pushed up my throat and exploded from my mouth before I could stop it, my head dropping into the pillow in surprise and embarrassment. My ass burned; surely his hand throbbed as well.

"I told you to be quiet." Leaving no room for argument, or another mistake, his voice dipped in the utmost seriousness. "If you speak again, I'll make good on my promise that you won't sit for two days. Nod if you understand." I complied, excited yet fearful he'd make good on his threat if I said a word.

His ragged breaths spread over my shoulder when he leaned over me. "Spread your legs. Wider. That's it." His finger disappeared inside me and I bucked against him. "Do you want more?" I nodded, realizing that response was the only safe one. He inserted a second then a third finger, pumping leisurely until I started to see stars, quivering around him. I struggled to catch my breath, the start of an impending climax spreading through my limbs, but then suddenly, he withdrew his hand. I groaned, but even though I hadn't spoken, I tensed for another hit to my bottom. But it never came. In fact, for several seconds nothing happened. I turned to look behind me, but due to my compromising and restrictive position I couldn't see him.

I opened my mouth to speak, prepared for the consequences when he flipped me back around to face him, slamming into me with brutal force and pushing me up the bed. My rough gasp made him still.

His jaw clenched as did every muscle in his neck and chest. Eli looked like he was barely holding on, which only served to wash away the pain he'd inflicted, my body tightening around his thickness. I parted my lips several times, only the sound of air escaping.

"You can speak," he said, staring down at me with such adoration, an odd expression during the midst of our experimental tryst. Experimental on my part, at least.

"I swear you've gotten bigger."

"You just make me unbelievably hard." Face-to-face, every emotion erupted inside me, but the only one I clung to was love.

It wasn't just sex between him and me. There was an undeniable, pulsating attraction between us, always had been, but there was a deep, insatiable devotion encasing us both. No amount of time or distance apart had stifled our need for each other. It was ingrained so deep, only death could break its bond.

No more overthinking.

No more running.

No more hiding.

We were it for each other, and after tonight, our fate was sealed. Once and for all.

"I can't believe you're really here." His affectionate sentiment didn't erase the look of dominance that danced over his features. Before I could reciprocate the sentiment, Eli pulled out, tugged me down the bed and threw my legs over his shoulders, careful of my restraints. He grabbed my hips and anchored me to him, rocking back into me with such intensity, I shuddered as the pain cradled my need for more. But the more he moved, the gentler he became. I supposed this was what he referred to earlier when he told me he was conflicted. Each leisurely stroke of his cock ignited the flame which had been burning since my last orgasm, stoking the fire to new heights.

"You're close." It wasn't a question. Even years later, he remembered my body, the small telltale signs I was closing in. "Your face always scrunches up ever so slightly, like you're trying to hold off longer. And your fingers curl into your palm." I looked up toward where my hands were restrained, and sure enough they were clenched. I started to laugh, was going to make some sort of comment about our past, and how well he knew me, but my body trembled, each perfect catapult into me striking the most delicious nerve. The moment Eli lowered my legs, I wrapped them around his waist. He captured my mouth, making love to me, soft and gentle, a way he said he hadn't done with anyone since me.

"You're mine now, Kalista." *Thrust.* "All mine." There was no point in arguing because I was indeed his. Then, now, and forever.

We'd come a long way, and although more time would pass before we were back to where we once were, hope bloomed in my heart at the prospect of us being, well... us again. My sentimental thoughts were torn apart when Eli picked up his pace. I moaned, writhed beneath him and wanted nothing more than to touch him, to hold him, to dig my nails into the tight muscles of his glorious ass. But with my hands tied, I succumbed to the desires screaming to life through every cell, every nerve, every pulsing beat of my heart.

I panted and squirmed.

I silently begged for his forgiveness, directing the sentiment back at myself for the same.

I vowed to love him with a fierceness that put my younger self to shame.

No more words were spoken as the pressure built higher and higher until my orgasm barreled over me, my release rendering me a wanton mess of pleasure. Eli chased his own climax, whispering a mixture of sweet and dirty sentiments in my ear before coming undone, the quick prick of his teeth into the soft expanse of my neck sending us spiraling together.

"So much for us being quiet." I laughed, but mortification would overshadow my amusement if Holden had indeed heard us at any point. There were moments, many, in fact, when I forgot all about our son being two doors down, wrapped up in Eli and his words, demands, punishments, and reverence. But the fact of the matter was, there was an impressionable young man close by, which served as a reminder to be more diligent going forward.

"We're bad parents." He nuzzled into the crook of my shoulder before removing himself from on top of me. He worked quickly to untie my hands, massaging my wrists for good measure.

Afterward, he disappeared into my bathroom only to emerge with a warm washcloth. When he was near, I spread my legs because I was familiar with the act I'd become accustomed to from when we were younger.

"I didn't hurt you too much, did I?" he asked, his tone full of surprising worry.

"Not at all." I smiled to ease his slight case of unwarranted nerves.

Once he'd finished cleaning me up, he tossed the cloth in a nearby hamper then climbed back into bed on top of me, his body completely flush with mine.

"Are you okay with me staying over?" He sucked my bottom lip into his mouth while he waited for me to answer, although any reply I gave would be garbled. Something told me his question wasn't really a question at all but a polite way of telling me he would be spending the night.

With my lip still captured between his, I deepened the kiss, nodding to give my approval, not that any was required. I wanted nothing more than to wake up next to Eli in the morning. He soon switched positions and tucked me into his side. I rested my head on his chest, the smooth hardness of his muscles cradling me while I inhaled his addictive scent.

"I want to talk to you about something," he said, tightening his hold around my shoulder, "and I don't want you to clam up." I tried to move back so I could see his face, but he kept me close, essentially immobilized against him.

"What was his name?"

There was no use in lying or even trying to avoid the topic. "John Kellison," I answered, hoping that was the end of it, but I should've known better.

"Did he go to jail?" His heart kicked up a notch during the brief silence.

"Yes. He was sentenced to two years."

"Is he still in there?"

"Yes." My answers were short, not wanting to elaborate or

spend any of my precious time or thought on the man who'd hurt me and my son.

Kissing the top of my head, he pulled me impossibly close. "I'll always protect you both, you know that, right?" His fingers trailed over my side, trying in his way to comfort and soothe me, attempting to erase what had happened.

"I do," I whispered. I pulled back, and that time, he let me. His eyes were sad, but as soon as they connected with mine, some of his sorrowfulness disappeared. Our lips met once more in a healing kiss. I laid my head back down on his chest, his heartbeat falling into sync with my own, the rhythmic sound calming me until I drifted off into another state of existence.

One which held all the possibilities in the world.

ELI

$\mathcal{T}$he rush of hot water washed away any uncertainty I held about giving Kalista another chance. Having woken up next to her had been the best moment of my adult life —right next to finding out I had a son, of course. There were some things we needed to work on—trust being the biggest— but after last night, I had a feeling everything would fall back into place in due time. She was the only woman I wanted to spend the rest of my days with, so the decision was easy. For my heart. But my head was taking a little more time to catch up.

I'd finally found a place of peace where she was concerned, and I didn't want anything to ruin that, myself included. She'd apologized for leaving me all those years ago and for hiding Holden from me. She'd said so on several occasions, and if her words hadn't convinced me, then the look of despair and anguish painted on her face every time she said so cinched the deal. We'd both been in pain during our time apart, and while I'd numbed my heart with meaningless, short-lived relation-ships, she'd done her best to survive and raise our son.

Stepping from the shower, I wrapped a towel around my waist before heading back into the bedroom, stopping several steps later to visually devour the beautiful woman sprawled across the bed. Naked. Her hair fanned down her back as she lay on her stomach, her face turned away from me and toward the window, the soft glow of the sunrise streaming through and illuminating her every curve. My cock jumped at the thought of taking her yet again. Sore or not, I could bet the second I laid my hands on her, she'd beg me to fuck her. Unable to restrain myself, lost to the images of taking her in every possible position, I moved closer, but a soft rap on the door halted my steps.

"Mom? Are you awake?" The handle twisted, but thankfully, I'd been smart enough to lock it before I'd fallen asleep last night. There was no way our son needed to walk in on us getting "reacquainted." Not only would that scar the poor kid, but it would also confuse him to no end. We hadn't had the chance to discuss what we were going to tell him, let alone what we were going to do pertaining to us as a couple. Our relationship. We certainly had a few things to discuss, living arrangements for one. Perhaps I was moving fast, but I didn't want another second to go by and miss any more than I already had.

Striding toward the bed, I pulled the covers over her in case he sidestepped around me and walked in when I answered the door.

His next knock barely sounded before I stepped into the hallway, crowding his space while closing the door behind me. Holden glanced down at my towel then back up to my face, his features scrunching slightly.

"Hey, bud."

He looked past me at the door before asking, "Did you stay over? Like, sleep in there with Mom?"

Not wanting to say too much without Kalista present, I gave him a short answer. "Yes."

Diverting his eyes, he appeared anxious, but after several moments, he looked up at me and asked something I never expected to come out of his mouth. "Did you have sex?" He shuffled from one foot to the other, but he never withdrew his eyes from mine, curious and concerned for his mom.

"That's a little inappropriate for you to be asking me, don't you think?" I wasn't upset, just stunned by his bluntness. I leaned against the doorframe and waited patiently for him to answer me.

Normally, Holden was a very easygoing kid. We'd bonded easily and our relationship continued to grow stronger each day. I'd left the discipline to Kalista until my established role in his life had more impact, although the harshest thing she had to do with him was remind him to finish his homework. He was a good kid, through and through.

"That's my mom," he all but whispered, fidgeting with his hands as he continued to stand in front of me.

"And I'm your father."

"I know. But…."

"But what?" *Where is he going with this interrogation?*

He puffed up his chest, stood taller and asked, "What are your intentions with her?" If I hadn't witnessed the harshly serious look on his face, I would have burst out laughing.

Trying my hardest to hide my smirk, I placed my hand on his shoulder. "Son, my intentions are good. There is nothing for you to worry about where that is concerned." I gave his shoulder a squeeze. "Do you trust me?"

A mixture of sadness and relief deflated his posture. "I do trust you, Dad. It's just that Mom has been really sad these past few years, and I don't want her to feel that way anymore. The few times I asked about you, she told me I looked just like you but then would disappear to her room and cry." The corners of his mouth turned down. "She didn't know I heard her, but I did. All the time."

A lump formed deep in my throat. I hated hearing that they both struggled without me, but there was nothing I could have done. I'd had no idea why Kalista had left, or that Holden even existed. If I had…

No, I can't go back there. No more what-ifs.

"I understand your concern for your mom, and I love that you're so protective over her, but I'm here to tell you that I won't hurt her. Not intentionally."

He relaxed, believing I spoke the truth. "Are you moving in with us?" he asked, his handsome young face brightening. "Are you guys getting married?"

"Whoa, one thing at a time." I laughed. "I still have a lot of things to talk about with your mom. But I'll tell you what, as soon as we figure them out, you'll be the first to know. Promise." I pulled him in for a hug, my hand cradling his head to my chest. I loved him more than I could ever express in words, but words were all I had. "I love you, Holden."

"Love you, too, Dad."

Giving him a quick squeeze, I pulled back. "Are we good?"

"Yeah, I guess so." He turned to leave but stopped when I called after him.

"Why did you come to your mom's room in the first place?" Gripping the edges of my loosening towel, I was curious what had brought him to her door.

"I wanted to remind her I have to be at school early today. I volunteered to help clean up the grounds with a few other students for extra credit. Gotta keep the environment clean for the next generation, right?" He laughed at his own joke before shutting the door to his room.

KALISTA

*S*tretching my arms above my head, I yawned, wiping away the cobwebs of a restful sleep. For the first time since I could remember, I looked forward to what the day would bring, my renewed romantic relationship with Eli at the very top of the list.

I wasn't naïve. There was plenty we still had to discuss, and several decisions that had to be made, but for the first time in years, my heart wasn't heavy with sadness. Finally, I could breathe again.

Stirring in bed, I heard voices outside my door. I sat up and craned my ear, but I couldn't make out any of the words, and as I swung my legs over the side of the bed, clutching the covers tightly to me, the door swung open. Eli stood there with nothing but a towel slung low on his hips, his dark hair still damp from an apparent shower. My hormones raged to the surface at the sheer sight of him, and it was everything I could do to stop from tackling him to the ground and ravaging him. I needed something else to focus on or else I would do just that.

"Who were you talking to?"

"Holden."

He locked the door behind him and prowled toward me, a hunger flashing behind his beautiful eyes. The way he watched me made me feel sexy, wanted, and the way I imagined him taking me again was enough to cause me to tremble all over. I stood and dropped the covers, baring myself before meeting him halfway, counting my breaths until I reached him, all inquiries about the muffled conversation in the hallway falling to the back of my mind.

He reached for my waist and pulled me flush to him, his heat intensifying my own. "You're so beautiful."

Feeling like a thousand butterflies took flight in my belly, I gasped for air right before he lowered his mouth to mine and I wasted no time in claiming what was mine. The urgency of my need drove him to deepen the kiss, our tongues dueling for ownership of the other.

My fingers fumbled with the corners of his towel, untangling it before tossing it to the ground behind him. I needed to feel the weight of him in my hand, but before I could touch him, he gripped my backside and pulled me up his body. He didn't need to tell me what to do, my legs instantly wrapping around his waist, his cock rubbing against me and driving me insane with the need to recreate last night. Parts of it, at least.

"Does someone want to go again?" he asked, his voice dipping low as he mustered his way toward the bed.

"Can you do gentle and easy?"

"I proved to you I can. Sort of." He smiled then pressed his lips to mine again, tossing me onto the bed and prying my legs apart before nestling between them. Before I could utter a word, he pressed deep, sliding slowly into me until he was completely sheathed. "I've missed you so much," he moaned against my mouth, hitching my leg over his waist as he began to move. "Tell me you've missed me just as much." The uncertainty in his voice tore me apart. I would never fully realize what I'd done to him when I left, but I vowed right then to make it up to him for as long as he would have me.

He had me pinned underneath him, my body his to do with as he pleased. "I missed you so much." My lips sought out his, but his face rested in the crook of my neck, inhaling my scent as if he was burning it into his memory.

I had a tendency to overthink, but right then, I vowed to put a pin in my insecurities and just feel.

Feel the gloriousness of him claiming me.

Feel the passion pulling us together.

Feel his forgiveness flowing through him and into me.

His thrusts bordered on punishing, but I welcomed the hint of intensity. "I love your pussy," he growled, spreading my legs wider to accommodate him. "I could lose myself inside you forever."

"Then do it," I said, my words almost indiscernible to even me. If I could have stayed wrapped up in him endlessly, I would have. I never wanted to leave my bed. I never wanted to feel his absence again, not for one single moment. But life didn't work that way, so I had to revel in our special times as much as possible. For as long as they lasted.

"Tell me you love my cock, Kalista. Tell me how good I make you feel. I need to hear you say it." The corded muscles of his chest twitched in exertion the harder he fucked me.

"I love the way you feel," I replied, my mind blanking on forming any other words. He grinned wide, as if he found what I'd said amusing. But he didn't say anything before kissing me hard, his tongue entangled with mine and adding to the bliss of our writhing bodies.

Eli's head dipped and his mouth was close to my ear. "I know you're close, but you have to be quiet." He nipped my lobe. "Our son will hear."

"I ca... can't." I had no control over my body, the familiar tingling taking hold and rocketing me toward my orgasm. I tangled my fingers into his thick hair right before I hooked my ankles around his waist, pulling him closer. The friction of him against my clit and his cock nudging the trigger spot inside me had my lungs seizing in no time at all. I threw my head back, but before I could scream, he covered my mouth, my cries muffled into the palm of his hand.

"Breathe," he whispered, powering forward several more times before losing himself in his own climax, his grunts deep and formidable.

Soon afterward, Eli moved his face closer and his facial hair tickled my cheek. I laughed, and he purposely rubbed his beard against me again. I tried to move away, but his body imprisoned mine to the bed. When he did finally pull back to look at me, his face deadpanned. My heart jumped into my throat. He parted his lips, and a million things ran through my mind of what he would say, but nothing prepared me for what came out of his mouth.

"We need to get you to dirty up your sex talk while I'm ravaging you." I expected him to at least smile afterward, but he didn't, his face still expressionless.

Not knowing what else to say, I blurted, "I can't think straight when I'm so full of you. I shouldn't be held accountable for my lack of sexy talk." I attempted a laugh, but the sound came out muffled and awkward. A wave of embarrassment hit me, and I ducked my head to the side, trying to hide from his intense stare. But he was having none of it. He pulled my face back towards his.

"I'll get it out of you yet. Don't worry your pretty little head." It was then he flashed me a genuine smile, chuckling afterward for good measure.

After he'd cleaned up in the bathroom, he returned with a warm washcloth, wiping between my legs, just like the night before, just like he'd done a thousand times in years past. Then he reached for his clothes and dressed in record time.

"Where are you going?" I did believe I pouted.

"Holden has to be to school early this morning, so I thought I'd take him."

"Oh my God. I completely forgot." I hopped out of bed, but when I moved toward my closet, he grabbed my wrist.

"Don't worry about it. Seriously. I'd love to take him." He pulled me into him and gave me the sweetest kiss. "Oh, and wait until I tell you about our little conversation this morning." He winked before disappearing from my room, leaving me to decipher just what he meant by that.

Moments later, I relaxed under the hot spray of the shower, closing my eyes and thinking I was the luckiest woman in the world right then.

KALISTA

"*I*f you give me one more excuse, I'm coming over there and kidnapping you. For real." Jasmine huffed into the phone in what I hoped was exaggerated irritation. She'd been trying to convince me to meet for drinks for the past three weeks, but I'd been so wrapped up in Eli and our rekindled relationship, I kept making up excuse after excuse. Feeling awful about pushing my friend to the side, I decided to finally take her up on her offer.

"Okay, no more cop-outs. I'm yours tonight." Silence departed down the line. She was probably so shocked she fell over. "I promise."

"Holy shit, woman. I didn't think you would ever agree." Her tone was light, but I knew her and my blowing her off had hurt her feelings. I wasn't one of those women who forgot all about her friends once she was in a relationship, but my situation with Eli was precarious. I wanted to spend as much time with him as possible to make sure we were on the right track and moving forward.

"I'm sorry I've been such a lousy friend, Jas. I'll fill you in on everything when we meet up. Which reminds me, where were you thinking of going? And please don't say a dance club or some shit like that," I groaned. That was the last place I wanted to be. A loud, crowded place with obnoxious people who were barely in their twenties wasn't my scene. Never had been. Besides, I had too much responsibility before I was legally able to drink.

"Cynthia told me about this place called The Underground. Said it was great."

"Cynthia who?" Before she answered, I fired back with, "Not Cynthia Smales? You still talk to her? Wasn't she always getting into some sort of trouble back in high school? Hanging out with questionable people?"

"If you would let me get a word in edgewise, I'll tell you." She paused, and I could picture her rolling her eyes at me. "Yes, I still talk to her, our kids go to the same school. And she's changed, for the most part." She mumbled the last few words.

"Uh-huh. I'm not so sure I trust a place *she* suggested."

"Oh, stop being a baby. I'll be there in an hour to pick you up." She quickly said goodbye before hanging up, knowing damn well I would've continued to give her a hard time about her dear ol' friend's suggestion.

Eli showed up ten minutes before Jasmine arrived, having volunteered to watch Holden. I would have asked my mom, but he insisted. He'd been working late most nights recently and I didn't want him to be stretched too thin, but he told me he wanted the time with his son, that nothing would make him happier. How could I argue with that?

"You look beautiful." He wrapped his arms around my waist and pulled me close, flashing me a sexy grin. "Almost too stunning to leave me for the night. I don't like thinking men will be gawking at you." He teased, and while Eli wasn't a jealous man by nature, he'd been tested on occasion when we were younger.

"Don't worry," I said, fidgeting with the hem of my black skirt. "We won't be gone long."

"Ten minutes is too long." He covered my mouth with his, but the moment he wanted to deepen the kiss, I pulled back. "What?" He frowned and I couldn't help but find his expression amusing.

"I don't have time." I devoured the sight of him in his dark gray suit, and I wanted to rip it from his body, but like I just told him, I had no time.

"Time to what?" He had the audacity to look serious, until I pursed my lips. "Fine." That time he gifted me a quick kiss, sans tongue, of course.

"What are you two going to do?" I asked.

He released me and headed toward the refrigerator. "Going back to my house, maybe play a game or two." His eyes lit up talking about Holden, a brightness which reminded me he could have had this kind of relationship with our son all along.

Choosing to focus back on Eli was the best kind of distraction. He pulled out a bottled water from the fridge, twisted off the cap and took a big gulp. Why did I find it sexy when the muscles of his tanned throat worked together to swallow? One simple and natural action and he'd drawn my complete attention. He caught me watching him and his mouth kicked up into a heart-stopping smirk. Slowly licking his lips to catch any remnants of the water, he took the few steps necessary to put him directly in front of me. He was so damn gorgeous; it was a real pity I had to leave the house at all. A sudden rush of heat bloomed over me, the urge to squeeze my thighs together too much.

Before I could even think of settling myself down, Eli pulled me into him. "I'll miss you, too, baby," he said. "But don't rush on my account. Enjoy yourself. Just not too much." He finally pulled back. "Where are you two off to, anyway?"

"Ummmm." I stalled, trying to remember the name of the place Jasmine told me. "The Underground. Yeah, I think that's what it's called." The blare of my friend's horn ended our conversation. "Gotta go." I gave him another quick kiss before reaching for my purse and keys.

"Call me if you need a ride home. No drinking and driving. I mean it," he warned, love laced with concern.

"I promise," I mock saluted before disappearing out the front door.

WE WERE an hour into our girl time together and feeling good. We weren't planning on getting drunk, but instead kicking back and celebrating finally finding the time to hang out. Me more than her.

"This is quite the place." I glanced around again as two people stepped through the front door, putting the total count of patrons at no more than thirty, which was fine with me because I wasn't a fan of big crowds. The Underground was nothing special, from the outside or the inside. It wasn't a dive, per se, but I wasn't sure why Cynthia had raved about it so much. The lighting was dim, seating was sparse, and the occupants were a bit on the rough side, men and women alike.

"Yeah, not really sure what all the hype was about." She took a sip of her beer. "But judging by the type of people here—ourselves excluded, of course—Cynthia fits right in. A little rough around the edges."

While I hadn't talked to Cynthia since high school, these were the types of people she hung out with back then, and I guessed nothing had changed. Even though Jasmine had told me she had matured a bit since our teenage years.

The tattooed, bald-headed bartender returned to our end of the bar. "Another?" he asked. We nodded and he placed our refills in front of us. He was a man of few words. His exterior was rough, just like everyone else, but he seemed pleasant enough. Although, seeing as how my friend and I were obviously not a threat in any way, and so out of our element, he didn't have any reason to be otherwise.

"So, when are you and Eli going to make it official?" Jasmine bumped my shoulder with hers, then toyed with the label on her bottle, tearing a piece of it away before taking another sip.

"What do you mean?"

She swiveled in her chair until her knees trapped me in my seat. "You know damn well what I mean, woman. Why are you two putting off the inevitable? You have a son together and are back to being madly in love with each other." She reached over and squeezed my leg. "So, I ask you again. When are you going to make an honest man out of him?" She smiled big, a gesture which was certainly contagious. I loved her optimism, but we just weren't there yet. Maybe someday, but we still had a lot of hurdles to overcome, none of which I could think of right then.

I opened my mouth to answer but snapped it shut when I heard the rumble of what sounded like a thousand motorcycles. The collective noise was so overpowering, if I didn't know any better, I would've sworn they were going to come right through the front door. Jasmine and I shared a "what the hell" look as we turned toward the entrance of the bar. After several very long minutes, the door burst open and in walked ten bikers, all dressed in leather vests. There was no doubt in my mind they were part of a club, their matching attire the obvious dead give-away. Shouting and laughter commenced as they dispersed, and it was then I became a tad nervous.

The men ranged in height, weight, and age, but they all looked like people I didn't want to cross. To judge by appearance was wrong, the sentiment was what I'd told Holden many times over, but the sudden intrusion of the raucous sound of their bikes mixed with their attire and the way most of them carried on and I couldn't overlook the stereotype.

I was so busy taking in the scene of it all that Jasmine practically yelled in my ear to turn my attention back to her. "Looks like we found out why Cynthia loves this bar." The corners of her mouth curved up, but I couldn't help but feel anything but unnerved.

Instead of giving in to my anxiety, however, I turned back toward the bar and played with the top of my bottled beer. Before I could say anything to Jasmine, the door opened again, only that time a flock of women filed in, scattering among the room to consort with the men. Most of them were young and pretty, although there were a few who looked weathered, like they'd been partying a bit too much. The one thing all of them had in common was their barely there tight fitted clothing, leaving nothing to the imagination.

We were clearly out of our element. While I wore a black skirt that flared out at the hips and hit just above my knees, paired with a pink sleeveless blouse and three-inch heels, Jasmine wore dark skinny jeans, heels and a black lacey top, the collar a sheer material, the most revealing piece either of us wore.

Moments after the men arrived, several of them flanked us on either side, yelling to get the bartender's attention.

"Yo, Barlow!" one of them shouted, pounding on the bar. "We need some fucking drinks over here."

Keeping my head down, I avoided any and all contact with the questionable-looking patrons. Jasmine had other ideas, however. She blatantly stared at each and every one, daring them with her eyes to speak to her. To us. Something I found surprising, but then again, she had always been one up for a bit of adventure. Not that I would call being in the middle of a bar of bikers an adventure. I considered that shit nerve-racking, uncomfortable at best.

Chills covered my skin when a throaty rasp sounded in my ear. "Well, look at what we have here," he grumbled, the smell of liquor invading my nostrils before I could move away. I refused to look up, praying he'd just think me rude and move on.

No such luck.

"What? You not gonna talk to me, sweetheart?" His speech slurred. "You certainly don't look like the regular wannabes we see in here. You lost?" He chuckled to himself, but still I ignored him, not only because I had no idea what a wannabe was but engaging in conversation with this guy was not something I wanted to undertake. Until he laid his hand on my shoulder. Once he'd made contact, there was no way I could continue to pretend he hadn't dived headfirst into my personal space.

Finding a sliver of courage, I jerked away from him, his hand falling to his side seconds later. "My friend and I were just leaving." I didn't want to insult him, fearing our encounter would somehow escalate, so I blurted out additional, yet unnecessary information. "It's late and we both have a busy day tomorrow." I kept my head down the entire time.

"You could have a busy night if you stay." He brazenly ran his finger up and down my arm, his gesture eliciting a swipe of fear to burn through me. This guy didn't know the first thing about social cues, and it appeared my resistance only encouraged him. Again, I pulled away from him, but he just laughed then moved closer.

When I finally turned to look at him, he took that as a sign I was interested, which I most certainly was not. While he had a handsome face hidden beneath his shaggy beard and dark shoulder-length hair, there was a darkness behind his eyes. I couldn't explain it exactly, but my gut told me this guy had done some bad shit in his life. Then mix in him being intoxicated and our interaction wasn't going to go well. For me, at least.

Strained seconds passed and he still hadn't taken the hint. He was close. Too close for any kind of comfort.

"Any chick in here would love my attention." He grabbed a lock of my hair and twisted the ends. It took me a moment to realize that he touched me again, and once that registered, I swatted his hand away.

"Please don't touch me." While my voice was low it was firmer than before.

"I like a woman who plays hard to get." He crowded so close I almost fell off my seat, bumping into Jasmine before doing so. She'd been texting on her phone and hadn't noticed what was going on, until now.

Looking at me and seeing the worry plastered all over my face, she peered over to the side and saw the reason for my concern. "My friend isn't interested."

"I think she is," he replied, reaching down and squeezing my knee. I jumped and pushed closer to Jasmine.

"Don't touch her again." I didn't have to look at my friend to know she scowled at the guy. Jasmine had no patience for drunk, handsy men.

I dared to look back at the biker and that's when I saw his lip curl. A flash of anger painted his face right before he roughly grabbed my arm, completely ignoring Jasmine. His eyes darkened right before he shouted, "Why the hell are you here if not to fuck one of us?"

His raised voice prompted some of his buddies to surround us, leering and smiling at the impromptu entertainment.

"I'm gonna kill Cynthia if we ever get out of here," Jasmine mumbled next to my ear. Her leg started to shake, and although she tried to hide her nervousness, it bled through, making me even more anxious, our precarious situation quickly spinning out of control.

"Don't you know where you are, darlin'?" someone yelled next to us.

"You a damn fool if you don't know who we are," another man shouted.

Darting my eyes all over the place, I couldn't identify who spoke, just that there were many pairs of eyes staring at us and grinning, clearly amused with our uneasiness.

Some of the women stalked closer to us, the looks on their

faces mirroring their body language. They were not happy that we'd drawn the men's attention. So, not only did we have to contend with the guys, but now I was worried about what the women were going to do, as well.

Good luck to us.

ELI

"*H*ang on, buddy. I'll be right back." Holden and I were right in the middle of the newest spy game when my doorbell rang. As I walked toward the front door, I wondered who in the hell would show up unannounced. The last person to come to my home unexpectedly was Beth but seeing as how she was no longer in my life, I tossed aside any uneasiness associated with her dropping in on me again.

When my eyes landed on Mike, I stepped to the left and welcomed him inside.

"You busy?"

"Just hanging out with Holden." Mike had met my son twice before, and each time told me what a great kid he was. I couldn't agree more. "Looks like you need a drink," I said, turning to walk toward the den, Mike following me. I gestured for him to proceed, stopping and telling Holden I'd be back in a few minutes.

"How's Sierra doing? Find the unlucky son of a bitch who's responsible?" I teased, knowing full well he was still searching for the man who knocked up his baby sister.

"Pour me a drink," he grumbled.

Handing him a glass of my best scotch, I took a seat opposite him. "What's going on?" Eyeing him up, I noticed he looked a little worse for wear. His hair was as unruly as usual, but there were dark circles under his eyes, his face drawn as if he hadn't slept in days. "You look like shit. No offense."

"None taken."

"Is it the whole thing with Sierra?"

"I wish that's all it was, but no." His nostrils flared right before he sighed. "It's a woman who's got my head all twisted up. Can you believe that shit, man?" He tossed back half his drink in a single gulp.

"Actually... no." I leaned back on the couch. "The great Mike Hawkings is all messed up over a woman? Someone call Ripley's."

"You're an ass, Warner. Besides, that show isn't on anymore." He frowned. "Is it?"

"Hell if I know." It was nice to be the one on the other end of the spectrum. My life had finally fallen back into place, which in turn allowed me to focus solely on Mike and his issues. At least for the evening. "Wanna talk about it?"

"I don't even know where to begin. I've never met anyone like her. My charms don't work on her, which just makes me want her even more." He tried to smile but was only half successful, the side of his mouth curving up before falling flat.

"Seems to me you like the challenge. Could that be the only reason you're intrigued?"

"I'm more than intrigued. I'm all twisted up." Mike rubbed his chest and groaned, concerning me in a way he never had before.

"I think it's weird you can't lure her in like all the others." My tone was serious, but I was clearly mocking him, although Mike didn't seem to pick up on my sarcasm.

"Right?" he asked. "I don't get it, either." I contemplated throwing something at that thick head of his, but he finally grinned, giving way to the fact he was pulling my leg. "No, seriously. It's more than that. The first time I laid eyes on her, I knew she wasn't like every other woman I've met. I don't know how to explain it, but she's... she's just... different."

Frustrated with his lack of articulation, he threw his hands up and blew out a puff of air. "Fuck it. I don't want to talk about it anymore." Reclining in his seat, he rested his head on the back of the sofa. Moments passed in silence, but it was all good. Sometimes, buddies needed to just be, to sit with each other without feeling the need to fill the empty quiet.

After checking in on Holden before rejoining Mike in the den, I started to ask him about the garage, but he cut me off.

"I'm surprised you let the little woman out of your sight for a few hours." Deflection was Mike's specialty, but I didn't mind. Any excuse to talk about Kalista was most welcome. "Where did you say she went again? Out with Jasmine?" Suddenly springing forward, he asked, "Have you *seen* Jasmine lately? Holy shit, brother. She is one fine piece of ass." He wiggled his eyebrows and nodded.

"Don't you have enough issues with women? Besides, she's married. And has two kids."

"Yeah, you're right. I have enough problems. I don't need to be adding any more to my plate." He refilled his drink before taking his seat again. "So, where did they go?"

"They went to some bar called The Underground. Ever heard of it?" Mike was in midswallow when he spit out his drink.

Wiping the remnants from his shirt, he answered precariously. "The Underground? Is that what you said?" I nodded. "Yeah, I've heard of that place, although I've never been there. I'm not that dumb."

My pulse quickened. "What the hell does that mean?" I sat up straighter. "What kind of bar is it?" If he didn't answer me in the next two seconds, I was going to lunge at him and strangle the life out of him.

"The Knights Corruption MC owns that bar. You already met the prez. Marek." Shaking his head, he continued to stare at me incredulously. "They went to a notoriously dangerous biker bar."

I'D PLACED a call to Kalista's mom, making sure she was home before I dropped off Holden. I told her I'd explain everything later. I took off before she could argue.

I'd never driven so fast before in my entire life, Mike tagging along in case I needed backup. From what I'd heard about the club, they didn't take kindly to strangers, Kalista and Jasmine surely sticking out like sore thumbs. Or, worse yet, because they were women, were they in a different kind of danger?

My only hope was that Marek was there. We weren't friends or anything of the sort, but I hoped he had enough respect for me to allow me to gather the women and walk away without incident.

Another reason I had brought Mike with me. Since he'd done the guy a favor as well, it would go a long way to smoothing things over… if they escalated beyond the norm. If the president of the MC was there. If the women were even still there.

I tried over and over to call Kalista, but there was no answer. Either she couldn't hear her phone, or she couldn't get to it. I was praying for the former.

"What the hell were they thinking going to that place?" I kept repeating, more rhetorical than anything. Mike shrugged, having no idea what to say.

"Everything will be fine, Eli. We just have to hope they left once they found out who owned the bar." He drummed his fingers on the tops of his knees, attempting to conceal his agitation.

"But that's the problem, man. I don't believe either one of them know who the Knights are or what they're capable of. Especially not Kalista, since she's been gone for so long. Fuck!" I yelled, striking the steering wheel twice before gaining some semblance of control. "That woman walks through life with blinders on. There is no way in hell she knows who those guys are."

Kalista's naivety was somewhat endearing, in most cases. But it was her obliviousness that would most likely cause quite the issue tonight.

Stepping on the brake so I didn't plow right through the bar, I swerved into an empty parking space. The place was packed and in full swing when we arrived. We counted fifteen bikes all lined up out front.

Son of a bitch!

Mike placed a hand on my shoulder to calm me before we walked inside, proverbial guns blazing. Shrugging away, I bottled in the anger and nervousness until it mixed into something I could later use when faced with danger.

I hope to hell I'm blowing this way out of proportion.

Even as the thought careened through my head, I knew I wasn't.

Exhaling a deep, pent-up breath, I stepped inside first, my eyes darting throughout the darkened space, looking for the one woman who made my heart beat faster, in both anticipation and anger. Yes, I was angry with her, but more so with myself for not finding out more about the place when she'd first told me. But there was no time for regret right now, so I shoved all self-deprecating thoughts to the side and focused on my one true agenda.

To locate and remove both women without incident.

I felt like we were on some kind of stealth mission, our targets located somewhere within the vicinity of the bar. Laughter mixed with shouting immediately put us on high alert. Mike moved past me and walked a step ahead into the rough crowd of people. He had never been afraid of anything, oftentimes rushing into situations without a second thought. At least that time, we had some sort of plan. We agreed not to pull any unnecessary attention to ourselves, but that went to shit as soon as we stepped inside.

All eyes were on us as we waded through the throng of people flanking us on both sides. The muffled shouting became clearer the farther in we walked, and it took us all of about three seconds to find out why.

"Why don't you leave us alone?" I heard a woman ask, setting my heart on full blast once I recognized who it belonged to.

Jasmine.

Which meant Kalista was nearby.

"Goddamn it!" I cursed under my breath. They were still here, even though I prayed like hell they weren't. We were a few feet from the bar when I saw her, shrugging away from some asshole. She was practically in Jasmine's lap, trying to get away from the fucker's hands pawing at her.

Without another thought, I sprinted through the remaining people blocking my way, grabbed hold of the guy touching my woman, and slammed him against the corner of the bar.

The entire scene reminded me of a bad movie, the one where the music skids to a stop and everyone stares at the person causing the disruption. In those scenes, either boisterous laughter would erupt, or a deadly bar fight would break out.

I doubted I was going to hear anyone laughing, so I braced myself for fists to start flying.

"Don't you ever touch her again, do you hear me?" I roared,

spit flying from my lips and hitting him in the face. I'd lost all sense of decorum and manners when I'd seen him touching her. But more than that, it was the look in her eyes I'd seen. She was scared and unsure of how to escape unharmed.

How long had she been subjected to the likes of this guy? These men?

A second was too damn long in my book.

Someone gripped my shoulder from behind, and at first, I thought it was Mike. However, I quickly realized it wasn't my friend when a sinister voice sounded in my ear. "If you want to walk out of here alive, you better unhand him." Before I could think of telling the intruder to fuck off, I heard a sound that slammed my heart to a stop inside my chest.

The click of a gun being cocked.

Right next to my ear.

For as much as I tried to control how the night would play out, convincing myself to keep a cool head no matter what I saw, all my rationale flew out the goddamn window as soon as I saw Kalista in distress. I'd gone on autopilot, simply reacting and no longer thinking.

The man I held was similar to my height and build, but for some reason, he wasn't fighting back against me. I thought it odd he was still, but then I'd discovered he was a tad more than intoxicated, his reflexes gravely inhibited as his body tried to catch up to what was happening.

But it was enough of an advantage, and I welcomed it with open arms.

"Do you want your precious little lady to wear your brains all over her? I won't ask again," the man behind me growled, pushing the muzzle of the gun into my temple. Hard.

As if coming out of some sort of trance, I unclenched my fists from the guy's leather vest, shoving him back just as he started to stumble toward me. Lowering his gun, the mystery man turned his attention to the asshole I'd just accosted.

"Maybe you should stick to the whores you already know, Breck." He moved to stand in front of me, all without blocking my view of the guy. "Otherwise, you could've ended up fuckin' your sister."

KALISTA

*E*verything happened in slow motion. Everyone surrounding me seemed to stop breathing, the delayed motion of their eyelids fluttering closed a thing witnessed only in a warped dream. Voices carried through the air around me, the muffled sounds so incoherent I couldn't focus on a single word.

My eyes scraped over Eli's body, his rigid posture poised for a dangerous fight. The muscles of his arms bulged while pinning the creep against the bar, his eyes boring holes into him as if they held the power to incinerate him where he stood. Jasmine's breath tickled the tiny hairs on the back of my neck. She spoke to me, but I couldn't focus on anything except the man I loved. A man who could be killed right in front of me. And it was all my fault. We should've left the second we saw the bikers enter.

I was responsible for jeopardizing Eli again, first with his heart and now with his life. *Only this time, he might not survive.*

I was so tuned in to watching my son's father, I almost missed what the man with the gun said.

Almost.

Surely, he couldn't have said what I thought I heard.

"Otherwise, you could have ended up fuckin' your sister."

What exactly did he mean by that? I was an only child, had been my entire life. My mother would have told me if I had a brother. *Unless she doesn't know.* But that's impossible. The only logical scenario was if my father had... if he was... but how would he...?

Thoughts pinged so rapidly inside my brain, I'd become dizzy from the overload.

Pushing off my seat and gripping Eli's arm for support, I leaned closer to the man still holding the gun, although thankfully, it was at his side and not pointed at Eli's head any longer.

"What did you say?" I only possessed enough mental energy to speak those four simple words.

With a flick of his head, most of the men walked away, dragging with them any woman who hung around strictly out of curiosity, quite a few of them still shooting daggers at me and Jasmine.

There was something familiar yet foreign about him. His high cheekbones and almond-shaped green eyes were just like mine, although his nose and mouth bore no resemblance at all. His graying hair was short, shorter than most of the men who accompanied him to the bar. If I didn't know any better, he looked like any other average man in his late fifties, attractive and able to blend in with the masses.

Tucking the gun into his waistband, he extended his arm toward the back hallway. Clearly, he wanted us all in a more private setting—to do what, I had no idea.

Eli wrapped his arm around my shoulder and pulled me into him, positioning his body in a defensive stance. "We aren't going anywhere with you. You have to be out of your mind, especially after you put a gun to my head." His heart hammered away inside his chest, but no one except me noticed. To everyone else, Eli Warner looked in control, ready to throw down with the best of them if it meant protecting me. I hated putting him in yet another situation he had no choice but to follow through with.

Before the man spoke again, someone pushed past him and blocked him from our view. The biker who had stepped forward was extremely handsome, although just as threatening as the rest of the men. His dark hair was also cut short, and the patch on the front of his jacket said President, which was fitting since he seemed to demand respect with a simple glance.

He placed his hand on Eli's shoulder as he leaned into his ear, whispering something I couldn't hear, but whatever he said made Eli relax some.

"Fine," Eli responded, before turning around and addressing both Mike and Jasmine. "Take her home."

"Fuck that, man. There's no way I'm leaving you two here alone." Mike stepped forward, but before he could protest further, the president of the club caught Mike's eyes and a silent exchange passed between them.

Without another word, Mike grabbed Jasmine's hand and led her away, her head twisting over her shoulder and mouthing, "Call me," before he dragged her out the front door.

Who the hell is this guy?

I didn't have time to contemplate before we were ushered toward the hallway, then to a small office at the end. The president, as well as the man who threatened Eli, made their way toward the center of the room.

"Sit," the leader of the club said.

Glancing at Eli, I noticed he didn't seem as wound up as he was moments before, although his demeanor was still on point, prepared for anything to happen.

"We'll stand, thanks."

"Up to you," the older man said, moving toward the desk. Sitting on the edge, he locked eyes on me, parted his lips and told me what I feared to be true.

"Kalista… I'm your father. I never intended for you to find out, but here we are."

There was no sorrow or disappointment in his voice. There was no happiness or expectation, either. His tone was flat, emulating his expression. He was stating facts, facts that had no bearing on him or his life but had flipped my world upside-down.

I think I'll sit down after all.

Separating myself from Eli, I took a seat in the middle of the couch. Hanging my head low, I tried to find the strength needed to ask the questions I'd wanted answers to my entire life. "How?" I uttered.

"I think you're old enough to know how," he said, his tone no longer harsh and dangerous. "I think your boy is proof of that."

"Cutter…" the younger man warned. "Take it easy. She didn't ask for this." A hint of sympathy rushed forward, but it did nothing to dispel the harshness of the situation.

The mere mention of my son put me on a dangerous edge. Shooting up from my seat, I crossed the room until I was face to face with my *father*. "How do you know about him? How do you even know about me? You took off before I was even born." The air around us suffocated me.

"Yes, I did leave. I told your mother it was over, and I didn't want anything to do with either of you." His words were matter-of-fact.

"Because you were married and already had a family," I reminded him.

"No. Because I wasn't about to drag Justine and an innocent child into this life. Make no mistake about it, I loved your mother. We had an affair for two years, but I knew I had to end it." Looking as if the past caught up to him, remembering a time from another life, he quickly averted his eyes. But I saw what he tried to hide from me—a flicker of sadness.

The words spilled from my mouth before I could filter them.

"And what? You felt guilty about abandoning us, so you've kept tabs on me? Do you think I'll ever want any kind of relationship with you after the way you treated my mother?" Tears welled behind my eyes, but I refused to allow him to break me. "You want me to call you Dad now?" My tone was sarcastic and filled with hurt and anger. It was a lot to absorb, and I wasn't sure I was doing so well with all the information.

"Hear me now, girl. I don't want any kind of relationship with you. If I had a choice, you still wouldn't know about me, but you just had to waltz yourself into my club's bar." His eyes remained glued to mine while he continued his surprising revelation of a speech. "I stick by the decision I made back then. It's safer for you and your family that way." He elaborated when he saw the confused look on my face. "We have many enemies, and they will use any weakness they can to cut us down." He drew a breath before exposing his soul. "And you, my dear, are a weakness."

As if snapping himself out of a delusional, emotional trance, he shook his head and walked toward the door. "Don't ever come back to this bar. And don't ever try to contact me. Ever." His back was to me the entire time. "I don't exist to you, just like you don't exist to me." He disappeared before I could say anything else.

BARGING THROUGH THE FRONT DOOR, I screamed my mother's name over and over until she came running down the stairs. She cinched her robe closed, all while doing her best not to tumble over her hurried feet.

"Oh my God, Kalista. What's wrong?" She reached me in record time and tried to touch me, but I backed away, the look on my face telling her not to try again.

"Why didn't you tell me?"

"Tell you what?" Her brows pinched together, and her bottom lip trembled. She had no idea what I was talking about, yet she was worried.

"Kalista, sweetheart... calm down," Eli said, but it was no good. Adrenaline pumped through me, coating over all of the other emotions I refused to recognize.

Turning fierce eyes on him, I shouted, "I won't calm down! She has to answer me. Once and for all." My eyes shot to hers. "No more goddamn lying."

"Honey, what are you talking about?"

"My father!" I roared. "Why didn't you tell me about my father?"

All the air deflated from her lungs. She stumbled toward the wall, bracing herself so she didn't fall over. Before she spoke, however, we were interrupted when Holden appeared at the bottom of the stairs, eyes wide in concern. For who, I wasn't sure. It was a rare occasion when Holden had seen me angry enough to shout, so I could only imagine what ran through his head.

"Hey, buddy." Eli walked up to him. "Why don't we go back upstairs and let your mom and grandma talk?"

"Okay," he whispered before glancing back at me to make sure I was okay. The only thing I could do was curtly nod.

Once they were out of sight, I laid back into my mother. "How could you not tell me my father was part of a dangerous motorcycle club?" I spoke so quickly, cutting her off every time she tried to respond. "Do you have any idea what it's like to go your whole life not knowing who your father is? To feel like there is a part of you that's missing, and to have the answers at your fingertips, only to be shut down every time I brought him up?" She straightened her posture, glaring at me as if I had two heads. "Well... do you?" I shouted again.

"Are you serious right now?" she asked, trying her best to remain calm. "You of all people do not have the right to come at me like this. Did you not do the same exact thing to your own son? Hide him from his father, never giving him any of the answers *he* deserved?"

I stopped pacing as soon as her words registered, all my outrage dispersing only to have my guilt and regret sheath me once again.

She was right. I'd done the same exact thing to Holden.

Same. Exact. Thing.

The only difference was that Eli was a good man and he never even knew his son existed until I was forced to move back home.

"Oh my God," I whimpered, collapsing to my knees. Holding my head in my hands, I cried. "I d-did the s-same thing." It was all too much, and I had no idea how or what to feel anymore.

ELI

*W*hen the yelling had finally subsided, I decided it was safe to emerge from Holden's room. He'd asked me why his mom was yelling, and the only thing I could tell him was that it was between her and her mother, and when she wanted to tell him, she would.

He shrugged and focused back on the game he'd been playing, my explanation enough to placate him for now.

Walking into the living room, I saw Kalista lying on the couch, her arm slung over her eyes. She was crying, and there wasn't a damn thing I could do to take away her pain. I moved to squat down by her to see if she needed me, but Justine's voice halted me.

"Eli." Once I was close enough, she reached for my hand. "Can you stay here with her tonight?" She motioned toward her daughter, but the gesture was moot. "She needs you to try and work through this, her own decisions making everything worse."

I had no idea what she was talking about, not being privy to their fight, but there was no way in hell I was going to leave her. "Absolutely. I'll look after her." There was nothing left to say, so she kissed my cheek and disappeared up the stairs and back to her room.

As I stood over Kalista, giving her a few more minutes to succumb to whatever emotions plagued her, I thought of what the night's events meant to her. Growing up, she'd often talked about her father, wondering who he was, if he thought about her... if he was even alive. Only to come to find out he was closer than she knew. Hiding in the background, his own justifications shielding him from his daughter her entire life.

Finally reaching for her hand, I pulled her from the couch. She never said a word as she followed me up the stairs, down the hall and into her bedroom. She was defeated and it showed, not only on her face but in her posture as well. Her beautiful eyes were red and puffy, her nose stuffed up from continuously crying.

Quickly undressing her, I pulled the covers back and helped her to bed. Once all my clothes were shed, I joined her, pulling her close to comfort her, to show her she was safe.

She would always be safe with me.

"But you don't understand. How can I be upset with my mom when I did the same thing to Holden?" She turned on her side because she didn't want to face me, her shame eating at her the more she looked me in the eyes.

"You came home, baby." I turned her onto her back again. "You told me about Holden, and him about me. It's different." I struggled to convince her that her situation wasn't the same, but there were too many similarities. And we both knew it.

"But if I hadn't been running away from John, you still wouldn't know you had a son." Tears fell from her own admission.

"Don't do that. Don't play out a scenario that doesn't exist.

You returned home. We know about each other now. I've forgiven you, Holden holds no grudge against you, and we're all in a better place because of everything that's happened."

I wanted nothing more than to forget the night before, but it had to play out. Kalista needed to work through it in order to heal. And I would be there for her every step of the way.

"What did your mom say? About your father?"

"He's not my father," she said through gritted teeth.

"Sorry. You're right." Stroking her hair, I remained silent until she wanted to talk about it.

Thankfully, it didn't take long.

"She told me the same story, that they had an affair for two years, got pregnant with me and he ended it. She said she left out the part of him being involved in that club on purpose, knowing I would try and find him at some point, and she didn't want me anywhere near those people." She paused for a moment before continuing. "I guess she was trying to keep me safe, just as he was doing by forgetting all about us." Her lip trembled.

"It'll be okay," I said, wiping away her distress with my thumb. "I'm here for you."

She reached for my hand and placed my palm on her cheek, leaning into it to find comfort. "How did I get so lucky?" she whispered.

I was the lucky one. No doubt about it.

I caressed her cheek before pulling my hand away. I needed to discuss something with her, something I pushed to the back burner because of everything that had just happened, but I didn't want to delay the conversation any longer. Besides, she could probably use the distraction.

"There is something I want to talk to you about." Sitting up in bed, she pulled her knees to her chest, her eyes focused on mine. "I want you and Holden to move in with me." *There. I said it. Finally.* I'd been thinking about it ever since the night we'd had sex, the night I finally let go of my hurt and anger and forgave her. I wanted nothing more than to be with my family. To go to sleep each night next to the woman I loved, and to wake up next to her beautiful face. To be able to make breakfast for Holden in the morning, take him to school and hang out with him—with them both—after work was something I desperately wanted. No... *needed* to move forward.

Hesitation tripped her words. "Eli... I... I don't think we're there yet." A strand of her hair fell over her eyes, but she tucked it behind her ear before speaking again. She looked hesitant but pushed forward, realizing I wasn't going to let up until we'd had this conversation in its entirety.

"I beg to differ," I responded, keeping a light tone to my voice. Touching her chin, I tilted her head so she couldn't look away. "Kalista, do you love me?" It was a simple question, and I prayed she gave me the answer I longed for.

"Yes, I do. But is it enough to take such a big step so soon?"

"We belong together. Always have. And I want nothing more than to have you and Holden under the same roof with me. If I had my way, I would take you there right now."

"Let me think about it, okay?" she asked. However, as soon as she saw my fallen face, she quickly added, "I just don't want to ruin anything."

"Okay, think about it. But in the meantime, let's take a shower."

I pulled her toward the bathroom, but she stopped me and turned me around to face her. "Eli? Do you love *me*?" Her lip disappeared between her teeth as she waited for my answer. But didn't she already know?

Bringing my lips to hers, I professed my feelings for the woman who had once destroyed me, but then brought me back to life.

"Yes. I love you. I loved you then, I love you now, and I'll love you forever."

KALISTA

"*H*olden, help me with the last of the boxes, please!" I yelled, pulling him away from my mother. Looking around her house, my childhood home, I was sad to leave. But my future looked bright. A smile appeared rather easily as I thought of all the possibilities of a life with Eli. We would all be under one roof as of that evening, and while I was nervous, I was also thrilled.

When I'd returned to California, I never envisioned the path my life would take, not only for me but for my precious boy, as well. He'd been gifted the opportunity to know his father and build a strong bond of love and trust. And I'd been given a do-over, it seemed.

While I'd laughed in Fate's face years before, she came back around and gave me everything I'd ever hoped and dreamed of. I was proof it was never too late to make things right. Although the situation with John had been dire and extremely dangerous, I wouldn't change a thing. It was because of him, and what he'd ultimately forced me to do, that I returned home and started living again, for the first time since I'd left as a scared, pregnant twenty-year-old. Thinking I knew what was best for Eli back then only proved how naïve I'd been.

I should have trusted in our love for each other... for his undying love for me.

"This one?" he asked, pointing to a large box on the dining room table.

"Yes. Those are my books." I would have grabbed the box myself but my hands were filled with a few bags of toiletries as well as some clothes. I was adamant about doing as much for myself as possible, even when Eli and Holden both insisted otherwise.

Eli wanted to be there to help move what little belongings we had, but he was kept late at work. The irritation in his voice was quickly dismissed once I told him he could make it up to me. When he asked me how, I remained silent. Mainly because I wanted him to use his imagination, but also because our son was standing close by. But he didn't have to know that fact.

"Oh, no," Holden teased. "Are you sure you trust me with your precious books?"

"Very cute," I said, nodding toward the front door. "My books are precious to me, but not as precious as you."

"Love you, too, Mom," he called over his shoulder as he walked out of the house.

AFTER A LONG DAY of reorganizing Eli's house, making room for my things as well as settling in Holden, I was beat. Luckily, Holden didn't have much, already having his own room at his father's house long before we moved in.

"What shall we eat for dinner?" Before my son could give me a suggestion, my cell rang, a picture of Eli and Holden appearing on the screen. I'd taken the photo two weeks ago, and

I loved it so much, I'd immediately made it Eli's caller ID picture.

"Hello," I answered breathlessly, reaching into the fridge to grab some grapes.

"Well, hello there," he said, his raspy voice instantly making me crave him. Desperately. "Are you alone? Are you naked in our bed, touching yourself?"

Straightening up, I popped a grape in my mouth, silence greeting him until I figured out what to say. His questions didn't shock me. Not anymore. He was very brazen with me, whether it be over the phone or in person. No matter where I was, alone or not, he found ways to entice me. A soft whisper in my ear, a possessive caress, or a ravaging kiss. No one was any the wiser, at least I thought so, anyway.

Swallowing the piece of succulent fruit, I licked my lips and moaned, "How did you know I was touching myself?" The dead air was proof I'd shocked the hell out of him. I knew he wanted me to up the ante with the sex talk, but this was the first time I felt comfortable enough to say something back to him.

Holden had disappeared to his room when my phone rang, so I was, in fact, alone. Taking the stairs quickly, I hurried down the long hallway until I came upon Eli's bedroom—*our* bedroom.

Closing and locking the door behind me, I kicked off my shoes, yanked my jeans down, bouncing on one foot then the other, all while trying to appear calm and not as if I was balancing the phone to my ear as I danced around like a crazy lady.

"Are you serious?" he finally whispered.

Placing the phone down while I tore off my shirt and bra, I laid on the bed before putting it back to my ear. In the sexiest voice I could muster, I gave him what he'd been hinting at for some time.

"I'm lying on our bed, naked but for my tiny, lace panties. Do you want me to take them off?"

His reply was instant. "No. Leave them on." I heard him shuffling some papers around and realized he was still at work.

"Are you alone?" I asked, hoping to God no one was in his office with him. I knew he wouldn't talk to me in such a way in front of clients, but if Mike or one of his brothers were there, there was no telling what he would do. He would probably say something dirty to me while ushering them out of his office.

"Yes, I'm alone. The door is locked, and my zipper is down. Now. Where were we?"

I heard the creak of his chair and my imagination ran wild. I envisioned his dress shirt pulled up, revealing his tantalizing stomach. His pants opened just enough so he could pull himself free, stroking his thickness each time I spoke.

The look on Eli's face when he was in the chaos of passion was a sight to behold. His eyes half closed, drugged in desire, his teeth working over his bottom lip, then popping it loose and accentuating its fullness. The pure image of him alone was enough to make me wet. Although his voice was lethal, as well.

"You wanted me to leave my panties on," I reminded him. "I'll just move them to the side while I stroke myself." His breath hitched in my ear. He was working on himself. "Ahh… Oh my God, that feels so good. I wish you were here with me right now. Your face buried between my legs, your tongue torturing me until I come in your mouth." My words made me slicker, bringing me closer and closer to detonating.

"Goddamn it, baby. That's so hot. Where the hell is all of this coming from?" His breaths came in short spurts. "Never mind. Just wait until I get home." The air in the room was suddenly thick with longing, the image of him pleasuring himself the best aphrodisiac. "I'm gonna fuck you so good. Do you want my cock, baby? Tell me now," he demanded. He was close; I could hear it.

"Yessssss," I moaned. I glided my fingers over my clit, back and forth, faster and faster, my orgasm just within reach. All I needed was his voice to push me over. "Tell me what you want me to do." The familiar pull barreled through me, the more I teased myself. "I'm so close. Tell me," I begged.

"Stick two fingers deep inside your tight pussy. Imagine they're my fingers as you fuck yourself." For a moment, the only sounds to be heard were our ragged breaths and the pounding of my heart as I chased my release.

Doing as he demanded, I filled myself, circling my clit with my thumb until pleasure struck me. Arching my back, the phone fell and laid on my shoulder. "Ohhhhh... I'm coming." I was careful not to cry out for fear Holden would hear. "Eli...."

Then I went silent.

My orgasm sent me into another world. I barely heard Eli as he shouted his own release into the phone, but it was only seconds later when I heard him say, "Breathe, baby. Breathe."

Every single time I came recently, my breath caught in my throat. I wasn't sure if ceasing to take in oxygen elongated my orgasm, or if it heightened it in any way. Either way, I was too consumed with the pleasure of it that expelling air from my lungs always seemed like an afterthought.

When we both were finally able to speak again, all thoughts of sex were gone. From me, at least. I was starving. "Babe, can you pick up some pizza on the way home?"

He chuckled into the phone at my request. "Sure thing. But make no mistake, I'm having you for dessert."

"You promise?"

"See you soon. Love you, baby."

An hour later, he strolled through the front door, hot pizza in hand and a salacious smile on his gorgeous face.

ELI

*T*hree weeks had passed since Kalista and Holden had moved in with me. And we were having the time of our lives. I'd never felt so alive. The air smelled different, food tasted better, hell, even the sun was brighter. I knew everything sounded like the cheesiest clichés, but they were all true.

Every time I looked at their faces, I realized how blessed I was. Yes, the path that led us here wasn't ideal, and it was paved with anger and resentment, but the end result was a woman I couldn't live without and the greatest son any man could ever dream of.

My life was complete.

Well, almost.

There was one more thing I needed to do to secure our future together. I was finally going to make an honest woman out of her, just as soon as I picked up the ring.

A month back, I rooted through the back of my closet and found the item I kept well hidden. Prying open the tiny box, I was hit with a weird sense of nostalgia. Staring back at me was the original engagement ring I'd bought for Kalista. The one I never had the opportunity to give her. For some reason, I couldn't bring myself to discard it. A part of me kept it as a reminder to be on guard, remembering the soul-shattering sadness I'd felt when she left. Reflecting back, I supposed I was a glutton for punishment.

I'd taken it to a jeweler and asked him to cut the small stone in half. I wanted the pieces to be placed on either side of the new stone I'd picked out. And boy, was it a big one. My income had greatly increased since then, so I could afford to give her a ring she would be proud to show off, even though I knew in my heart she didn't care about such things. But it made me feel good I could buy her something many women would be jealous of.

The added bonus was that you could see the sucker from a mile away, warning all men she was taken. I was claiming her for all the world to see.

Wanting to have a talk with Holden about what I was planning, I asked him to run to the store with me to pick up ingredients so I could make my famous meatloaf for dinner. Kalista had been busy with her new job at the hospital as a radiologist tech, even though I reminded her she didn't need to work. I quickly ended that conversation when she looked as if she was going to argue.

I kept forgetting how fiercely independent she was. After all, she'd managed to work full-time and raise my son all on her own. Loving them both the way I did, I hated the thought of either one of them struggling back then, even though it was irrational of me to feel that way.

We were a mile from the house when I started the conversation. "There's something I want to run by you." Even though I was staring straight ahead, I saw him twist his head toward me.

"You want to buy me a car when I turn sixteen? Why yes, I approve." He laughed, and I could tell he was only half kidding. Hopefully, he wouldn't be too disappointed.

"Nice try. How about we discuss it in a couple of years?"

"Okay," he said, mock disappointment in his voice, since he knew he was nowhere near the age where he could study for his permit.

"I wanted to know what you thought about me asking your mom to marry me." I swore to Christ, as the last word left my lips, he yelled excitedly, slapping me on the arm.

"It's about time, Dad! What took you so long?" His response was better than I could have ever hoped for. "Does this mean I get a brother or sister soon?"

And... there it was. His main motive for wanting us to get married, although I was sure he knew in this day and age, you didn't *have* to be hitched to have kids.

"One thing at a time, buddy. First, she has to say yes, then we can discuss having more kids. Actually, come to think of it, I have no idea if she wants any more children." I remembered having the discussion when we were younger, but that seemed like forever ago, young people in love wishing for a large family of six.

"When are you going to do it?" Holden asked, fidgeting next to me when we walked into the grocery store.

"I haven't decided yet. But until I do, no ruining the surprise." I pulled him close for a quick side hug.

"My lips are sealed, but you better do it quickly because neither one of you are getting any younger." Laughing, he ran ahead of me before I could catch him, smirking at me over his shoulder until all I could do was smile and shake my head.

I love that boy.

KALISTA

"*A*re you sure this is a good idea?" I asked, scouring through the closet to find something to wear. "The last time I went to your family's dinner, it didn't end so well." Eli had only attended one other dinner after that night, choosing to spend every spare moment he could alone with me and Holden. But it was time for me to show my face again and I was nervous about going, but he'd assured me he'd talked to Dray, as well as Cal and Dex. Everyone was on board with me being back in his life, more than simply the woman who was his son's mother.

"It'll be good, I swear." He gave me a quick kiss before scooting around me to find his own clothes. "Besides, if anyone says anything off-putting to you, they will have me to deal with." He winked before selecting a navy blue shirt, the color a shade darker than his eyes.

Deciding not to let my paranoia ruin our evening, I pushed all negative thoughts aside and dressed for the evening, enjoying our conversation on the way to his mom's house. Holden was in the back seat, chiming in when we asked him where he wanted to go on vacation in a few short months. It would be our first family getaway, and I was a little more than excited. It was a small thing to other people, but to us, it symbolized our lives were joined and moving forward.

Standing on the porch, I fidgeted next to Eli as he pushed the door open, ushering both Holden and me inside. I wasn't two steps in when he reached for me, linking our hands together and pulling me close. "I love you," he said, moving me toward an empty room off the entryway. Holden had walked on, looking back only to make a mock expression of disgust at our open display of affection. Secretly, I knew he loved to see us embrace and kiss, realizing our family unit was back on track.

"I love you, too."

His words made my heart flutter. It wasn't the first time he'd said them to me since I'd come back into his life, but every time made my soul soar.

His lips brushed over mine, his hands tightening around my waist as he pinned me against the nearest wall. "I can't seem to think straight when you're near." He devoured me with his skillful mouth before I could respond. At first, I wanted to bask in his light, to stare into his eyes and profess my love for him, but as soon as his lips made contact, I was a goner. Slinking my hands around his neck, I enticed him closer.

Pressing his body to mine, he moaned into my mouth, his tongue capturing mine and pushing me closer to becoming indecent with him in his mother's house.

"I want you so bad," I panted, tangling my fingers into the thick of his dark hair. "Why don't you make up an excuse and we'll come back for Holden." I was desperate for his touch, and I would do and say anything to get it.

His hand brushed over my breast before trailing down my side, only to move around and cup my backside, pushing me hard against him. His excitement was evident, and if we weren't going to leave, then he needed to calm down before anyone saw us. We both needed to, heat rising through me and no doubt making me flushed.

"For as much as I would love to ravage you right now, we *have* to stay." He tripped over his words. Something was up, but I wasn't sure what.

Loud chatter drifted in the air the closer we came to the kitchen. It sounded like everyone was already there. I stood tall and walked next to Eli as his entire family came into view. Children raced around the dining room, loud screams of delight as they all played with each other. Holden was playing with his two youngest cousins when his eyes found us.

"What took you so long?" he asked, Isla and Emma tugging on his arm for his attention. He smiled at them and they giggled, running around the table and wanting him to chase them. They were so enthralled with him, they didn't even notice their uncle. Not yet, at least.

"I had to tell your mom something," Eli responded, leaning in to give me yet another tempting kiss.

"Sure." Our son smirked, looking so much like his father, before he took off chasing after the little girls, making them squeal in excitement.

"About time you two joined us!" Cal shouted, smacking Eli on the back before bending to give me a kiss on the cheek, his affection surprising me since it was the first time I'd seen him in years. "Hey, Kalista," he greeted. "How are you?" Cal had always been laidback, his demeanor remaining calm and unaffected when so many others would have been stressing out. I always liked that about him. The years had been good to him, the only visible signs he'd aged were a few lines around his eyes. The last time I saw him, he'd shaved his head on a dare from one of his friends, but thankfully he hadn't stuck with that look, the strands of his dark and wavy tresses now hitting just above his collar.

Returning his smile, I replied, "I'm good. Great, in fact." I stole a glance at Eli as I spoke.

Dex suddenly joined us, moaning in faux annoyance. "Oh,

good God, the sickly love is going to kill me," he teased, pulling me in for a quick hug before kissing my other cheek. "So good you could make it tonight," he said, running his hand through his short dark hair while he glanced back and forth between Eli and me, the corners of his mouth curving up.

While all the Warner men bared a strong resemblance to each other, Dex and Cal looked the most alike, in my opinion, even now after all these years. They were both clean shaven and shared the same oval-shaped eyes and straight nose, although Cal's looked to have a tiny bump at the ridge that wasn't there before. The two of them even sounded alike, but maybe I was the only one who thought so. The last time I'd seen either of them they were teenagers and while I realized that fifteen years had passed, it took me a moment to come to terms they were grown men now.

"It's so nice to see you both," I said, meaning every word. I really wasn't too worried about being around the two of them, knowing they weren't as intense as Dray. My heart skipped a beat just thinking about our future encounter, but Eli had assured me he was okay with seeing me again.

I guess we'll see.

ELI

"Where is my boy?" my mom shouted, stepping away from the stove. "Give your mother a hug, honey." She fussed about, acting like she hadn't just spoken to me the day before.

Running her fingers over my stubble, she shook her head, but for once didn't say anything about me shaving it. There was a new twinkle in her eye, and if I had to guess, I would say it was because I was truly happy again. I had the love of my life back and a wonderful son to make my life complete.

"Kalista, honey. So nice to see you," she said, drawing her into a loving embrace.

"Nice to see you as well, Mrs.... I mean, Vivian." She laughed, remembering my mother's scolding at being so formal with her the last time we were here.

"Dinner is almost ready. Everyone go wash up." I reached for Kalista's hand and pulled her beside me. We rounded the corner to enter the nearest washroom when Dray and Essie met us in the hallway.

A bristle of tension sprung up but was quickly dashed when I reached for my sister-in-law. Before I could accost her, as my younger brother loved to say, he blurted, "Hah! What are you gonna do now, Eli? You can't very well attack my wife now that you have a woman of your own." *Bastard.* But he was right. Turning to look at Kalista, I saw her smile, grabbing onto my brother's olive branch gesture with both hands. The fact he joked about her, in front of her, was a very good sign. The moment wasn't lost on any of us.

My mouth fell open, my eyes flicking from one person to the next, trying to decide how to respond to his smug ass. But I had no words. No moves.

And my speechlessness made Dray beam from ear to ear. Finally, he had me. No more shamelessly flirting with his wife. "Damnit," I muttered. "You're right, man. No more accosting your wife. But I can't be held responsible if she decides to attack *me.* You know, when she wants the attention of a real man," I goaded. His smile fell when he saw his wife move toward me.

"Well, I guess our fun is over now, Eli." She laughed, the grin returning to her husband's face.

"Finally," he whispered, whisking Essie down the hall, throwing me a wink over his shoulder before he disappeared.

Dinner was delicious, my mom's famous pot roast practically melting in my mouth. Conversation was good, laughter filling the air as we all relaxed into each other's company.

My two other sisters-in-law, Dela and Bridgette, chimed in, spreading their attention between the adults and their children. They welcomed Kalista and Holden with open arms, as I knew they would. Everyone was having fun, but I tensed as the slow tick of the clock's hand mocked me.

And for good reason.

I had something planned, and the closer the time came, the more nervous I was. Looking toward my son, I caught his attention with the flick of my head. I winked and acknowledgment soon graced his face. He was on board... just waiting for me to make my move.

"Kalista." I turned my full attention to her. "I want to change Holden's last name. What do you think?" Acting as casually as possible, I took a bite of my dinner, the sudden silence around the entire table almost deafening. All eyes were pointed at both of us, waiting for her to respond to my out-of-the-blue question.

"W-Well," she stuttered, realizing she was in the hot seat, "then he wouldn't have my last name." Her acute observation made me smile.

"Then how about we change your name, too?" Her brows knit tightly, her mouth parted and waiting for me to clarify.

Pushing my chair away from the table, I stood, reached down to take her hand and helped her to feet. I noticed the looks on my family's faces but was too nervous to really appreciate them for what they were.

Acceptance of Kalista back into our family as well as pure happiness for the man they thought was destined to never love anyone else ever again.

With her hand still in mine, I turned her toward me and spoke from my heart. "Kalista, you were my first love. And while our lives didn't turn out the way we planned, you were my only love. All the years we were apart couldn't break our bond. Of course, I would've liked to have had things happen a little differently, but I wouldn't change where we are now. I love you, more than I can express in words, and I dream of spending the rest of my life with you." Lowering onto one knee, I heard a collective gasp around the room. Nerves wracked me, but my deep-rooted feelings for her spurred me on. Looking deep into her beautiful eyes, I said the words I'd practiced for weeks. "Will you do me the honor of marrying me and making me the happiest man in the world?"

"Yes," she cried, a tear streaking down her cheek as her hand shook in mine. "Yes," she repeated, "I'll marry you."

Everyone applauded as I placed the ring on her finger.

Rising from the floor, I took her into my arms and kissed her passionately, audience be damned. I did my best to keep it PG, but once our lips met, it was hard to pull away. Thankfully, Holden had walked around the table to hug us both, interrupting our moment before we were unable to control ourselves.

"It's about time, Dad. Now you can start on that sibling I wanted." Kalista looked back and forth between us, eyes wide.

"I'll see what I can do, buddy."

KALISTA

*S*ix months in the making, I never thought this day would come. We'd dreamt about it when we were younger, envisioning where we would do it, what we would wear and who would attend always a favorite subject of ours.

Then I'd left… and those dreams died.

Standing at the edge of the beach, realization dawned on me. Our lives had come full circle. Yes, as Eli said when he'd proposed, our lives turned out differently than we'd planned, but the place we found ourselves and how we felt about each other were worth everything that happened.

My fingers fiddled with the ring he'd given me. He told me how he'd included the original ring he had for me, and at first, I was upset, not wanting to wear a constant reminder of my betrayal. But when he explained how the two rings melded together tied our past and present as one, the sadness lifted, and I saw his offering as the true gift it was.

Forgiveness and unconditional love.

"Are you ready, honey?" Mom asked, fluffing the back of my wedding dress. The strapless, cream gown fitted me like a glove, lace beading stitched into the fabric from the waist down. It was simply gorgeous, and as soon as I saw it, I knew I had found the one. Because I wanted to show off my neckline, I decided a classic up-do hairstyle would work best, my dark tresses pinned in stylish curls all around the crown of my head.

Securing my veil in place, I nodded and looped my arm through hers. She was walking me down the sandy aisle, and I didn't know who was more nervous.

Our wedding was an intimate affair, only family and a couple of friends invited to share the day with us. We decided to get married in Tahiti, on the beach at sunset. I asked Jasmine to be my matron of honor, and Eli had asked Dray to be his best man, both people truly happy to stand with us when we pledged our lives to each other. My relationship with Dray was pretty much back to normal. We had a long talk a week after the proposal and hashed everything out.

Taking a step toward my future, my eyes roamed the scene in front of me, thankful everyone was able to make it to share our day with us. When I found his mother, a sudden burst of emotion fired off inside me. She was dabbing her eyes with a handkerchief, her lips curving while she watched me walk toward her son. Vivian Warner was like a second mother to me. She'd always been accepting of the serious relationship Eli and I had when we were young, even though she was concerned we were too wrapped up in each other. Then when I'd finally returned home, she'd embraced me back into her family with open arms, realizing I was young and scared when I'd made the biggest mistake of my life by leaving the only man I ever loved. We had a long talk, and she'd seen the sincerity in my eyes, realizing she could trust me with his heart once more.

When my eyes finally landed on the man who made my heart soar, it was as if time stood still. His gaze penetrated my soul as I walked toward him. He'd decided to finally give in to his mother's wishes and shave for the occasion. Stubble or no stubble, my future husband was the sexiest man I'd ever laid eyes on.

"Are you okay?" Mom whispered, our steps falling in sync the further we walked.

"Yes, just really excited." My hand shook, but it was only partly from nerves. Radiant happiness poured from me, my heart skipping a beat the closer I came to marrying Eli.

Finally, I stood in front of him, my eyes trained only on him and his gorgeous face. His blue eyes shone brightly, but the closer I looked, I saw a tiny crack in his otherwise stoic appearance. He was truly happy, as was I, his eyes glassy from the overwhelming feelings zinging back and forth between us.

The part of the ceremony where we listened to the meaning of marriage then recited our vows was a blur. Before I knew it, we were being introduced as husband and wife.

With our hands entwined, we stepped closer until our lips connected. All the heat and passion I felt for him poured forth from my kiss, but I had to restrain myself; otherwise, our display wouldn't be fit for spectators. I felt Eli stiffen a little, holding himself back from fully showing me how much he loved me.

Our lips opened and we allowed each other the smallest of tastes before we parted. *There are children present, after all.*

"I love you more than life, Kalista," he murmured in my ear as we walked past our guests.

"You do, do you? How about you show me just how much you love me. Whisk me away and make love to me... your way." His eyes widened the second my plea registered.

"The first moment we're alone together."

THE CELEBRATION WENT ON WELL into the evening. We enjoyed everyone's company, regaling tales from our youth as we sat around one of the rented cabanas. The slight breeze felt wonderful on my skin and as I breathed in the tropical air, I felt more alive than I had in years.

I was married.

To Eli.

To the man who had stolen my heart when I was just a girl.

To the father of my son.

To my best friend.

To my soul mate.

I was the happiest woman in the world, and I wanted nothing more than to show him just how much. Yawning, I stretched my arms above me and wiggled around on my husband's lap.

"I hope you're not too tired, Kalista." Dray winked from across the way, his arm circled around his wife as he swayed into her. He'd had a few drinks, and although he wasn't drunk, he was certainly feeling good.

"Not *that* tired."

Eli's fingers tightened around my waist, moving underneath me as he tried to adjust himself. I'd felt him harden against me some time ago, but I refused to acknowledge it because that would have meant I would have dragged him off to our room, guests be damned.

"Yeah, that would really suck for my man," Mike shouted, laughing while he busied himself with his newest conquest, a woman he'd met not two hours earlier at the resort. He was relentless in his pursuits, and I only hoped he found a woman strong enough to tame him. He deserved happiness, and I hoped one day he'd find what he was so desperately searching for. Whatever that may be.

After another half hour, my simple display of exhaustion triggering the end of the festivities, everyone said their good-nights as we all walked toward the hotel.

Once inside our suite, Eli trapped me against the door, his

hips pinning my body while his lips tasted my skin, nuzzling into the crook of my neck. "I can smell your arousal, sweetheart." He kissed along my jaw until he found my mouth. "I can smell how much you want me," he growled before brushing his mouth over mine. His taste was addictive, the way his lips parted just enough to tease, his tongue sneaking out to lick and torment before disappearing again.

He worked me up until I couldn't see straight. Every time I tried to deepen the kiss, he pulled back, silently telling me he was running the show.

Yeah? We'll see about that.

"Honey," I mumbled, feigning exhaustion once more. "I'm really tired. Do you think we could just go to sleep?" My hands rested on his chest, pushing him back so I could see his face.

He looked stunned. "Are you serious?"

Reaching lower, I gripped him, feeling his thickness through his tuxedo pants. I squeezed gently, licking my lips before dropping my hand. "No," I said, lightly shoving him back and laughing as I raced toward the bedroom. He gave chase immediately, the sound of his laughter booming through the room.

He caught me and picked me up in midstride, a shriek of surprise falling from my mouth.

"You tease," he rumbled, tossing me on the bed before covering me with his body. As he lowered his head, he stopped to stare into my eyes. A moment of silence passed between us, each of us professing our love with a simple look. Then it was gone, both of us lost to a sea of pleasure and want, longing and desire so unbridled, if we didn't join together in the next few seconds, we were both going to combust.

Rolling off me, he situated himself until he laid on his back. He'd removed his jacket earlier but was still dressed in his shirt and pants, his bowtie untied and hanging around his neck. Kicking off his shoes, the thudding sound they made when they hit the floor brought me back to the realization that we were about to have sex for the first time as husband and wife.

His hand found his zipper, drawing the metal through the teeth until he had enough room to free himself. Fisting his cock, he gave me a sexy-as-hell smirk. "Wanna take a ride?"

He doesn't have to ask me twice.

I tried to swing my legs off the bed to stand and remove my dress, but he grabbed my wrist and pulled me back toward him. "What are you doing? I have to take this off," I said, waving my hand over my wedding gown.

"No way. We're going to have sex fully clothed. Don't you know you're supposed to leave your dress on the first time you make love to your husband?" I loved nothing more than feeling Eli's naked skin pressed against mine, but the thought of having sex with all our clothes on *was* kind of a turn-on.

"Okay," I conceded, positioning myself so I was hovering over his exposed length. "But first I want to taste you. Is that all right with you, *husband*?" I asked, my desire shining bright for him to witness. His answer was a sultry lick of his lips and a small thrust of his hips. With his thumb placed at the base of his cock, he held himself upright for my mouth.

The sight was erotic.

It was perfect.

A single moan escaped before I made contact, the tip of him rubbing against my lips. He was so hard I was sure it was painful, but I wanted to take my time, explore the steely length of him and taste his essence as a drop of pre-cum appeared.

I licked his excitement, my warm breath coating him and making him writhe underneath me.

"Stop teasing me, woman." His pleas were muffled, his tone gruff while he waited for me to suck him.

"Because it's our wedding night, I'll give you what you want." I flattened my tongue and ran it over him, from root to tip. "Do you like that?" Closing my lips over the top of him, I pulled him in deep, tasting as much of him as I could fit, which was only about half. He was rather wide, and long, and if I had any hope of not gagging, I had to take it slow.

"You have no idea how sexy the view is from up here." He tilted his hips and pushed himself further into my mouth. He restrained himself enough so he wasn't rough, but his body screamed at me to pick up the pace or else he would have no choice.

"Patience," I whispered, but he didn't hear me, too many expletives falling from his mouth while he tried to control himself. Circling my fingers around him, I pleasured him faster, my hand aiding my attempt to make him fall apart. I was hungry for him, wanting his release more than anything right then, but for some reason, he tried to stop me.

"No... Kalista... stop." He twisted about. "Don't... don't make me come yet," he shouted, but I was on a mission. I lifted my eyes to meet his and almost came myself from the look on his face. The muscles of his neck strained, his bottom lip disappearing between his teeth as he held on to the last strand of sanity. He was close... so close that if I didn't slow down, he would explode in less than ten seconds. But I was greedy, and I wanted all of him.

Taking him as deep as I could, the hollows of my cheeks sucking him hard as I pulled back, I flicked the tip of my tongue over his head, twirling it around and around until he filled my mouth, hot salty ribbons of his climax shooting down the back of my throat. He grabbed the back of my head and pushed himself in and out, over and over again, milking every last bit of pleasure he could.

Once he'd come back down, he fell from my mouth with a small popping sound. Sitting up straight, I wiped the corners of my mouth proper-like, as if I was dining in an upscale restaurant and had just devoured an expensive meal.

He laughed at my display, the sound low and sexy, sultry

music to my ears. Then his expression morphed to seriousness. "I wanted to come inside you, not in your mouth. Not the first time, at least."

I straddled his waist and held his eyes with mine. "But I was hungry," I pouted, a mock apologetic smile kicking up my lips. "You wouldn't want me to starve, now, would you?"

"Of course not." He pulled me up his body until I hovered over his mouth. "And now it's time for *me* to eat. But first, I want you to brace your arms on the headboard." I did as instructed, gripping the solid wood to anchor myself.

"Hmmm... I'm very hungry, but I'm going to make this fast because I have this incessant need to bury myself inside you." Without another word, he moved my panties aside and licked me, gripping my ass and pulling me closer, his assault quick and mind blowing.

"Yes... yes. Right there," I moaned, the feel of his tongue, teeth, and lips pushing me closer to the edge. My husband feasted on me, swift teasing flicks, then hard and hungry until I rocked back and forth, chasing my orgasm faster than ever before. I was so overwhelmed with pleasure, my body convulsing on his tongue that when I shifted forward, I hit the headboard. Not hard, but enough to make a sound. But a little knock on the noggin was nothing compared to the feeling of losing myself to him.

"Are you okay?" he asked, placing his hands on my waist to move me back an inch. "I heard that."

"I'm fine. But know I would smack my head again and again if it means I'm going to have such powerful orgasms." I moved down his body until I straddled his waist. He helped me lift my gown, multiple layers of tulle underneath momentarily hampering my ability to own and possess him with my body.

Finding the seam of my white lace panties again, he shifted them to the side, lined himself at my entrance and pushed inside me as I continued to grip the hem of my dress. I let go of the material and placed my hands on his chest, digging into his shirt as I steadied myself.

Eli reached up and traced his fingers over my collarbone, teasing my flesh as he ran his hand up and behind my neck, bringing me down to meet him. "You feel so fucking good, wife." His eyes became hazy the more he moved, the seduction of his hips pumping into me, sending my pleasure into overdrive.

I met him thrust for thrust, his resolve weakening the closer he came to flying off the cliff with me. "Baby," I purred, my gyrations creating the perfect friction to bring me that much closer.

His sweet breath danced over my face as he looked lovingly into my eyes. "I love you so much," he groaned, driving himself deeper into me with each word.

"And I love you." I captured his mouth and owned him, showing him with my kiss what I couldn't express with mere words. "I'm so close." I impaled myself on his cock as the shards of pleasure threatened to destroy me.

"In that case." He grabbed hold of my hips and rocked me back and forth on top of him. He was unbelievably deep, hitting every sensitive nerve he could, driving me closer to the brink. His movements came faster and faster until we both spiraled out of control, my head thrown back and my breath stifled in my lungs.

His hand circled my throat as he roared out his release moments later. He never applied much pressure, but the possession he demonstrated was intense, enough to draw out my pleasure a few seconds longer.

I truly belong to this man, as he belongs to me.

Later, as we lay in each other's arms, he asked me a question I wasn't expecting. "Do you want more children? Because we can certainly work on it as soon as you're ready." His lips tickled mine and it was the most welcome feeling. I loved having him close, feeling him against me, the air he breathed mixed with mine. A tiny piece of our souls joining for all time.

"Funny you should ask me that," I said, turning to see his expression. "Because you're going to be a father again sooner rather than later."

EPILOGUE

KALISTA

"*B*reathe, baby," he whispered in my ear, the warmth of his words doing nothing to distract me. "Breathe," he repeated, grasping my hand tightly in his. I tried my hardest to focus on something. Anything. But the pain was too great.

I supposed what they said was true: a woman remembered the pain of childbirth like that of a migraine. You know what it felt like but forgot the intensity until you were experiencing it again. Although to compare a headache to pushing a tiny human out of your body was simply ludicrous.

When I'd been in labor with Holden, there was pain, yes, but it never lasted as long, his birth having been rather quick, comparatively speaking. Four hours to be exact. My water had broken, but because of complications, I'd been rushed into surgery to have a C-Section.

This delivery was much, much harder. I was older, for one, the toll of the pregnancy having greater effects on my body. I was constantly exhausted, barely having enough strength and energy to get out of bed in the morning the past two weeks. While I was thankful the day had finally arrived, I was a little scared, as well.

Agony ricocheted through my body, a cry hurling from my mouth before I even knew it was coming. "Oh my God!" I screamed, squeezing Eli's hand so hard I saw him wince. I'd been in labor for ten hours already, and it wasn't going very well. The doctor said I was only two centimeters dilated, so I had quite a way to go. The thing was I didn't know how much longer I could do this. I had no other choice, I realized, but wishing away the day was soon becoming my favorite fantasy.

Because I'd had a cesarean before, I could've opted for another one this time around, but I'd had too many complications when I'd had Holden. My incision had gotten infected, I'd developed blood clots in my legs, which were thankfully dissolved before reaching my lungs, and my recovery time took much longer than I'd anticipated, several weeks longer.

"You're doing good, baby." Eli brushed the hair from my forehead. "Real good," he repeated.

While I loved my husband dearly, the sound of his voice grated on my last nerve. "Honey," I said, turning to face him right before another contraction ripped through me. "If you say one more word, I'm going to kill you." I clenched my teeth and struggled to breathe through the pain.

My mother walked through the door as he was probably about to apologize, bringing a cup of ice chips with her. She witnessed the distressed look on my face and quickly rushed to my side. Handing me the cup as soon as my body relaxed, she ushered Eli away from the side of the bed.

"Why don't you go and get something to eat? You haven't left her side since you two arrived last night."

"I don't want to miss anything. I wasn't there when Holden was born, so I want to experience everything right along with her," he told my mom. The subject of him not being present when his son was born was a topic we'd discussed a few times, working through the regret on both sides. So, when he said the words aloud again to someone else, they didn't quite have the negative effect they had months before. I'd forgiven myself for the decisions I'd made back then. Although Eli hadn't given me much of a choice in the matter, hounding me to acknowledge that our lives worked out exactly as they were supposed to.

Who can argue with destiny?

"The only thing you're going to miss out on is seeing your wife in pain, and while I admire you wanting to help her through this entire process, you need a break. Plus, I'm sure she's threatened you already. Right?" She arched a brow, waiting for him to tell her what she already knew. Was she standing outside the door when I said that? I loved him with all my heart, but right then, I could only take so much.

"Your daughter threatened to kill me if I said another word." He smiled, letting both of us know he hadn't taken it to heart. "But you're right, I *am* hungry." He kissed my forehead before retreating. "I won't be long."

Once he left, I allowed my guard to shift and fall. If I broke down in front of him, he would feel helpless, and it would cause more stress on the both of us. He hated when I cried. He said it broke his heart. I could see it in his eyes, the sadness my own tears caused him. Luckily, I didn't cry in front of him often, only when the hormones had done a doozy on my emotional state.

I relished in the release my mother's visit offered. One tear after another slipped down my cheek until I was full-on sobbing. She didn't say a word, simply offered her love, wrapping me in her arms while she stroked my hair. After a bit, I'd calmed down enough to collect myself again, pushing away from her so I could lie back. And no sooner did I shift my position than another wave of pain had me doubling over.

"Mom, please... please ask." I blew out a couple breaths. "The doctor if I can have the epidural now," I huffed, coming off the last wave of the toe-curling contraction.

"I will, honey. I'll ask for you. But be prepared for her to say you can't have it until you're a little more dilated." I nodded, but I had to try, nonetheless.

"ARE WE READY, KALISTA?" Dr. Albrecht asked, securing my feet into the stirrups. Nudging my knees apart, she wheeled her stool closer.

I'd been able to receive the epidural an hour before, coming right when I was ready to give up. Or at least that was exactly what I felt like doing. Sixteen hours and I was finally ready to start pushing. I swore if Eli asked me about having another child anytime soon, I was going to have some more choice words for him.

Clutching my hand, he was sitting next to me and coaxing me through what was about to take place. Since Dr. Albrecht assured me both of my babies were head down and in the right position, and being thirty-five weeks along, both weighing four pounds, I was cleared to deliver without surgery.

Thankfully, triplets don't run in his family.

Eli and I found out we were having fraternal twins, a boy and a girl, early on, and when we told Holden he was going to have two siblings instead of just one, he was ecstatic. Eli, on the other hand, took more time to come to terms with having two newborns in the house. He was scared and told me as much; his fear of not knowing what to do with one baby, let alone two, had him peppering me with questions until I calmed him down.

I assured him he was going to be a great father, just like he was to Holden, to which he reminded me that Holden was self-sufficient when he came into his life.

To further placate his worries, I encouraged him to talk to Dray because he knew exactly what his older brother was about to go through, him being a father to his own twin girls.

His talk with his brother proved successful, thankfully reassuring him enough to where he wasn't freaking out the closer I came to my due date. There was still concern and worry in his eyes, but a simple, soothing touch from me was enough to quiet his erratic nerves.

"On the count of three, I want you to start pushing. Okay, Kalista?" Dr. Albrecht instructed, her brows raised in expectation of my answer.

I inhaled a quick breath and nodded, ready and willing to finally bring my babies into the world. Locking eyes with my husband, I smiled for the first time in hours while I listened to the doctor count to three.

<hr />

Eli

I'D ALWAYS THOUGHT my wife was a strong woman, and after watching her give birth to not one but two babies, I was sure of it. My son Aiden was born first, a full five minutes before his sister, Addison. Both were born healthy and with a full set of lungs. I'd never been so happy to hear babies cry in unison before. It was as if they knew they were no longer joined inside the safety of their mother and were speaking to each other, letting the other know they were all right.

"Are you ready?" I held Aiden in my arms and waited for Kalista to situate herself in the rocking chair. It was feeding time, and although my wife looked tired, I'd never seen her so beautiful.

"Yes, you can hand him to me now," she said, reaching out her arms to take him. Aiden was being breastfed, while Addison had to be bottle-fed because of her allergic reaction to my wife's milk. Kalista had been saddened she couldn't provide for her daughter like she could for her son, but she soon realized it was a wonderful bonding opportunity between father and daughter.

As I looked around the nursery, I counted my blessings, giving thanks that fate had stepped back in and brought Kalista and I back together, for giving me Holden, and now the twins.

I used to think my destiny was to live that of a desolate man, one whose heart had been shut down, never to love again. But I quickly realized I was simply preparing for a life more precious than I could have ever imagined.

The End

**WANT MORE OF DRAY AND ESSIE?
THEN GRAB YOUR COPY OF STOLEN FATE, AVAILABLE
NOW.**

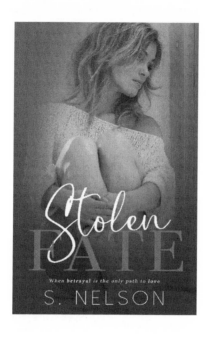

WANT MORE OF MAREK ?
IN THE MOOD FOR A SEXY, GRITTY, DARK SAGA?
THEN GRAB HIS STORY TODAY, BOOK ONE IN THE
KNIGHTS CORRUPTION MC SERIES.

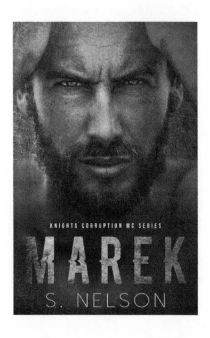

With the weight of the club on his shoulders, Cole Marek, president of the Knights Corruption MC, had only one choice: Turn their livelihood legit.

Everything was falling into place until one unexpected, fateful night. With an attack on his fellow brothers, Marek had no choice but to retaliate against their sworn enemy. Swarming their compound, he comes face-to-face with the daughter of his rival club, making an astonishing decision which would change his life forever.

STAY INFORMED

Did you enjoy Torn?

Want to find out about S. Nelson's next novel?

Each month she sends out updates on upcoming books, sales, cover reveals and awesome giveaways.

Get her FREE monthly newsletter by going to: www. subscribepage.com/snelsonnewsletter

WANT A STORY THAT WILL LEAVE YOU BREATHLESS?

THEN GRAB YOUR COPY OF ADDICTED, BOOK ONE IN THE ADDICTED TRILOGY.

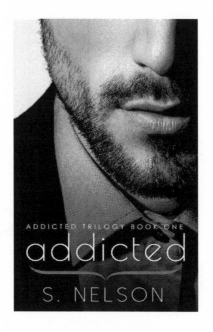

She intrigues him.

She challenges him.

She threatens the secret he's been hiding for years.

Will a promise made long ago be the very same thing that destroys their chance for happiness?

ABOUT THE AUTHOR

S. Nelson grew up with a love of reading and a very active imagination, never putting pen to paper, or fingers to keyboard until 2013.

Her passion to create was overwhelming, and within a few months she'd written her first novel. When she isn't engrossed in creating one of the many stories rattling around inside her head, she loves to read and travel as much as she can. She lives in the Northeast with her husband and two dogs, enjoying the ever changing seasons.

If you would like to follow or contact her please feel free to do so at the following:

Website: www.snelsonauthor.com
Email: snelsonauthor8@gmail.com

Also on Facebook, Goodreads, Amazon, Instagram and Twitter

Note to Reader

If you are a new reader of my work, thank you so much for taking a chance on me. If I'm old news to you, thank you for continuing to support me. It truly means the world to me.

If you've enjoyed this book, or any of my other stories, please consider leaving a review. It doesn't have to be long at all. A sentence or two will do just fine. Of course, if you wish to elaborate, feel free to write as much as you want.

ACKNOWLEDGMENTS

Thank you to my husband for taking care of everything else while I immersed myself in the countless hours of re-edits for Eli and Kalista's story. I love you!

A huge thank you to my family and friends for your continued love and support.

To my wonderful editor, Becky. You continue to challenge me and I'm forever grateful. Thank you for everything!

Clarise, CT Cover Creations, I'm in love with this new cover for Torn. You're amazing, lady!

To all of the bloggers who have shared my work, I'm forever indebted to you. You ladies are simply wonderful!

To all of you who have reached out to me to let me know how much you love my stories, I'm truly humbled.

And last but not least, I would like to thank you, the reader. Without you, I'd just be some crazy lady with a bunch of characters in my head. I loved revisiting Eli and Kalista and I hope you enjoyed this tweaked edition of Torn.

S. Nelson

Standalones
Stolen Fate
Redemption
Torn
Blind Devotion
Massey Security Duet
The Assignment
The Score
Addicted Trilogy
Addicted
Shattered
Wanted
Knights Corruption MC Series
Marek
Stone
Jagger
Tripp
Ryder

KCMC Complete Series
(all five MC books in one: Marek, Stone, Jagger, Tripp, Ryder)

Knights Corruption MC Series-Next Generation
Kaden

Made in the USA
Middletown, DE
11 October 2020